SAVING MISS SWAN

Hearts of Cornwall

K. LYN SMITH

Epigraph Image in the Public Domain: British Library digitized image from page 417 of "Tales of Shipwrecks and Adventures at Sea: ... with celebrated voyages, amusing tales ... and ... anecdotes. Illustrated with ... engravings ... Edited by J. L. No. 1-59"

Epigraph Quotation in the Public Domain: Mackenzie, James S. *The Wrecker's Light*. United Kingdom: n.p., 1876.

Davenwood Press, USA
Paperback ISBN: 979-8-9911573-0-8

GET A FREE BOOK

Subscribe to K. Lyn Smith's newsletter at klynsmithauthor.com/dw and receive a free copy of the Hearts of Cornwall prequel novella, *Discovering Wynne*.

LOSS OF THE COMMERCE, CAPT. JAMES RILEY, AUG. 29, 1815

"The medical men who examined the
body… believe a foul murder
has been committed."

- J. S. MacKenzie, *The Wrecker's Light*

PROLOGUE

DRAYTON-MARSH, SOMERSET
APRIL 1820

MARI TALBOT'S WEEK had begun like many others, with no hint of the turn her life was about to take. As teacher of deportment and drawing, there'd been lessons in perspective and scale, posture and elocution, though the girls were eager for their holiday.

At last, the end of the term arrived for Mrs. Sherwood's Seminary. Most of the teachers had taken their leave, and after seeing the last student bundled off, Mrs. Sherwood herself went to visit an aunt in Wiltshire.

Though Mari had no home to which she might return, she looked forward to the quiet days ahead.

She would revisit Garth's translation of Ovid's *Metamorphoses*.

Her personal library was modest, only a dozen carefully selected books on a shelf in her room. Next to them, on the small desk where she prepared her lessons, she kept a portfolio with her latest drawings. Soon, she'd have another collection to send to her publisher.

The illustrations were mostly done in ink, with a few watercolors of some of her favorite scenes—Hector defending Troy against Achilles and Hippolyta leading the Amazons. Her latest illustration of Perseus battling the sea monster needed more work to properly capture the hero's rescue of Andromeda.

But before she could indulge in the ancients, she would write her sister again, though Hannah had yet to reply to her last three missives. Her sister was an irregular correspondent at best, so one or two unanswered letters had not been cause for concern. *Three*, however, were beginning to test the limits of sisterly affection.

As Mari assembled ink and paper, there was a knock at her door. "Yes?" she called.

The housekeeper, Mrs. Armstrong, poked her head round the door. "Mr. Petersham and another fellow have come to call."

"Did you tell him Mrs. Sherwood has gone?"

"I did, miss, but he says as how he'd like to speak with you especially."

Mari's brows drew together. She wasn't dressed for receiving visitors, but Mr. Petersham was the local magistrate. She didn't think his call was meant to be a social one. "Please have tea brought to the front parlor, Mrs. Armstrong. I'll be there directly."

She replaced the lid on her ink then stopped before the mirror to smooth her skirts and secure a few locks. It was a futile effort, though, as her hair was forever escaping its pins and would soon come down again. She descended to the parlor, wondering what matter of Mr. Petersham's would keep her from Garth's translation, and for what length of time.

Morning sunlight pushed through the thick-paned windows to throw patterns across the wool rug. Through the glass, a cart waited on the drive. Mr. Petersham stood before the fireplace with another man she didn't recognize. Both were simply dressed, hats held at their waists.

"Mr. Petersham, I'm afraid Mrs. Sherwood has gone to visit her aunt. She won't return until Tuesday next."

He gave her a kind, though tight, smile. "It's you we would like to speak with, Miss Talbot. May I present Constable Bragg from Eventon?"

Mari exchanged pleasantries as her confusion grew. "What brings you to Drayton-Marsh, sir?" Though not but a few miles farther along the Bath road, residents of Eventon rarely had occasion to visit Drayton-Marsh unless they came on school business.

"I've come to speak with you regarding your sister," he said.

"Hannah has gone to Bath," Mari explained. It had, in fact, been more than a year since Hannah left Mrs. Sherwood's employ. When the men exchanged a frown of puzzlement, she added, "She's been engaged as chaperone to a young lady there this past year—a former student." Holding her sigh, she said, "If she's found a spot of trouble…"

It would not tax the imagination to believe her sister had found herself in a difficult situation. Turned out, even, from her employment. Of the Talbot twins, Hannah was the more impulsive—charming and outgoing to a fault—while Mari's manner was more reflective. Some might even say dull, though she hardly thought bookish and dull were the same. She could easily believe Hannah had spoken too hastily or engaged in some lark that had not gone as planned. But to bring the constabulary to her doorstep…

"Won't you have a seat, Miss Talbot," Bragg said with a nod toward the chair behind her. The suggestion was given as a statement rather than a question, and Mari's unease grew.

"I prefer to stand, thank you."

Bragg tucked his chin before saying, "Very well. It is with regret that I must inform you…"

The rest of what he said came to Mari as if through water. "A regrettable tragedy… your sister… truly unfortunate… drowned herself."

Mari stared at him, noting the gap between his front teeth as her mind tried to make sense of his words. When it failed to do so, she said, "I'm sorry, Constable, but there's been a mistake."

"I'm afraid there's no mistake, Miss Talbot. The evidence is quite clear." Bragg cleared his throat and, as if just recalling the requirements of polite discourse, he added, "You've my condolences for your loss."

The room tilted as Mari swayed. Her legs felt like they belonged to someone else, and Mr. Petersham took her elbow as if she might faint. Dimly, she heard him ask, "Do you have salts?"

Mari straightened and strode toward the window. Drawing a long breath, she forced a firmness to her voice she was far from feeling. "My apologies, Constable. This is quite a shock, and I'm still not certain I understand. Why have you come from Eventon if my sister was in Bath?"

Bragg exchanged another frown with Petersham

before replying, "Your sister has been residing in Eventon these last six months, Miss Talbot. Were you not aware?"

"No," Mari said with a shake of her head. Then, seizing his words, she said, "Six months? But I have more recent letters from Bath, so you see, there's been some mistake. I'm sorry for your trouble—"

"I assure you, there has not been a *mistake*." A bit of impatience colored Bragg's tone, and when his gaze went to the mantel clock, she wondered if her questions kept him from another appointment. "Mr. Petersham identified your sister's cor—that is, he's identified the body," Bragg said. "As for the manner of death, a coroner's inquisition reviewed the facts and made a ruling of suicide. I realize that's not what a young lady such as yourself might wish to hear—"

"Of course not!" Mari said. "None of this makes any sense." Her sister found too much enjoyment in her life to end it. And Eventon... if what the constable said was true, then Hannah had been living no more than a few miles from Drayton-Marsh. Why had she said nothing of her change in circumstance?

"Miss Talbot, I did not wish to tell you this, but your sister was living in Eventon under a false name. May I suggest she was not the person you believed her to be?"

Mari pulled her head back and stared at him. She heard his words but they made little sense. The men took their leave, and below, the front door opened and closed. Numbly, she watched from the window as the driver of the cart unloaded her sister's trunk. Next came a long box, set carefully onto the gravel by Bragg and the driver. It wasn't until the men stepped away that she realized it was a coffin, and her limbs began to shake.

Her sister lay in a box on the drive. Hannah had died, and Mari hadn't known.

As her sister's twin, Mari ought to have felt *something* in that moment when life left her sister's body. They were as different in temperament as they were in looks—indeed, it had been years since she and Hannah had been like-minded in anything—but that didn't make them any less sisters.

What had she been doing when Hannah took her last breath? Reading Virgil? Painting scenes from some long-ago battle?

The footmen left her sister's trunk at the end of Mari's narrow bed. She opened it to Hannah's favored lavender scent. Inside were colorful spencers and pelisses, walking dresses and simpler morning gowns. Stays and petticoats and white lawn chemises. All the fine things a lady—even a chaperone—needed for moving about in Society.

Mari ran a hand over the soft fabrics. It was a simple thing to picture Hannah wearing the blue cloak, smiling as if she held a secret or laughing with genuine pleasure. What was *not* so easy to imagine was her sister walking into the river at Eventon.

She prepared Hannah's body alone, despite Mrs. Armstrong's protests. Her eyes remained dry as she untangled her sister's hair, then again as she exchanged her sister's gown for grave clothes. She lamented the loss of Hannah's necklace, a ruby pendant that matched one Mari wore. She shouldn't be buried without it.

The baubles were naught but glass, but they had been their mother's final gift to them years before. Three ruby pendants for three Talbot ladies. "As long as we have these to bind us," their mother had said, "we will never be parted."

Now, with growing desperation, Mari searched every corner of Hannah's trunk, but the necklace was gone, probably lost to the river as her sister had been. The realization brought an ache to her throat.

Hannah was buried the next day at the crossroads two miles north of Drayton-Marsh. The service was done discreetly in the early morning and witnessed only by Mari, Mrs. Sherwood's head groom and a lone gravedigger.

There was no cross or marker, but Mari gathered what stones she could carry and, with the groom's assistance, placed them in a small mound atop her sister's grave. Had she means or influence, she might have persuaded the vicar to allow Hannah a consecrated plot in the parish graveyard, but she had neither.

Afterward, Mari wandered the school until she found herself once more at Hannah's trunk. Pushing aside a lace-edged nightgown, Mari found the shawl her sister had sewn two years before, wrapped about Hannah's diary.

Mari set the book aside and unfolded the shawl, smoothing her thumb over the small rose embroidered in one corner. It was finely done, evenly stitched and wrapped with a slender vine of pale green ivy. While Mari preferred drawing to embroidery, Hannah had always had their mother's talent for stitching the most delicate leaves and flowers.

She lifted the wool against her cheek and inhaled its soft lavender scent. Sinking back onto her bed, Mari curled herself about the shawl, numb to the passing of time. When she rose, night had come and the room was dark. She stood on shaky legs, lit a lamp, then opened Hannah's diary.

———

"Constable Bragg," Mari said, "you must agree the circumstances of my sister's death are irregular. Her diary—"

"The coroner's inquest has made their ruling, Miss Talbot."

Mari resisted a very unladylike urge to growl and said instead, "Could you not ask more questions? It doesn't seem anyone has spoken yet with my sister's neighbor—"

"Miss Talbot, I am not insensitive to your grief, but are you aware the position of constable is an unpaid one?"

"I—I was not aware," Mari said.

"As such, I have neither the time nor the resources to ask endless questions about an affair that has already been decided by men far more versed in these matters than you."

"I do not expect you to ask 'endless questions.' Only that you ask *some*."

"Miss Talbot, there is no evidence that a crime has been committed. May I suggest you return to your teaching duties and put this unpleasant experience behind you?"

"No, Constable, you may not." Mari's patience had found the end of her tether. Despite her very rational appeals, Bragg refused to look beyond the fact that the coroner's inquest had ruled her sister's death a suicide. Despite the evidence of her sister's diary, the man refused to acknowledge another, more criminal explanation. And despite Mari's pleas, he refused to investigate what had become of Hannah's *child*, a niece Mari had never known existed.

No, she would not—*could* not—put the matter behind her.

CHAPTER 1

NEWFORD, CORNWALL
JUNE 1820

GAVIN KIMBRELL HEARD the shouts long before he came upon the upset blocking the lane. The early summer's day had dawned warm beneath a crisp blue sky, but a cooling breeze had begun to blow in from the sea. They would have fog by dusk. He might have considered it a portent, but little of portent-worthy interest ever happened in Newford.

Ahead, where the road narrowed at the top of Widow Chenoweth's farm, a line of carts and wagons sat immobile in both directions, locked between the stone hedgerows that bordered the lane. Mr. Clifton had already tried to turn his baker's cart with unfortunate results. A basket of cakes now lay tumbled on the lane, and the man waved his arms as Mr. Morgan's hound greedily ate the spoils.

Gavin led his horse through a gap in the hedge and cantered along the low stone wall, passing the knot of carts until he found two familiar figures at the source: Trevik Pengilley and Bertie Evans. Newford's chief sea pilots had been at odds, on the water and off, for longer than Gavin had been alive. Whenever Pengilley and Evans crossed paths, the result was certain to be more quarrelsome than the meeting warranted.

Now, Evans' crimson face was nearing apoplexy. "Move yer blimmin' wagon, Pengilley, afore I move't meself!"

Pengilley stood in front of his own wagon, hands fisted and blood streaming from his nose. Evans, apparently, had already landed a proper thump. "Ye'll not be havin' yer way today, Bertie, mark me words."

Around them, men grumbled for the pair to move their carts. Gavin had to raise his voice to be heard above the din. "What's the trouble this time, lads?"

"Constable," Evans said, "I insist ye arrest this blighter."

"Hold yer clacker, ye great gaukum—"

Evans' and Pengilley's voices clamored one over

the other as they argued about who'd been wronged the most. Gavin closed his eyes on a sigh. Regrettably, scenes like this one passed for a constable's lawful duty in his quiet corner of Cornwall. He wondered again if he ought to remove to Truro or Falmouth. Bath, even—anywhere he might try his hand at sorting something of significance.

"Gentlemen," he said forcefully, and was surprised when the men ceased their hostilities long enough to turn sharp glances on him. "Now, which of you arrived at the bend first?"

Predictably, both men claimed that honor, and since their carts were equally blocking the narrowest part of the lane, it was unclear where the truth lay. Gavin appealed next to their sense of community.

"I can't have you upsetting the good commerce of our neighbors. To be sure, Mr. Hammett has business to see to at the smithy, and now Mr. Clifton's orders are ruined. One of you must give way."

Loud rebuttals met this statement as neither man was willing to give an inch of the lane to the other. More shouts rose from the onlookers, and at least one was of the opinion that Gavin ought to, "Arrest the pair of'm!"

"The magistrate won't like that," another said.

"Aye. Carew's 'ad a perfect record all year, and 'e makes no secret of't."

They weren't wrong in their assessment. Squire Carew took uncommon delight in attending the quarter sessions, where his lack of anything to report was as loud a boast as any to his fellow magistrates. He wouldn't appreciate a blemish on his perfect record, and certainly not for an infraction as minor as disturbing the peace.

But the lane needed clearing before a minor disagreement became a brawl. Fortunately, Gavin had a long acquaintance with Evans and Pengilley. The only thing the long-feuding pair enjoyed more than arguing with one another was the attention of the Widow Chenoweth. And that fair madam had a soft heart for moderately roguish, slightly scandalous gentlemen.

Pitching his voice lower and directing a stern glower at each man in turn, Gavin said, "Aye, you know 'tis true enough—Carew won't welcome any arrests marring his record. Our magistrate is of the opinion that the stocks are a measure of last resort, meant only for the worst out-and-outers. Rogues of the most… roguish… sort."

The crowd considered this, and murmurs of agreement rose as Gavin continued.

"But you also know I'm oath-bound to uphold the law. I can't allow disturbances like this to upset Newford's peace. To be sure, the wives and widows will sleep better to know the scoundrels among us are duly called to account for their raffish ways." He stressed the word *widows*, and predictably, the men grew pensive at the sound of it. Both of them glanced in the direction of the nearby farm, where the widow herself watched the fracas occurring across her field.

"Raffish?" Evans said.

Pengilley straightened his bony frame and puffed his chest. Removing his hat, he ran a calloused hand through his thinning hair. "Aye," he said with a curt nod, and Gavin lifted his brows in question. "I'll have me time in the stocks," Pengilley said.

Evans jabbed a finger at his rival. "No, I'll not hear of't! If anyone be in the stocks, 'twill be me!"

Pengilley bristled. "Over me dead body, ye daft old man!"

Gavin stifled a laugh that the men would argue over the *privilege* of the stocks before allowing the other any quarter. "You're to be commended for your eagerness to set our ladies' minds at ease, but to be clear, you're *both* volunteering for the stocks?"

The men nodded.

"And you realize the alternative is for one of you to simply yield the way to the other?"

"Never," Evans said with a mulish tilt to his jaw.

"Not while there's breath left in me body," Pengilley vowed.

Gavin eyed the pair of them. Newford's stocks could only accommodate one man—they weren't in Truro after all—so he said, *"I'll* decide who will grace the stocks today." Then, with a nod for Pengilley, he said, "Come along then. Evans, you may recover your neighbors' goodwill with a donation to the vicar's children's fund. Twenty shillings ought to be sufficient."

"Twenty shillings! But that's—"

"Generous and charitable," Gavin finished for him, "and likely to earn a smile from the ladies at Sunday services."

Evans grumbled, but his protests were weakening. Gavin directed the vehicles closest to Newford to back down the lane until they reached the crossroads. Pengilley did the same, and Gavin followed on his horse as the man pointed his cart toward the stocks.

When the lane widened enough to allow them to ride abreast, Pengilley turned to Gavin. "Ye can take a swing if ye're so inclined," he said.

"Aye?"

"'Twill give us a tale to tell the lads."

Gavin couldn't help his grin. "And garner the sympathies of a certain widow?"

"That too."

"I'm not thumping your brain box without cause." At the man's speculative gaze, Gavin gave him a narrow-eyed stare. "Do *not* give me cause."

Moments later, he was fastening the man's wool-clad feet into the stocks near Newford's harbor when his cousin emerged from the Fin and Feather Inn.

"The stocks *again*, Mr. Pengilley?" Wynne said.

"Aye, Mrs. Teague. 'Twould seem I found meself a spot o' trouble." The man's grin was unrepentant, and Gavin wondered when he'd lost his authority in the parish, or if he'd ever had any.

"And what offense have you committed this time to earn such cruel treatment?"

"Disturbin' the peace, I believe the constable said. Though to be sure, 'twas that ill-bred lout Evans what kicked up first."

Gavin gave the strap securing the wooden yoke a final sharp tug. "Aye," he grumbled, "and you're innocent as a babe."

"Oh, but you'll be missing your ale, to be sure," Wynne said. Gavin had never known his cousin to miss an opportunity for an extra bit of revenue, so he wasn't surprised when she added, "Per'aps you'd like me to send Peggy with a tankard from the Feather."

"'Twould be a kindness, Mrs. Teague, thank ye."

Gavin tossed his cousin an exasperated look, to which she only shrugged. "I won't apologize for making a bit of coin, Gavin Kimbrell."

Wynne left, and Gavin went next to the church at the end of the high street. After using the boot scraper, he entered to find the vicar overseeing a collection for the St. Lawrence parish home near Falmouth. The benches lining either side of the nave were stacked with baskets and crates, and a dozen of Newford's matrons were filling them with castoff linens and foodstuffs.

"Constable, you've come earlier than expected. The boxes won't be ready for another day."

"I'll bring the cart around then," Gavin said, "but I thought you'd wish to know Mr. Evans will donate twenty shillings to the children's fund."

The vicar's bushy brows climbed above the rim of his spectacles. "Indeed? I wonder where he came by such a sum."

"I hear he had a lucky night with the dice in Truro."

"Did he now? I can't approve of gaming, but I can't fault such a noble gesture. Now, we'll be able to send more toys, and Newford will make a fine showing for St. Lawrence's new administrator."

Gavin replaced his hat and left the church. The air had cooled even more, and a distant smudge of fog blurred the horizon above the sea. With the matter of Pengilley and Evans settled, Gavin thought to join his cousins in the Feather's coffee room. Wynne would have a cheery fire burning in the grate and pastries fresh from the oven. He'd not gone more than a dozen steps, though, when the magistrate found him.

"Walk with me, Kimbrell," Squire Carew said as he fell into stride with Gavin. "What's this I hear about Pengilley? Have you arrested the man? I can't say I'll be pleased for the paperwork, to say nothing of the quarter sessions—"

"I've not arrested him, sir." As briefly as he could, Gavin explained the day's events. "I merely persuaded the men some form of penance was owed for upsetting their neighbors, and Pengilley volunteered for the stocks."

"He *volunteered*. Again?"

"Aye."

"And Evans?"

Gavin jerked a thumb back toward the church. "The children's fund will be twenty shillings richer."

Carew shook his head. "I don't know how you do it, Constable, but as long as you keep the arrests to a minimum"—by which Gavin surmised he meant zero—"I won't question your methods."

"Aye, sir."

When Gavin passed the stocks again, Pengilley saluted him with a meat pie and a grin as the Widow Chenoweth strode away.

HANNAH'S DIARY
13 APRIL 1819

Bath is everything I ever imagined and so unlike Drayton-Marsh. It may be foolish of me to say, but I can almost believe I'm living the genteel life Mother planned, before Father left us to beg employment from Mrs. Sherwood.

I cannot indulge myself for long, though, as my charge reminds me of my duties at every turn. Chaperoning Miss Elizabeth is a task easier said than done. The lady seems determined to give me the slip, but I am becoming wise to her tricks. Indeed, I might once have used them myself, had I enjoyed a season of my own.

But my days are not all work. In the course of my duties, while guarding Miss Elizabeth's virtue at Lady Haverstock's soirée, I made the acquaintance of a gentleman. He is handsome and engaging, and yesterday, quite by accident, I chanced to encounter him again while visiting the shops.

Mr. K—for that is how I shall think of him—is a merchant, and though I know nothing of shipping manifests and contracts, our conversation comes easily. It's as if we've known one another for ages.

CHAPTER 2

THE ENGLISH CHANNEL, NEAR CORNWALL
JUNE 1820

THE SEA CHURNED as the *Destiny*, a sleek merchant vessel out of Bristol, rounded Land's End. The sky, which had begun the day brilliantly, was now veiled behind a thickening white fog that crept ever closer. The ship took each swell with ease, but Mari would be glad to have solid earth beneath her feet once more.

She tapped the door of the Kingsley cabin, and after some moments, it was opened by Lady Philippa herself.

"Miss Swan," Lady Philippa said, not bothering to hide her disappointment. "I thought you must be Beatrice come to help me dress."

"Beatrice is still feeling poorly," Mari told her employer as she bent in a shallow curtsy. "Every motion of the ship sets her stomach to rolling. With your permission, my lady, I'm prepared to stand as your maid." Mari kept her eyes soft and hesitant, hands folded demurely before her as she waited.

"Have you any experience with the curling tongs?" Lady Philippa asked. Then, with a narrowed eye for Mari's own hair, which had never held a curl, she answered her own question. "No, I can see you have not."

"I often arranged my sister's hair when we were girls," Mari said. She spoke the truth, but she would have claimed an acquaintance with the Queen Consort if it meant she might have access to the Kingsley cabin. Once Lady Philippa left for supper and Kingsley's valet retired to his own cabin, Mari would be alone and free to continue her investigation.

Lady Philippa released a sigh of long suffering. "Kingsley and I are to dine with Captain Henderson and Tate in less than an hour, so I don't suppose I've any choice at this point. Well then, let us see the extent of your skills."

Lady Philippa moved away from the door, and Mari followed her through the receiving salon and into the lady's bedchamber. Though the Kingsley cabin was near to Mari's own berth in distance, the two couldn't have been further apart in distinction.

Mari's accommodations were spartan, with barely enough room for a body to turn about—suitable for a paid lady's companion, in short. By contrast, the Kingsleys shared a well-appointed suite that spanned the width of the ship. Beyond the salon, the sleeping quarters were separated by a shared dressing room larger than Mari's cabin and a bathing room complete with copper tub.

They might have been in a fine townhouse, if not for the motion of the sea beneath their feet. Here, there were no indications the *Destiny* had once served as warship. Indeed, the square gun ports that lined the hull, one of which took up most of the outer wall in Mari's cabin, must have been hidden behind the fine walnut paneling. But that, Mari supposed, was a distinction due the owner of a successful merchant enterprise.

In the gentleman's berth beyond the dressing room were the sounds of someone moving about. Smith, the valet, she supposed. Mari wondered how much longer he might remain in the cabin. In the lady's chamber, Lady Philippa arranged herself at the vanity, chin up and shoulders back as Mari took up the silver-handled brush.

Her employer, whom Mari judged to be of an age with herself, was neither beautiful nor plain. She had light brown hair and a slim nose that tilted up slightly at the end. Her hazel eyes were clear, though they lacked animation or warmth.

If Lady Philippa's looks were ordinary, so too was her character. She seemed neither cruel nor kind, clever nor dim-witted. Mari had never heard her laugh, but neither did she seem overly morose. The only trait Mari could identify with any certainty was a tendency toward vanity, but that was hardly unexpected in a lady of Philippa's background.

Mari wondered again if she'd made a mistake in attaching herself to the Kingsley household. Although she'd changed her name, her attire and her manner to fit that of paid lady's companion, she'd found little of interest so far. But she couldn't ignore the fact that Hannah's diary pointed her squarely in the Kingsleys' direction. Or rather, in the direction of *Victor* Kingsley, Lady Philippa's handsome and wealthy husband.

No, Mari would hold her course. She would have the truth of what happened to Hannah and her child. She only wished the truth were swifter in coming. She willed her impatience to settle and went about the business of seeing Lady Philippa properly outfitted for supper with the captain.

"The burgundy makes me look sallow," Lady Philippa said. "Wouldn't you agree, Miss Swan?"

And Mari, who knew what was expected, replied, "I don't believe there's a shade that could do you a disservice, my lady."

Lady Philippa gave a low hum of agreement as she adjusted an already-perfect curl at her temple. "Nevertheless," she said, "Kingsley doesn't prefer it. Perhaps we should try the green silk."

Mari retrieved the green silk from the dressing room, passing Smith as she did so. He gave her a superior nod as he went through to the salon, and she breathed a sigh to hear the front door close behind him. Soon, she would have the cabin to herself.

As Mari fastened the final hook on Lady Philippa's gown, the outer door to the cabin clicked open, and male voices could be heard entering the salon. Victor Kingsley and his man of affairs.

"I don't like the terms," Charles Tate said to the sound of rustling paper. "I'll press Langston for a lower fee."

Lady Philippa's mouth tightened at the sound of her husband's trade being conducted not more than a dozen feet away.

"He won't agree to it," Victor said.

"Perhaps we ought to remind him we can find another supplier—Bullington, perhaps. Your marriage has given you a formidable advantage—"

"Bullington will cost more in the long term."

There was a long pause before Tate responded. "The purpose of your marriage was to improve your position, and yet you disregard the advantage at every turn. Langston only charges a larger fee because he thinks he can."

"Do whatever you think is best," Victor replied, his words clipped.

Lady Philippa's form was unnaturally still as her husband's conversation continued in the salon, and Mari busied herself selecting a shawl from the wardrobe to suit the green silk. It was a well-known fact that her employer's marriage to Kingsley was one contracted for mutual benefit rather than mutual affection, but no lady wished to be reminded of it. Mari emerged from the wardrobe and silently extended a wrap to Lady Philippa. Her employer took it with pale fingers.

As they entered the salon, Victor looked up from where he'd been adjusting his cuffs. The gentlemen made their greetings, Victor's glance barely taking in his wife's appearance. He wore a dark suit and pale grey waistcoat. Tall and clean-shaven with hair the color of polished walnut and a cleft in his firm chin, Mari admitted Victor Kingsley was precisely the sort of gentleman who might have attracted her sister's interest.

Were circumstances different, he might have attracted *Mari's* interest, at least until he revealed himself to be an unprincipled knave.

Behind Victor, Charles Tate sent an appreciative,

none-too-subtle gaze around the richly paneled cabin. He stood a few inches shorter than Victor, the paisley silk of his waistcoat done in shades of lavender. With an elaborate stock and silver-headed cane, his appearance was more showy than that of his employer.

Despite his efforts, though, Mari thought he must always fall short in the comparison as Victor Kingsley had some undefinable attraction that couldn't be purchased—a fact for which ladies everywhere should be grateful.

"Shall we go?" Victor said. His manner was cool. It was certainly not that of a man who held any fondness for his wife, but how could it be when only months before, he'd kept another young lady in a cottage in Eventon?

Lady Philippa nodded with the merest tightness to her jaw. Mari knew a moment of unexpected pity for the woman who'd attached herself to Victor Kingsley for a lifetime.

"This blasted fog is thick as wool," Tate grumbled as he looked to where white mist swirled beyond the salon's window. "I don't know how Henderson's men can see to navigate."

Just then, the ship gave a mighty roll over a steep swell. They braced themselves against the motion, and the bell could be heard clanging midship.

"Do you think we're in any danger?" Lady

Philippa asked. "Should we delay our supper?"

"I'm sure Henderson has managed worse conditions," Victor replied.

Mari held her breath until Lady Philippa nodded in vague agreement and pulled on her gloves. As companion to Lady Philippa, Mari had expected to have access to much more of the Kingsley household, but there were always servants bustling about the couple's stately home in Bath. Beatrice, the maid, was especially devoted to maintaining her lady's dressing room, and Victor's chambers had always been out of Mari's reach.

But aboard the *Destiny*, with Beatrice indisposed and Smith retired to his own berth, this would be her first—possibly her *only*—opportunity to properly inspect Victor Kingsley's things.

———

GAVIN STOOD IN the Feather's front window, a mug of coffee warming his hands as he awaited his cousins. Outside, a pale mist slicked the cobbles, and the day's breeze had fallen away. The Feather's red-painted signboard hung still in the cool, damp air, and flowers in front of the shops didn't so much as wave a petal. It would be a bad night for sailors, with no wind to fill their canvas or dispel the fog that banked up on the horizon.

Across the way, Pengilley remained in the stocks, but someone had draped an oil coat over his shoulders against the damp. The man had enjoyed another pie, and now he drank from a tankard of ale, pausing to wipe his beard with the back of his hand. He seemed altogether too satisfied with his lot.

"Your punishments are lacking." His cousin Alfie lifted his own mug to indicate the stocks.

"I think Pengilley would disagree," Jory replied, "given the female attention his situation has earned him."

"'Twas proper kind of you to give him a coat," Gryffyn said to Gavin, whose reply was a snort of disgust.

"That'd be the widow's doing," he said, though he couldn't say as much for the ale. That, he was fair certain, had come from the Feather's stores, and he cast an irritated eye on Wynne behind the bar.

He left the window to take his seat at his cousins' table as the room began to fill. Soon, more of their relations joined them, drawn to the Feather's warm glow in the misty gloom like moths to a lamp. As the fire popped in the hearth, Gavin resigned himself to more of his cousins' jests.

"'Twould appear Pengilley's been watered, fed

and sheltered from the cold," Merryn said as he pulled a chair. "Are you thinking to entertain him as well? Per'aps we could persuade Rowe to play his fiddle."

"What Pengilley needs is a bit of theater," Jory added.

"And a cushion. I imagine that bench must be hard on a lad's hindquarters."

"Your suggestions are duly noted," Gavin said drily. "I shall recall them if one of you should ever find yourselves in such a position."

His cousins laughed, and the edge of Gavin's scowl twitched despite his efforts to maintain it. But all laughter ceased when the door to the inn banged open to admit Alfie's youngest brothers. Daniel and Matthew hurtled through, their hair damp with mist.

"A ship!" Daniel exclaimed when they reached Gavin.

"Aye," Matthew added more soberly. "You said to keep our weather eye up, and we spotted a ship not a mile from the Devil's Teeth."

Daniel brushed wet curls from his eyes. "She's going for the straits past the old smugglers' path, but no captain'd be daft enough to sail'm in this fog!"

The room quieted. Daniel was correct. No captain worth the title would go anywhere near the Devil's Teeth in this weather unless he had no choice.

Jory spoke first. "With no wind, she'll be at the mercy of the sea. If the current doesn't dash her on the rocks, the tide will."

"If the captain can land at Copper Cove," Merryn said, "she might not go to pieces."

Gavin stood. "We'd best see what's to be done then."

Several of the coffee room's patrons rose with him, and Roddie Teague, Wynne's husband, left his place behind the bar. The Feather would be empty of customers soon enough if a ship were in trouble.

Though it had been some months since the last wreck along their shore, the experience was as familiar to every Cornishman as the taste of salt in the air. Coats were hastily donned and hats jammed low as they ventured out. The fog was closer now, a steep, towering bank that advanced from the sea. As Gavin passed the stocks, he paused to unlock them.

"What's this then?" Pengilley said.

"Step lively," Gavin said gruffly. "I've a notion all hands will be needed afore this day is done."

Pengilley fell into step with them, pulling the oil coat tighter about his thin frame. After gathering ropes and lanterns from the Feather's stables, they rode as swiftly as the fog allowed to the cliffs above Newford.

Indeed, as Matthew and Daniel had reported, the

outline of a ship could be seen just ahead of the fog—a former warship turned merchant, judging by the even row of empty gun ports dotting her side. A lantern shone at the masthead. The captain appeared to be holding a course for the beach at Copper Cove, but the dark jagged shape of the Devil's Teeth waited ahead. The rocks were close—too close for a ship with no wind to steer by.

Gavin raised a glass to his eye, squinting to make out more of the ship's condition. She rode broadside to the sea, her sails slack. The captain hadn't ordered the distress flag run up yet. He still thought he could manage his vessel, but they could all see from this vantage point that was not the case.

"The tide," Alfie said, "'twill turn soon…"

There were sounds of agreement. Any hope for a successful landing on the sand was tempered with the knowledge that time was short. The sea was at slack tide—that narrow period between ebb and flow—and the currents were at their weakest. Soon, though, the flowing tide would threaten to dash everything in its path against the rocks.

"We haven't time to lose," Gavin said. "If she misses the beach or the tide turns before she lands, I fear all souls will be lost. Gryffyn and Alfie," he said, "ride ahead and light the fires to guide the captain. If he's any wind at all, he'll need to make the most of it." Stone windbreaks had been built atop the cliffs for just this purpose, directly above the cove. As his cousins rode off to see the fires lit, Gavin shouted orders to the rest of the men.

"Merryn, set up a watch against the wreckers. If word gets to Truro, it won't be long afore they come to see what spoils can be had."

To Bertie Evans, he said, "Get your boat and organize the others. If this fog lifts, we'll need barrels and plenty of rope."

"Aye," Evans said, his eagerness no doubt bolstered by the tale he'd have to share with the Widow Chenoweth. That, or the possibility of a salvage reward if the situation turned.

"I'm coming, too," Pengilley said to Evans, to no one's surprise. "Just to be sure ye do a proper job of't."

"What can we do?" Daniel said.

"Take Matthew and fetch Dr. Rowe. And bring blankets!" he called as the twins raced off.

"Teague and I will go with you to the beach," Jory said.

Gavin agreed, and then, in case it needed to be said, he called after Evans and Pengilley. "Your argument stays behind, lads."

"Aye, Constable," Evans said, "so long as this codger don't muck things up."

CHAPTER 3

MARI STUDIED THE Kingsley cabin. The dressing room held two wardrobes and a chest of drawers. She'd return to it later, but first, she must see what she could find in Victor's chamber. The bed—a four-post affair with crimson bolsters—took up most of the space. One corner held a privacy screen for the chamber bucket, and opposite the bed was a desk with a brass-bound writing box.

She wasn't certain what she was looking for, but that seemed as good a place as any to start. She lifted the lid on the box to reveal an ink-stained writing slope and a leather pocket for documents. She sifted through the contents to find business correspondence and a tradesman's receipt.

Her fingers found a slim book of some sort, and a quick glance revealed it to be Victor's appointment book. A ribbon marked the current date. Glancing through the pages, she found most of the entries brief to the point of being useless. *Confirm contract. Call at Lloyd's. Inquire about shipment.*

She opened to the ribbon and found a note for "Falmouth" with the names St. L and Harris next to it. The *Destiny* must be planning to put in at the port town. She knew Victor maintained interests around Bristol, Bath and London, but she hadn't realized he also had his foot in Cornwall.

Turning back to the start, she thumbed through the earlier months. These entries were more detailed than the later ones, with clear explanations in Victor's even hand. He described at length the design of a new warehouse in London and plans for a canal expansion in Bristol. His earlier notes were so detailed, the change to his current style so abrupt, it was easy to see it had occurred not long after Hannah's death. That couldn't be a coincidence.

Had her sister discovered something in Victor's business dealings and been killed for it? Was he involved in something irregular? Nothing in his appointment book indicated as much, but Victor would hardly write *Negotiate illegal contract* or *Confirm shipment of illicit goods*, would he?

When she came across an entry shortly after Hannah's death that read *Lady Philippa—wedding,* she held the book closer to the lamp, uncertain whether she'd read it correctly. But no, she'd not been mistaken. Victor had made an appointment in his book for his own wedding, which was followed an hour later by an appointment with *Westbrook, timber contract.* She checked the date. She knew the Kingsleys' marriage was a recent one, but he'd married Philippa mere *days* after Hannah died. If Mari didn't already have a distaste for the man, she would now.

His wedding appointment wasn't the only one to catch her interest, though. As she continued turning the pages, advancing closer to the present, she was startled to find her own name scratched in the narrow margin, next to another entry for Falmouth dated just three weeks before. *Marianne.*

Her heart hammered, her pulse loud in her ears. Mari had never been to Falmouth, and she couldn't imagine why Victor Kingsley would have written her name in his appointment book. Lower on the same page was a reminder: *One hundred pounds to C Harris.* Harris again.

Taking up Victor's pearl-handled quill knife, Mari carefully removed the page from the book. The entry was old enough that Victor might never notice it was missing. Folding the paper into a hasty square, she tucked it into a pocket in her skirts.

The ship's timbers creaked and moaned as another swell lifted the *Destiny* then brought it back down. When the ship settled and she had her balance again, she returned Victor's appointment book to its leather pocket and resumed her search of the writing box.

There were compartments for a pen and jar of ink. She pushed the ink aside and stopped when she heard a small click. It was faint beneath the sounds of the sea, and she moved the jar again, listening more closely. There it was: an unmistakable *snick* beneath the leather writing slope.

She unfolded it to find a small wooden panel had been loosened, no doubt sprung by a mechanism in the ink compartment. Behind the panel were two small drawers. The first was empty, but the second held a small snuff box and a folded linen square. She lifted the handkerchief, her thumb grazing the embroidered rose in one corner. A length of finely stitched ivy twined about the flower. She *knew* that ivy, and bile rose in her throat.

Hannah's handkerchief was proof that Victor had known her sister, though, to Mari's frustration, it was hardly evidence of more. Closing her hand over the cloth, she added it to her pocket. She felt no remorse for doing so. As far as she was concerned, she had a right to anything belonging to her sister.

Outside the cabin, footsteps sounded in the companionway, and she stilled. It was only a member of the crew, though, hurrying about his duties. She swallowed and released a slow breath.

Her heart, which felt as if it had climbed to her throat, was not made for skulking about in gentlemen's chambers.

She closed the writing box then returned to the dressing room. A quick rifle through Victor's wardrobe revealed nothing of interest, so she moved on to the chest of drawers. The first drawer was neatly arranged with velvet boxes for pearl sleeve-buttons and cravat pins. Expensive cologne—bergamot, perhaps—perfumed the air. More folded handkerchiefs lay to one side, but these didn't have her sister's ivy.

The next drawer held Lady Philippa's silk stockings and chemises. Victor's linen smallclothes, which in other circumstances, she would have been mortified to be rifling. Mari moved methodically through each drawer, working her way down the chest but finding little more beyond the day-to-day trappings of a wealthy merchant and his lady.

As she closed the last drawer, something tucked at the back caught her eye—another handkerchief, set apart from the rest. She unfolded it and there, nestled in the snowy linen, lay a small pendant. Her hand shook as she lifted it. The clasp was broken, and the paste ruby spun on its thin gold chain, over-bright in the wavering lamp light. Mari tried to swallow but her throat was tight. "Hannah," she whispered. "What happened to you?"

There was a sound behind her and she spun.

"Miss Swan, have you seen my wife's—" Victor Kingsley's words ended abruptly as he spied the pendant swinging from Mari's hand. The moment stretched for an impossibly long time, though it couldn't have been more than a heartbeat's duration. When Victor's surprise fell away, his jaw tightened, his brows pinching in a hard expression that sent Mari back a step until she felt the paneled wall behind her. His eyes still on Hannah's necklace, he took a step toward her.

"Does my wife know she employs a thief?" The words were low, spoken in a growl. Of course, he wouldn't acknowledge Hannah's necklace, but to accuse her of thievery—he could see her hanged, and she'd have no defense. No way to prove *he* was the villain, not her. But in that moment, seeing the intense anger in his eyes, she could well believe he'd committed murder against her sister.

Before she could think what to do next, the ship pitched again, this time more violently. The lanterns swung drunkenly on their hooks, and Victor's attention shifted. Seizing her chance, Mari darted around him. He called out, but she ran through the salon and fled into the companionway.

Her pulse thumped in her ears as she looked about frantically. She couldn't return to her own cabin. Victor would be certain to find her—and the necklace—and she wasn't about to let go of the only evidence she had to show for her weeks in Lady Philippa's employ.

On the deck above, the crew's shouts could be heard as the ship continued to pitch on the waves. She'd find no help in that direction. Then she chided herself for even thinking such a thing. The *Destiny's* captain and his crew answered to Victor. They wouldn't come to her aid, even without the fog and the sea demanding their attention.

"Miss Swan!" Victor called. With no other choice, she raced for the stairway leading to the hold.

Victor's call followed her as she descended. Her breathing was ragged as she found the heavy door at the bottom of the stairs, and she panicked to think it might be locked. Her fingers trembled and slipped on the latch until finally, she dragged the door open. Ducking inside, she closed it behind her and pressed her back against the wood. *Think!*

She had to hide. Victor would turn every inch of the ship over to find her if he were so inclined, but she couldn't remain hidden indefinitely. They were days from London.

Falmouth. They would dock there soon according to Victor's appointment book. She would hide until then and leave the ship when it was safe to do so. Her employment, she was certain, was at an end anyway. She'd have to find another way to continue her investigation, but now, with Hannah's necklace, she knew she was on the right course.

With a plan in her mind, her breathing calmed and she looked around. The hold's only illumination came from the ship's lanterns that flashed through the deck gratings high above. Her eyes adjusted slowly to the cavernous space.

In the center were a few wooden crates and burlap-wrapped bales, all lashed together with ropes tied to the floor through heavy iron rings. Some had shifted with the movement of the ship, creating crevices where a body might hide. Mari navigated the tethers, stepping carefully between the ropes and bales and pressed herself into the shadows.

The air was thick with the musty smell of cotton mixed with the sharp bite of salt and tar. She pinched her nose against a sneeze. The creaking of the ship's hull was loud in the enclosed space, but then she heard them: footsteps. Victor was coming down the stairs. Mari froze, her heart high in her throat as she clutched Hannah's pendant.

The door to the hold opened with a heavy scrape. "Miss Swan," Victor said, and there was a deceptive earnestness to his voice. "I must speak with you," he called.

His voice was closer now, and Mari wedged herself more firmly into the shadows.

Victor's footsteps paused, and she heard his exertions as he loosened one of the ropes. He began shifting the bales, searching. She held her breath as another sneeze threatened. Then came the sound of wood sliding on wood as he moved the crate closest to her.

The ship pitched steeply, and one of the bales tumbled from its place with a heavy thump. Mari stumbled, grabbing at the ropes to keep from falling as her hiding place was revealed.

"Miss Swan," Victor said when their eyes connected.

Mari finally found her voice, but it wasn't as strong as she would have liked when she said, "What did you do to Hannah?"

He jerked in surprise and peered more closely at her. Then, in the next wash of light from the deck lanterns, his dark brows lifted in recognition. "You're the sister, aren't you? Mari. You don't look much alike, but I can see it now in the shape of your eyes."

"You killed her," Mari said, amazed at her boldness.

Victor sucked in a sharp breath and his eyes narrowed. "I did not," he said.

Mari had to admire his acting talent as she almost believed him. But she'd just accused him of the vilest of acts. She didn't imagine he'd take her words lightly. She had a sudden image of his hands closing about her neck, squeezing until he choked the life from her. Or perhaps he'd simply toss her overboard and let the sea have her. Drowning, she thought, would be a worse fate than strangling. Her breath came swiftly, her chest rising and falling.

When the ship pitched again, she didn't waste the moment. Lunging from between the bales, she ran. The door was still open where Victor had come through. If she could make her way to the deck above and other people…

A wave struck the side of the ship. The force of it sent her sprawling, and pain shot through her elbow. The pendant fell from her grasp to skitter across the wood planks.

She saw Victor's intent a moment before his fingers closed around the thin chain. He pushed the necklace into his coat and reached a hand down for Mari as the ship leaned sharply again. The motion sent her pursuer stumbling against the crates with a pained grunt.

The ship's bell tolled above the sound of the sea. Mari scrambled to her feet and ran. Behind her, Victor grimaced as if he'd been hurt, but she didn't fall for his trick.

She scrambled through the doorway and up the stairs, only to pull up short when she nearly ran into Finnegan Doyle, the ship's chief mate. He smelled strongly of gin, but his words were steady as he said, "Ye'd best be makin' yer way back to yer quarters, Miss Swan. The fog's upon us, an' this stretch o' coast be rough enough as it is. Captain's ordered all passengers to remain below deck."

Mari answered automatically. "Yes, of course."

Doyle's eyes narrowed on her features, which she was certain must have betrayed her desperation. Victor couldn't be more than a few steps behind her. But any comment Doyle might have made was forestalled when Leo, the young deck hand, appeared in the hatch.

"Mr. Doyle! Sir!"

"Aye, what is it?"

"The aft pump's gone an' jammed again! Water's risin' fast in the bilge! Ye want me to fetch Mr. Blackwood to bring 'is tools?"

"Ah, blast and bugger! I'll see to't. Start bailin' straight away. Go on, quick as ye can!"

And then, opening the door to Mari's cabin, Doyle gave her a little shove inside.

———

MARI PACED THE narrow confines of her cabin. Three steps, turn, three steps and back again as waves lashed the side of the ship. Her heart fluttered in her chest as she waited. How long had it been since she'd escaped Victor? An hour? More? She'd heard sounds in the nearby cabins, but there'd been no sight of him. Surely, he would come for her. He didn't seem the sort of man to give in easily, and certainly not if he thought her a thief. She sank onto the end of her cot and tried to think.

As soon as she'd closed her door on Doyle, she'd lowered the lock, but it was little more than a scrap of wood. Next, she'd slid her small trunk to bar the way. Neither the lock nor the trunk would protect her from a man determined on entering, but there was nothing else with which to secure the door as her cot was bolted to the floor.

She was trapped. If Victor found her, there was no escape unless she meant to go through the gun port to the sea below. The thought of all that cold, dark water closing over her head made her shiver despite the sweat that gathered at her hairline. She thought again of Hannah and wondered what her sister's last thoughts must have been as the river took her life.

The ship's bow dipped low to plow the sea ahead, and urgent shouts sounded from the main deck above. Next came footsteps in the corridor outside her cabin. They paused, seemingly just beyond her door, and Mari froze, listening. She imagined she could hear Victor breathing on the other side. Only when the steps resumed, did she release her breath. She gripped her hands tightly and tried to recall what Ovid had written of Poseidon's son, who, though he was caught and bound with a hundred chains, "will escape his fetters and, changing his shape, will make himself what forms he will." If only she might find her escape so easily.

A moment later, she was jolted as the ship struck something hard. A horridly slow, grinding scrape echoed through her berth, drowning the sound of the waves. Wood creaked and splintered, and the entire vessel gave a tremendous shudder before pitching sharply to one side. Stunned, it took Mari a long moment to realize what had happened.

The *Destiny* had run aground.

HANNAH'S DIARY
28 APRIL 1819

Victor (yes, he is no longer the obscure Mr. K in my thoughts) has well and truly captured my affections, but I learned today he is betrothed and has been these last three years. Three!

She is the daughter of a marquess and so far above me in station that I dislike her immensely, though we have never met. The union was agreed upon by their fathers, and Victor assures me neither party feels any affection for the other. As if that changes the fact that he will soon be married and beyond my hopes.

I cannot credit my ill fortune. I must guard my heart, but I fear it may be too late.

CHAPTER 4

GAVIN AND THE others left the cliff, taking a small cart path at a pace far too dangerous for the conditions. The riders quickly outpaced those driving carts, hooves sliding and churning up cold mud in their wake.

As they neared the cove, they passed the leaning ruin of an abandoned croft, its walls half-hidden by brambles and ivy. A low-ceilinged stable crouched in the nearby shadows. It wasn't more than a crude linney, but it would serve as shelter for the horses while the men went ahead on foot.

As children, Gavin and his cousins had delighted in their grandfather's tales of hidden cellars and secret tunnels that ran beneath cottages like this one, but many of the smugglers' crofts were abandoned as the Crown's revenue men and lower taxes chipped away at the trade. Now, they sat crumbling and faceless, and the horses snorted as they were secured in the stable's dubious shelter.

Gavin led the way to the beach, and the roar of the waves crashing against the cliff drowned out any words they might have exchanged. Finally, they emerged onto the sand. The cove was sheltered from the worst of the fog, and the sight that greeted them was grim.

The ship had run aground some fifty yards from shore. She listed heavily, and her stern rode deeper than the bow. Waves pounded the hull and sent falls of water over the main deck. At least one beam was splintered, and the light at the masthead was dark.

Jory muttered an oath, and Gavin couldn't disagree. "Can you make out the name?" he asked.

"It looks to be the… *Destiny.*"

"Fateful," Gavin replied, though he didn't intend it as a jest.

He wiped mist from the lens of his glass and trained it on the vessel. Several men shouted and scrambled over the main deck. There was also the figure of a youth, possibly a cabin boy. Gavin moved the glass along the length of the deck and spied females huddled near the capstan.

Gryffyn and Alfie, having got the fires lit atop the cliff, joined them on the beach with more oil torches. Soon, they had stakes placed in the relative shelter of the cliff's brow, the flames writhing and hissing in the mist.

Gryffyn pulled Gavin aside. "'Twould seem we weren't the only ones who thought to signal," he said, opening his palm to reveal a broken scrap of mirror. It shone clean, as if it hadn't been atop the cliff for long. "There were footsteps in the mud," Gryffyn added. "At least two sets."

"Did you warn Merryn?" Gavin asked. If wreckers had lured the ship to shore, they'd arrive soon enough. He was surprised they'd not already done so.

"Aye. Alfie's adding to the guard."

Gavin gave his cousin a grim nod.

"What's keeping the captain from firing his lines?" Alfie asked.

Gavin had been wondering the same thing. In recent years, more ships had begun carrying Mr. Trengrouse's life-saving apparatus. The device consisted of rocket-fired cables and a chair to ferry passengers and crew to safety. It was an ingenious bit of invention, but it only worked if the crew deployed it.

"She's taking on more water," Roddie said.

Indeed, the ship's stern was considerably lower now. The tide had begun flowing, and the sea grew rougher by the minute.

The *Destiny* wouldn't last much longer.

"Find out where Evans is with the boats," Gavin said to Gryffyn. Newford's gigs were small, and they managed the currents well. They were the only hope of towing the *Destiny* off the rocks before she splintered completely, but he'd not risk it while people remained aboard. The captain needed to clear his ship.

Had it only been hours since Gavin had wished for something more exciting in his day?

——

MARI HUGGED HER arms about her in a futile effort to ward off the chill of the fog that wrapped the ship's deck like a living thing. The *Destiny* continued to moan and shudder while the tide battered its hull.

After the ship ran aground, Finnegan Doyle had come through, pounding a fist on all the doors and shouting, "Ho! Ev'ryone, to the deck with ye! Lively, now!"

Mari had been the first of the passengers to reach the deck, but now she stood with the ailing Beatrice near the capstan. The maid was pale, her skin damp from the fog. Their employer didn't fare much better where she stood near the forecastle. The green silk gown drooped about Lady Philippa's frame, and the poor woman didn't even have her wrap. She must have been frozen through.

Despite Doyle's calls, there'd been no sign of Victor, though his valet, Smith, stood near the bow. With every movement at the hatch, Mari's stomach lurched. Between her terror over drowning and waiting for Victor to appear, her nerves were near to breaking.

"Lady Philippa should have worn the burgundy silk," Beatrice murmured, heedless of the waves that washed over the deck to wet their feet. Her face was the color of chalk. She was in shock, Mari realized.

"Are you well?" she asked the maid.

With a crease pleating her brow, Beatrice said, "Why did you dress her in the green? She will think it was my suggestion."

Mari blinked. In her short time in the Kingsley household, it had become clear how much Beatrice valued her position as lady's maid. As the person responsible for attending to the personal needs of the lady of the house, Beatrice commanded more respect than many of the staff, but now hardly seemed an appropriate time to worry over their employer's attire.

"I—it was her preference," Mari said.

She noted then that Lady Philippa watched them. Her gaze slid from Beatrice to Mari where it remained for an uncomfortably long time. Mari swallowed, certain the lady could not have heard their words above the thrashing sea. Did she know about Mari's encounter with Victor? A tightness gripped her chest as the lady crossed to them, then eased when Philippa addressed the maid.

"Beatrice," she began. "I left my wrap—"

"I'll see to it, my lady," the maid said, and Mari was relieved to see a bit more color return to her features.

Doyle, who'd passed them in time to hear Beatrice's offer, growled, "No one goes below deck."

"My lady," a masculine voice said from behind them. Mari jumped, but it was only Charles Tate. "I couldn't find Kingsley below," he said.

Lady Philippa's brows slanted as her vacant expression yielded to worry. Lifting a hand to her throat, she said, "You don't think he's fallen overboard, do you?"

Tate's gaze flicked to the sea churning beyond the ship's deck before he said, "Most assuredly not. There are others at the quarter deck—I imagine he's taken refuge there."

Mari recalled Victor's pained grunt when she'd fled from him in the hold. It had been a trick, surely, nothing more than a play on her sympathies to make her stop.

She held her silence, her thoughts warring with her conscience, until she blurted, "Did you check the hold? Perhaps"—she licked her lips—"perhaps he's gone there for something."

"There's no reason for him to be in the hold," Tate said with a sharp tug on his sleeve.

"Captain," Doyle said, drawing their attention to a place in the fog as he lowered a sailor's glass from his eye.

Mari squinted until she could see the dim flicker of torches off the port side of the ship. The fog shifted, revealing the shadowy forms of several people as shouts came to them over the noise of the sea. Another ship? Or were they so close to shore?

"There be a dozen or more men on the beach," Doyle said, answering her question. "I'll fire the lines."

"Hold the lines," Henderson said, his dark beard shifting with his frown. "We don't know if we can trust their intentions."

"You don't think they mean to rob us?" Tate asked, to which Beatrice gave a startled gasp.

Henderson considered his reply before saying, "'Tis a possibility we can't ignore."

"We should wait then, for aid to arrive from another quarter," Tate said.

Doyle's mouth thinned as he stared at the man. Hands on his hips, he said, "D'ye see more ships? We should ask Kingsley—'tis his cargo at stake."

"It may be his cargo, but it's my vessel, and I'm still the captain," Henderson reminded them as the ship moaned loudly.

"Captain," Doyle pressed, "foul intentions or not, we've no other choice. No aid be comin' from 'another quarter.' 'Tis the beach or the sea for us."

As if to offer its agreement, the sea sent a wave thundering over the side of the ship, spraying them with icy water. The *Destiny* chose that moment to shift on its rocky perch. The sound of splintering wood was loud. The ship was breaking apart.

"Aye," Henderson relented. "Fire the lines, then."

Doyle moved to do so and soon, a bright streak whistled along the white belly of the sky, trailing a plume of sparks and a sturdy cable toward the figures on the beach.

Two more rockets were sent up in rapid succession from the quarter deck. Tension was applied at the other end until the lines were taut, holding the *Destiny* firm.

"Leo!" Doyle bellowed, and the cabin boy hurried across the tilting deck.

"Aye, sir!" Leo stood tall and straight before the seaman and lost his balance only once when another wave struck the ship. Despite his bravado, Mari detected a small quiver in his chin.

Doyle removed a crude wooden contraption from a sea chest and thrust it at the boy. "'Old fast to the chair," he said, "while I set the pulleys on the line."

"My lady," Henderson said, "you'll cross first."

Lady Philippa's eyes narrowed. "What do you mean, 'cross'?"

Tate indicated the chair clutched in Leo's hands. "Once Mr. Doyle has fixed the chair on the line," he said, "it will carry you across to the shore."

"On that? It's not but a bit of wood and rope!"

"That wood and rope will be our saving," Henderson said gruffly.

The ship rolled again, threatening the cables that held it and knocking Mari into the capstan. Just as she regained her balance, another wave swamped the deck. When the water finally fell away, Mari dashed a hand across her eyes to clear the salt from them. Then, softly, she heard a shout from somewhere below. She looked over the edge and there was the cabin boy, holding fast to the rail.

"Help!" Mari shouted. "Someone, help!" She held fast to the boy's shirt, but she wasn't strong enough to pull him up on her own. She held onto him as she continued to call for help.

Finally, Doyle heard her shouts and yanked the boy up and over the rail. "Ye clumsy fool!" he shouted. "Now ye've gone and lost the chair!"

Tate darted a glance between Doyle and Leo. "What—what do you mean, he's lost the chair?"

Everything about them was silent, save for the relentless pounding of the waves. And there, bobbing on the surf as the tide pushed it along, was the chair. The waves pulled it under, but it rose again to taunt them, floating ever farther away. Beatrice moaned, pressing her hands tight against her middle.

Doyle rounded on Leo. "I'll see ye lashed for this!"

The boy's thin frame shrank, and before Mari could think better of it, she stepped between him and the sailor. "Lashed!" she said sharply. "You will do no such thing."

Doyle snarled at her, but she stood her ground. Now was not the time for arguments, but neither could she remain silent while grown men threatened a young boy.

Beatrice moaned again. "What's to become of us?" she said breathlessly.

No one had an answer. Mari looked toward the shore again. The fog had shifted, and she could see the line of figures more clearly now. They might have been miles away rather than yards, though, for all the aid they could offer. The sea was too rough, and now, without Doyle's chair…

One man strode away from the rest to where the sea met the sand. He tossed his hat aside and, drawing a length of rope about his waist, he began to knot it. Mari's breath caught. He meant to brave the sea. He was a fool to think he might succeed, though she couldn't help but admire his courage.

Surely, though, his companions would make him see reason. Three of them strode to his side. They conferred there on the beach for a long moment before, against all reason, the others went for their own ropes. They were *all* going in the water. It was a town full of idiots.

As those on board the *Destiny* watched, the first man entered the surf, the rope that tethered him to his companions paying out slowly. Mari pressed cold hands to her mouth as he went under time and again, drawn beneath the waves by the flowing tide.

Once, she thought he must have succumbed, so long did he remain beneath the surface. When he finally emerged, her breath escaped her in a dizzying rush.

He was Perseus braving the sea monster, and Mari kept her gaze trained on his head, praying for but not expecting his safety. Finally, he drew alongside the *Destiny*. Clinging to the gunwale with one hand, he lifted the other in which he held, miraculously, their lost chair.

Doyle caught it, and shouts went up from the men on board, but they were premature. A strong swell lifted the ship, straining the cables and sending crew and passengers tumbling.

Perseus disappeared from the side. Mari held fast to the rail to maintain her footing, but a piece of timber swung down in a long arc, catching the side of her head. The last thing she remembered was Perseus's arms coming about her as the sea closed over her head.

HANNAH'S DIARY
16 AUGUST 1819

I can no longer ignore the signs: I'm in a family way. The smile that appeared on Victor's face when I told him was one I shall treasure, despite the fear that swirls inside me.

I wish to return to Drayton-Marsh, to Mari, but I know I cannot. My situation will ruin us both, and Mari will despise Victor. She's sure to tar him with the same brush she's used for Father, though Victor and Father are nothing alike. Victor would never abandon me, nor would he leave our child penniless. I am certain of it.

Victor suggested I remove to a village where I might pose as a widow. His visits will be those of a brother. This deceit weighs on me, but I see no other path.

CHAPTER 5

GAVIN LAID THE female on the sand and wondered if his ham-handed rescue had drowned her, or if the force of the mast striking her head had done her in. There'd been no chance of getting her back on board the *Destiny* safely, where she might be ferried by means of the chair, so he'd been left to return to shore with her.

The sea was rougher than he'd anticipated, and he'd shielded her from the rocks with his body as he fought to get them both to dry land. Now, she lay cold and pale on the wet sand, dark hair clinging to her cheeks like seaweed. Spiky, wet lashes lay unmoving against her waxen skin.

"Rowe!" Gavin called, but the doctor was already running to his side with a blanket. Gavin took it and covered the woman, chafing her arms beneath the wool to warm them as Rowe bent to check her pulse. "Is she—?"

"She's alive," Rowe announced as the woman began to cough. The surgeon rolled her on her side as she expelled water.

When the coughing subsided, Rowe eased her back on the sand, and she opened her eyes. Her gaze bounced over the faces watching her until she found Gavin's.

"Thank you," she whispered.

Her voice was soft and earnest and raspy from her coughing, but he felt it all the way to his center, like a tuning fork had been taken to his ribs. He couldn't speak. It might have been the cold seeping into his bones, or the fog. Perhaps it had clouded his brain. He simply dipped his head once in reply.

Color soon began to return to her cheeks. When a commotion at the edge of the surf drew Gavin's attention, he left her in Rowe's capable hands to learn another figure bobbed on the waves. He waited while Jory strode in. His cousin dodged floating timbers and debris, and Gavin lost sight of him for an uncomfortably long time. When Gavin thought to go in after him, Jory surfaced with the figure, and Gavin hurried to lend his aid.

The man was limp but alive, his skin ashen. Gavin estimated his age at some thirty years. With trimmed hair and fine clothes, it was clear he'd been a passenger.

Together, Gavin and Jory settled the man in the shelter of a large boulder, away from the surf. "I have him," Gavin said as Jory left to watch for more swimmers.

Gavin covered the man with a blanket, and he coughed once, then again. He tried to speak, though his voice was faint. Gavin had to bend to hear him.

"Miss Swan," he said. "Find Marianne." He lifted one hand before allowing it to fall back onto the sand.

"Can you tell me your name?" Gavin asked.

"Kingsley." The man's voice was thin and pained.

"Are you injured, sir?" Gavin asked.

"Find her," Kingsley repeated more firmly, his hand finding new strength to grip the edge of Gavin's coat.

From the edge of the beach, Jory called to Gavin. With the chair restored to the ship, the rescue of the *Destiny's* crew and passengers was in full force now. Gavin was needed, but the man's gaze remained insistent. Gavin gave him a slow nod before leaving to join his cousin, his boots squelching in the wet sand.

The process to clear the ship was slow and steady. Over and over, the chair brought another from the *Destiny's* tilted deck and was returned by way of the hawser's pulleys. While they waited for the next passenger, Gavin's eye sought the lady he'd pulled from the sea. Did she belong to the finely dressed man—was she his Miss Swan? He didn't examine the pinch behind his ribs that accompanied the thought.

The sand where he'd left her was now bare. His gaze returned to Kingsley, propped against his boulder, but the lady wasn't there either. Then he spied her standing in the shelter of the cliff's brow, her blanket wrapped tightly about her shoulders. Her hair hung limp, but it was her posture that drew his interest. She stood straight and alone, a bit wary perhaps, but he sensed strength in her as well. Curls of fog twisted at her feet as if they were hers to command. This was the sort of lady who inspired ballads, like fair Rosamond or the maid Marian.

The hawser bounced as another took the chair at the other end, drawing his attention. Gavin winced at the ridiculous turn his thoughts had taken. Ballads? Thank providence he didn't know any sonnets or he might begin spouting them.

The lady met his gaze for a second time. His skin warmed beneath his wet neckcloth to be caught staring. Not just staring—he was *mooning*. He gave her a polite nod and looked away, relieved when the chair returned with the ship's carpenter.

Over the next minutes, a wind came up from the Channel, loosening the fog until they could see the *Destiny* more clearly. The tide still pounded the hull, but the ship remained lodged on her rock, the taut hawsers holding her. The rescue was nearly at an end, but there was one more member of the crew to come across. The *Destiny's* master, Captain Henderson.

Long moments passed, but the hawser remained still. Gavin sent a frowning glance to Jory, who shrugged in reply. When Gavin thought he might have to go into the sea again, the hawser jumped, and a man came across in a weathered coat with brass buttons.

"Captain," Gavin said when the man landed. Henderson wore the tanned skin of a sailor. His dark beard was trimmed, and sun lines edged his eyes.

The captain acknowledged him with a short nod. "Aye. Captain Oliver Henderson."

Gavin introduced himself then said, "Your chief mate reports you had eleven souls aboard."

"Aye," Henderson said. "Four crew and seven passengers." He paused before adding, "Not a one of them were meant for this fate."

"The sea can be a cruel mistress," Gavin agreed philosophically. When Henderson remained silent, he continued. "It could well have been worse, though. Your arrival makes a perfect count, Captain."

Henderson's silence turned to surprise. "All are accounted for?"

The captain would have been counting on his end, and Gavin realized now, he must not have seen his missing two has been rescued. "Aye," he said. "We pulled two from the sea. With the eight you sent across and now yourself, that makes eleven."

Henderson closed his eyes, and his shoulders fell. "All are accounted for," he murmured.

It had been a trying night, and they were all cold and bone-weary. The captain leaned heavily against a boulder, his gaze turning to what remained of his ship. "Is she insured?" Gavin asked.

Henderson nodded.

"Send word in the morning. I imagine the company's agent can arrive in a few days' time to begin his assessment."

The captain sucked his cheek. "I expect so."

A bell tolled nearby, and Roddie called down from the head of the cove. "The boats have come!"

Soon, two gigs emerged from the fog to round the cove. They sailed with lanterns swinging fore and aft and a trail of barrels towed behind them. Despite their arguments, Evans and Pengilley were two of the most successful pilots in Cornwall.

Gavin didn't doubt they'd be regaling a certain widow with tonight's tale soon enough, though their memories of the events were sure to differ.

The gigs cut through the surf, sails snapping as the wind picked up. The small crafts were designed for speed, and for navigating treacherous waters to ferry men and goods to and from the larger ships. The pilots maneuvered alongside the *Destiny* and hove to, waiting.

"Do the pilots have permission to board your vessel, Captain?" Gavin asked.

Henderson hesitated long enough that Gavin wondered what manner of cargo he carried. Finally, the captain assented, and Gavin gave the signal.

Several figures boarded from the gigs. They worked swiftly to tether the *Destiny* to the smaller crafts before removing the hawsers binding the ship to the shore. Henderson watched in silence as barrels were lashed beneath the hull to buoy his vessel. Slowly, as the tide continued to flow, the ship was lifted from its rocky mooring, the gigs straining at their tethers.

"You run an efficient rescue, Constable."

"It looks like your *Destiny* may be saved," Gavin replied. When Henderson remained silent, he added, "The cove is deep and wide enough to careen her. Our shipwright will see that repairs begin as soon as she can be secured."

Henderson's nod was far less hopeful than Gavin expected for a man who'd nearly lost his ship, but a good night's work had been done. All souls were saved. The shipwright, John Nance, would welcome the work, just as those on the beach would welcome their portion of the salvage reward. He returned his attention to the gigs and held his sigh, certain he'd soon be called to mediate Evans' and Pengilley's shares.

———

MARI'S HEAD THROBBED with a dull but even rhythm. She pressed a hand to her temple to soothe it, but when the thumping continued without cease, she set her mind to ignoring the pain. She was alive. That was reason enough to rejoice, though every memory of the sea folding over her head made her think of Hannah. What fear she must have known in her last moments!

Mari shivered and wrapped the blanket more tightly about herself. She swallowed, and when tears threatened, she focused instead on the place where Victor now sat with his back against a large boulder. He was hatless, his fine clothes soaked through. Clearly, he'd been knocked into the sea as she had been, though that was all Mari would ever have in common with Victor Kingsley.

She didn't think he'd seen her. Certainly, he made no move to approach her. He spoke to the man who'd pulled her from the sea—Perseus—but they were too far away to make out his words. When Perseus left, Victor closed his eyes. He remained still, propped against his rock, his features slack in the shadows.

His coat was open. Did he still have Hannah's necklace? She shouldn't let something so small trouble her so greatly, but the fact that Victor was in possession of her sister's most prized belonging was the only tangible evidence Mari had that something untoward had happened. It was the only proof that her intuition was not mistaken. And knowing Victor had had the pendant while her sister was put in the ground caused her pulse to pound in time with her head.

He looked to be… sleeping. If there was any justice in the world, he'd suffered some mortal injury during his swim to the shore, but then she saw his chest move. She watched and waited, and when Victor still didn't awaken, she approached him slowly.

The torches' light barely illuminated Victor's boulder, and the cliff threw dark shadows onto the narrow beach. Everywhere people bustled about, but no one paid her any notice. She gave the toe of his shoe a tiny nudge. He still didn't move.

Emboldened by the evening's events and the reassuring presence of others on the beach, Mari knelt and inched a hand into Victor's coat. His clothing was sodden, his torso firm but cold. Mari winced at her task, but Victor remained still, with not even a flicker to betray his awareness. Keeping her eyes on his face for any movement, she felt his pockets, finding the edges of a watch and the weight of his purse but no necklace.

She carefully withdrew her arm, but his hand shot out to grab her wrist with surprising strength. Mari barely avoided an undignified yelp as she jumped, tugging hard to free herself.

Victor's eyes were open now, the pupils large in the shadows as he held her gaze. She waited for him to call out, to denounce her as a thief or draw attention to them at the very least. He did neither but remained silent, a grimace pinching his features. With creases lining his forehead, his shoulders slumped as if he bore an uncommon weight upon them. An uncommon sorrow.

Mari hesitated, caught by his pained expression despite herself, but when Victor shifted his legs as if he might try to stand, she didn't linger. Spinning, she crossed the beach to put as much distance between them as she could. Retreating into the cliff's shadows, she stood beneath a stone ledge, cold despite the blanket's dry warmth.

Glancing up, she caught the gaze of the man who'd rescued her. He'd been watching her, and her skin instantly heated. Had he seen her at Victor's side? He must think her some sort of adventuress, to be rifling a man's pockets as he lay on the sand. But her rescuer returned his attention to the chair coming across from the *Destiny*, and she released the breath she'd been holding.

The activity on the beach continued and soon, Mari became aware of the soft sound of… crying. How was it possible to hear such a faint noise above the relentless wash of the waves?

Then she realized the noise came from behind her, from the cliff itself. Investigating, she found a small opening just large enough for a person to pass through. The crying came from inside, amplified by the cave's entrance.

She looked around, but no one else had heard it. Moving slowly, she took a lantern from the sand and entered. The cavern was much larger inside than it appeared. Her light lit the front, leaving the back in the darkest of shadows. Everything was silent save the hushed noises coming from the beach. Had her mind deceived her? Of course, it must have been the wind, playing tricks on her ears as it blew in from the sea.

But as she turned to go, the sound came again. It was the soft, unmistakable tears of a child.

Already, the sea had begun to advance on this end of the beach. The tide would fill the cave soon, and anyone still inside would be trapped. A shiver chased across her skin, brought on more by terror than the cold.

She didn't give a thought for her slippers, which were already sodden. Splashing through icy, ankle-deep water, she advanced into the cave. A narrow path wound between the stone walls, and she let the lamp lead her way. The path continued for some yards, and she followed the sounds, ducking beneath low points in the ceiling. And there, just ahead, was Leo, the young cabin boy. His pace was hurried, but he turned when she called out.

"Miss Swan," he said with a sniff. "I thought ye be Doyle." Wiping his nose with his sleeve, he stood straighter, and his slight frame nearly touched the ceiling.

"Leo, are you well?" she asked.

He nodded, though his assurance was punctuated with another watery sniff.

"Are you injured?" she tried again.

"Nah."

"Well, then, the tide has already begun to fill the cave. We must return to the beach," she said in her best school mistress voice. That tone was sufficient to scold gossiping schoolgirls, but it seemed to make little impression on a determined ship's boy.

"'Tis too late," Leo said without any hint of concern.

"What do you mean, it's too—" Mari stopped and listened, and she could hear it now: water swirling and flowing over rock as it entered the cave. The volume of it was increasing, and she prayed the cave's acoustics were making it seem closer than it was.

"We must go!" Mari urged, but Leo ignored her to continue up the dark path. She considered hauling him back to safety beneath her arm. He was slight, and she was stronger than she looked. She could do it. But then she held up her lantern to dispel the shadows and saw that the path continued up and away, well beyond Leo and around a bend in the stone.

"Wait!" she called. "Where are you going?"

He motioned behind him with a thumb. "'Tis an old smuggler's passage, like the one me mam 'ad in Lancashire."

Mari had heard stories about such things, about natural tunnels in the cliffs that were used to ferry illicit goods to and from the sea. There were any number of things wrong with this scenario. For one, she had no wish to meet an actual smuggler. For another, if this path were an old one as Leo said, who was to say they wouldn't find their way barred by fallen rocks? But at the sound of the water's flowing advance behind them, she hurried after the boy.

"And why are you taking the smuggler's passage?" she asked.

Leo hesitated, digging the toe of one shoe in the gravel on the cave floor. The sole gapped from the upper where the stitching had come loose to reveal a stockingless toe. With a sigh, he said, "I s'pose you'll be tellin' I left anyways."

"I'd not thought to," Mari replied, earning her a sharp look of surprise, "but I'd like to know why you're going. And where."

Leo cocked his head at her, the light from her lamp reflecting in his eyes. Turning his gaze to the ceiling, he murmured, "Doyle means to see me lashed. I'll 'ave me punishment again, but mebbe if I find a mislaid bottle of somefing—"

"Lashed *again*!"

"Aye, for droppin' the chair this time. A ship without discipline be a rudderless vessel," Leo said. There was little inflection in his voice, as if he recited an oft-repeated lesson. He stood taller, or as tall as the low ceiling allowed, and showed no hint of the fear such a prospect must have wrought. Mari's heart tightened just the same.

"Even the strongest ship must steer clear of the rocks," she returned. "No one is lashing anyone," she said for the second time that day.

HANNAH'S DIARY
3 SEPTEMBER 1819

I've chosen Eventon for my new residence. It's as close to Mari as I dare, and it gives me comfort to know she'll be nearby. I'm ashamed to think how eager I was to leave Drayton-Marsh when now I wish only to return.

Victor has acquired a cottage. He says it is a charming property, with the River Frome flowing gently behind it. I will go there tomorrow and begin this new life of mine.

CHAPTER 6

GAVIN LEFT HENDERSON'S side to find Rowe crouched beside Kingsley. The surgeon allowed the man's hand to fall to the sand before looking up at Gavin. "He's gone," he said with a shake of his head.

"Gone?" Gavin echoed with surprise. The man had been alive only moments before. He appeared young and fit—not more than a year or two above Gavin's own age—and now he was gone. Gavin scrubbed a hand over his face as the surgeon closed the man's eyes.

"Victor?" A woman in a sodden green gown hurried across the beach, stumbling in the sand in her haste. Gavin recognized her as one of the first passengers to come across on the chair. Her arms, pebbled with gooseflesh from the cold, were held tightly about her middle, and Gavin motioned to Daniel to bring more blankets.

He recalled the dead man's worries over his missing lady. "Miss Swan?" he said as he stepped forward.

The woman gave him an arch look and knelt at the man's side. "I am Lady Philippa Kingsley," she said. "This man is my husband."

Gavin tucked his chin on an inward wince for his error.

"Victor?" the woman said again. She hesitated uncertainly before reaching for her husband's bare hand. Then, with another glance for Gavin and Rowe, she said, "Is he…?"

"I'm sorry, my lady," Rowe said gently.

The woman stared at him for a long beat, brows knit above her slim nose, before awareness eased her expression. She held one hand against her throat as she took in the full import of the surgeon's regret.

Gavin stepped away, leaving Rowe to see to the new widow. He'd never been comfortable with the grief of others, and he regretted he'd not thought to send someone for the vicar.

Alfie called to him then. "The tide comes in more fully now," he said. "Soon, there won't be any beach left."

His cousin was right. The cove had been steadily shrinking. The sea would soon flow over the sand

and fill the nearby caves. They needed to move everyone to dry ground and secure the area against wreckers—

"Still no trouble?" he asked his cousin.

Alfie shook his head. "All remains quiet."

News of a foundering ship usually brought the usual gang of wreckers from nearby Truro. Gavin could only assume they'd found better pickings elsewhere. He shook his head, but he'd not go borrowing trouble. There were too many other things to see to at the moment. Securing the *Destiny*, to be sure, but accommodations for the crew and passengers must be paramount.

He found Roddie and leaned close to ask, "Can the Feather accommodate these people?"

"Wynne will be glad to fill the rooms. You know she's happiest when the inn is full." Gavin gave him a wry look, and Roddie hurried to add, "I'll see that she provides a fair bill."

"'Twill be some time afore anyone can return to the *Destiny* to collect their things," Gryffyn said. "Keren and I will organize clothing for those who need it."

"Speak with the vicar about the boxes for the parish home," Gavin said. "To be sure, these poor souls are deserving of a bit of charity."

He thought again of the woman who'd just lost her husband, though he doubted the parish boxes held anything suitable for a lady of quality. An overdressed man in a patterned waistcoat sat with the widow, who was huddled tightly in a worn quilt some distance from Kingsley's body.

The man left her side and approached Gavin. "Sir," he said, "I am Mr. Charles Tate, Victor Kingsley's man of affairs. Lady Philippa has suffered quite a shock. I insist that she be given warm and dry accommodation immediately."

Gavin motioned to Roddie. "Mr. Teague will see that everyone is transported safely to the inn."

"In a private carriage, I should hope."

Gavin's brows drew together before he could remind himself these people had just suffered a tremendous ordeal. "I'm afraid we're unable to secure a private carriage," he said evenly, "but we'll do our utmost to see everyone is made comfortable."

Tate nodded, though it was clear from his manner that he wasn't pleased. "And what's to be done with the remains?"

The bald nature of the question, so soon after the man's death, caught Gavin by surprise. He opened and closed his mouth before replying, "We'll see that Kingsley is transported to the surgery and prepared for burial."

Jory joined them then. Catching Gavin's eye, he cleared his throat. His manner was thoughtful.

Cautious, even, though Gavin supposed that could be attributed to the grim topic. Still, he couldn't ignore the sense that Jory held his words. Gavin pulled him aside as Tate returned to the widow.

"What is it?" he asked.

Jory's jaw slid to one side as he considered the people milling about the beach. Then, with a quiet motion of his head, he led Gavin back to the dead man.

"There's something off about our friend's injury."

With a frown, Gavin said, "How d'you mean?"

Jory lifted his lantern and pulled Kingsley's dark coat aside. Beneath it was a waistcoat, pale grey silk by the look of it, and finely made. But what caught Gavin's eye was the large cut in the cloth over the man's abdomen, an inch or more in length, and the blood staining the fabric around it.

He closed the coat back over it and now, with the light of Jory's lamp, he could see a similar cut in the coat. The blood staining the dark cloth had been obscured by the shadows.

"'Tis an injury from the flotsam, per'aps?" Gavin said.

Jory shrugged one shoulder. "It could be, I suppose, but the cut—it seems too cleanly done."

Gavin couldn't disagree. He rubbed his jaw. "Bring Rowe," he said, "but be discreet about it."

His cousin brought the surgeon, who knelt in the sand next to Gavin.

After showing him Kingsley's injury, Gavin said, "D'you think this man was stabbed?"

"'Twould appear so, but I won't know for certain 'til I've had a chance to examine the body proper."

Gavin stood. "If 'tis true, it might explain why he was found in the water. Someone meant to hide their crime by hoisting him overboard."

Rowe tilted his head in agreement.

"Can we keep this between us until you know more?" Gavin said quietly. There was no sense upsetting anyone—the magistrate included—until Rowe had completed his examination.

With a wry snort, Rowe replied, "I've been surgeon in Newford for nearly forty years, Constable, long before you were even born and well before the smuggling ceased. I know when—and how—to keep a secret."

"Calm yourself," Gavin said. "I meant no offense."

He looked up, and the shadows on the narrow beach took on a more sinister weight. If they were right about the nature of Kingsley's wound, then one of the *Destiny* lot had committed murder. He studied the people scattered on the sand. Some were huddled in their blankets and others milled about anxiously, eager to quit the damp and cold for a warm hearth. It was then that Gavin noticed the female he'd brought ashore—Maid Marian—was no longer among them.

———

GAVIN FOUND NO sign on the beach of his missing female, nor the cabin boy, Leo. How they'd gotten past Alfie and the others who'd stood guard against the wreckers he couldn't say, nor had he any notion where they might have gone. But Newford was small, and he knew every household. He'd find her soon enough.

He and his cousins escorted the *Destiny* lot to the top of the cliff, where wagons waited to take everyone to the inn. They were an exhausted bunch as they retrieved their horses—cold and hungry and soaked through for their efforts—but as Roddie, Merryn and the others rode ahead, Gavin held back. He cast a long and speculative glance at the croft before leaving his horse at the edge of the trees.

The cottage was dark, deserted as expected, and the overgrowth didn't appear to have been disturbed. His coat caught on the thorns as he pulled a thick vine away from the entry until he found the knob. He didn't bother extinguishing his lantern. As loudly as the hinges protested when he entered, there was no point to any secrecy.

Inside, the cottage was still, the air close and dank with disuse. He lifted his lamp and swung it in an arc from corner to corner. Cottony webs clung to the ceiling, and vermin had chewed holes in the plaster. The room was empty, but just there, drops of water mingled with the dust on the floor to create a muddy grey trail.

Smiling, he looked more closely and saw that the corner of the rug was askew. He pushed it aside with the toe of his boot to find the edge of a wood-planked door—one of the secret tunnels of his grandfather's stories.

He left the rug and the tunnel door and followed the muddy trail to a room at the back of the cottage. It was a tiny bedroom with a bare cot and washstand. The window was open, but the sill was still dry, free of the night's damp mist. It hadn't been open for long. Poking his head through, he looked down to where thorny bushes lay beneath the window. They were thick and unbroken, the damp ground beyond them undisturbed.

Turning sharply, Gavin studied the room. There was nowhere for a person to hide except... He knelt to peer beneath the bed.

Two pairs of eyes looked back at him—one green and wary in the reflected light of Gavin's lantern, the eyes of the boy. The other pair was dark and thickly lashed. His missing female.

She gave an audible sigh.

"Miss Swan, I presume?" Gavin said.

"I tol' ye they'd find me," the boy whispered, loud enough for Gavin to hear.

Gavin assisted them from beneath the bed and gave them his name.

Leo's shoulders rounded. "'Ave ye come to lash me then?"

"Of course he has not," Maid Marian assured him as she stepped between Gavin and the boy. Though fierce, her features were pale, no doubt a lingering effect of her recent tumble into the sea. Or, he reflected, a queasiness owing to her hand in Kingsley's death.

"Miss Swan didn't have nuffin' to do wif me runnin' off," Leo said. "'Twas all me own doin', but I'm prepared to face me fate."

"And why are you running, Master Leo?" Gavin asked. Was *this* the culprit he was seeking? He couldn't imagine this thin scrap of a boy perpetrating such violence on Kingsley, but worse things had been done by younger boys.

"On account of losin' the chair," Leo said. "I didn't mean to, but the sea was somefin' fierce tonight. Doyle says 'e'll see me lashed. I don't fancy bein' lashed again, but I'll accept me due." He pulled his shoulders back at the end of this speech, a show of false confidence if Gavin had ever seen one.

"No one is getting lashed tonight," he said.

Miss Swan swayed a bit where she stood before the cot. In fact, she wasn't looking well at all. Gavin kept an eye on her as he crossed to close the window.

"Miss Swan, are you well?" he asked.

"I am fine."

Another show of false confidence, though Gavin couldn't miss the slight tremor in her voice. She lifted trembling fingers to her temple as if to ward off a headache, and as she brought her hand down again, she studied her sleeve. If anything, Miss Swan paled even more until she was the color of Newford's summer clouds. That was when Gavin spied the blood staining the pale blue muslin—a stain she might have gotten during an altercation, perhaps, whilst fatally stabbing a man.

"Miss Swan," he said sternly, jaw tight. "How did you come by the stain on your sleeve?" He took a step forward, fully prepared to apprehend the lass if she tried to run. But then she swayed again, and for a second time, the lady landed in his arms.

CHAPTER 7

THE PASSENGERS AND crew of the *Destiny* were given warm accommodations at the Feather, and Rowe was summoned to tend Miss Swan. Gavin waited impatiently for her to wake, but when the surgeon informed him it could be some hours yet given the good-sized lump on her head, he went in search of information. He found the captain installed in a modest room at the top of the inn's wide stairs. He knocked and after a long moment, the captain's gruff command came: "Enter."

Henderson sat by the window, eyes fixed on the darkness beyond the thick panes. A half-empty glass of amber liquid sat at his elbow. He'd shed his captain's coat to reveal a worn but clean shirt and trousers, and exhaustion added more lines to the man's already weathered face.

"Brandy?" Henderson said with a nod toward the bottle on the table.

"Thank you, but no," Gavin replied. "I find coffee allows me to keep my wits about me, and 'tis just as warming." He had no objection to others imbibing, but he preferred to be in full command of his faculties.

"What will you do, I wonder, when you wish to lose your wits?" the captain murmured.

Gavin had no answer for that, nor did he think the other man required one. Finally, Henderson looked up from his study of the window to examine Gavin in the dim light of the room's single lantern. "As a former naval man myself," he said, "I know another when I meet him. Where did you serve?"

"My final post was aboard the *Bellerophon*," Gavin replied. Five years later, the words still caused pride to expand in his chest, though he, along with many of his fellow sailors, had since been jettisoned by His Majesty's Navy.

"The Billy Ruffian," Henderson said with a low chuckle. "Were you aboard at Rochefort?"

"Aye. I witnessed Boney's surrender myself." Gavin still recalled the occasion of the *Bellerophon's* return to Plymouth Sound. They'd been met by countless boats, all filled with people eager for a glimpse of the Corsican. As they'd passed through, their colors flying from the stern, his companions had grumbled at the spectacle, though they'd all stood a little taller. Gavin wouldn't deny he'd felt like an important cog in an even more important machine. He'd been part of something larger than himself, and the sensation had been intoxicating.

But he'd not come to Henderson's room to reminisce. Turning them to the matter at hand, he said, "Captain, I need to speak with you regarding the events aboard the *Destiny*. You're aware that Victor Kingsley is dead?"

Henderson's gravity returned. "Aye. I saw him loaded aboard the surgeon's cart." He closed his eyes briefly before adding, "Some sort of injury, I take it."

Gavin nodded but refrained from revealing the nature of Kingsley's wound. "I need to ask you about the events leading up to his death," he said.

Henderson gave a weary nod and motioned for Gavin to sit. "I don't know that I'll be of any use, but I'll answer your questions as best I can."

Gavin sat and crossed one leg over the other before turning the page in his notebook. "You and the chief mate said there were eleven aboard the *Destiny*," he began. He read off his list of passengers. "Mr. and Mrs. Victor Kingsley. Charles Tate and his manservant. Kingsley's manservant Mr. Frederick Smith. Lady Philippa's maid Beatrice Jones and the lady's companion, Miss Swan."

"Aye, that's correct."

"For the crew, you had yourself and your chief mate, Finnegan Doyle. The cabin boy Leo, and Tobias Blackwood, who served as carpenter. Is that all? Was there no cook or boatswain?"

"Blackwood served as both cook and carpenter."

"Was that the usual arrangement?"

Henderson didn't answer immediately. Gavin didn't press but waited silently until Henderson continued. "No," he admitted. "But this was to be my final voyage. Many among the crew have already taken positions aboard other vessels."

"Your final voyage? How so?"

"I mean to retire," Henderson said. He poured another finger of brandy from the bottle and tossed it down in one swallow. He grimaced before adding, "My daughter is ill. Some sort of cancer, the physician says. She has a cottage north of Manchester and two young children she can no longer keep up with. I aim to leave the sea for the life of a respectable farmer."

"I'm sorry to hear of her troubles," Gavin said. "'Twill be quite a change, I imagine, for a man accustomed to captaining a vessel." He recalled his own adjustment on leaving the sea had been less than smooth. He'd returned to Newford, unsure of his place in the village that had always been his home. He still was, at times.

"Aye, a change to be sure, but a welcome one," Henderson said. "I've rarely had my feet in one place for more than a sennight at a spell. 'Twill be nice to have them rooted for once."

"Roots can be confining."

"Or they can be a steady anchor in an uncertain sea," Henderson returned.

Gavin leaned back in his chair and studied his notebook. "Where were you bound?"

"London."

He considered the captain's reply before saying, "Was the sea Kingsley's normal mode of travel? Wouldn't the overland route from Bath have been more direct?"

"Aye, if Kingsley wished to travel directly to London, but he had another destination along the way."

"Where?"

"Falmouth."

Falmouth wasn't far from Newford. In fact, the *Destiny* would have run aground shortly after leaving Falmouth's harbor. "Did you spend much time there?" Gavin asked.

Henderson took a long swallow from his glass before saying, "We didn't stop." At Gavin's raised brow, he added, "The fog altered our course. I thought to put in at Falmouth on the return, but... Well, I suppose there's no point to it now."

"Did Kingsley have business there?"

"I imagine he must have," Henderson replied.

Gavin rubbed the side of his jaw before puffing his cheeks on a sigh. It seemed his questions were only begetting more questions, and he felt like he wasn't asking the right ones. "How long have you sailed for Kingsley?" he said.

"Two years now." Henderson poured more brandy, and the bottle clinked noisily against the glass. Gavin wondered if he'd get through this interview before the captain fell asleep, but the man seemed no worse for his imbibing. If anything, the spirits seemed to loosen his words, so Gavin remained silent and waited.

Soon enough, the captain drew a long breath and explained, "I'd just put everything I had into acquiring the *Destiny*, and Tate was seeking a ship to make regular runs for Kingsley between London, Bristol and Manchester. A few jaunts to Dublin here and there."

"Is Tate an investor in the venture?"

Henderson snorted. "He's naught but Kingsley's man of business, to my knowledge. Not that he wouldn't like to be more."

Gavin couldn't forget the blood on Miss Swan's sleeve, but neither could he ignore such an intriguing line of thought as Henderson had opened. "What does Kingsley's death mean for Tate?" he asked.

"Does he gain any interest in the firm?"

"You'd have to ask him," Henderson replied.

"To your knowledge, was the association an amicable one?"

"They seemed agreeable enough to me…"

"But…?"

Henderson released a quick breath. "Kingsley has been—or *was*—more distracted of late. He's turned over more of the business to Tate."

"Distracted? In what way?"

"It seemed as if something weighed on him—something more important than his commercial interests."

"D'you know what that might have been?"

Henderson shook his head.

"What was he transporting to London?"

The captain stood and retrieved a folded sheaf of papers from his coat. "The usual," he said as he passed the papers to Gavin. "Silk, wine… wool from the mills."

Gavin opened the papers to find the ship's manifest. The ink was smudged in places, but the list of items in the ship's hold was brief. He committed the figures to memory before returning the papers to Henderson.

"It seems like a light cargo," he said.

Henderson's only reply was to empty the last of his bottle into his glass.

Gavin brought the conversation round to Kingsley's movements aboard the *Destiny*. He needed to establish the order of events and the timing of Kingsley's wound.

"Captain, when was the last time you saw Victor Kingsley alive?"

Henderson considered this with a lowered brow. "He was in my cabin for supper. The fog had already started gathering by then, but Tate always insists on formality, so we dine in full dress."

"This was shortly before the *Destiny* ran aground?"

"Aye."

"And afterward, did Kingsley join the others on the quarter deck?"

Henderson shook his head. "No. I counted to be certain, but I never saw him."

"Was Miss Swan above deck?"

"Miss Swan? Oh, the companion. Yes, I believe she was the first to arrive after we ran aground. When she went overboard, I assumed Kingsley must have suffered a similar fate." Henderson straightened, and his eyes sharpened. "Constable, why do I have the impression you believe Kingsley's death was more than an accident?"

"I'm just trying to sort the facts," Gavin said. After a long moment, Henderson leaned back, rubbing his hands once along his thighs, and Gavin continued. "So you dined in your cabin, even with the carpenter serving as cook?"

The captain released a short breath. "Aye. Blackwood did his best, but I dare say the fish soup and boiled vegetables were never going to measure up to Tate's standards."

"Tate's? Not Kingsley's?"

"For all his wealth, Kingsley isn't a pretentious man."

Gavin didn't correct his use of the present tense. "Who dined with you?" he asked.

"There were three others—Tate, Kingsley and his wife, Lady Philippa."

Gavin leaned forward. "And I gather Kingsley was uninjured at supper?"

"He appeared so, as far as I could tell."

"Where was Miss Swan during this time?"

"Why, I imagine she must have remained in her cabin."

Gavin slid his jaw to one side, considering. He was missing something, he was certain. "What was the nature of Kingsley's interactions with Miss Swan?"

Henderson's brows pitched into a steep V. "I can't say I paid any heed to his manner with his wife's companion. Why would I?"

"How would you describe Miss Swan's demeanor? Did she get on with her employer?"

"I imagine so. She seems a quiet thing, keeps to herself mostly."

"Have you encountered her on previous voyages?"

"No," Henderson said with a shake of his head. "But then, Kingsley was newly married, and this was the first time his wife traveled with us, so I wouldn't have."

Gavin considered all that Henderson had told him. There was nothing to point to anything unusual or suspicious regarding Miss Swan. By the captain's account, Victor Kingsley had been well and unharmed at supper. Then, after the ship ran aground, he'd not appeared with the others above deck, though Miss Swan had been the *first* to arrive. Perhaps Kingsley's injury *had* been nothing more than a casualty of the wreck. He held a sigh and asked, "How long were you at supper?"

"Not long at all. The bilge began taking on water, and I left to see to that. Kingsley had already gone by then as well."

Gavin, who'd been turning the pages in his notebook, lifted his head. "Kingsley left? In the middle of supper?"

"Aye. He went to fetch something from his cabin, I believe."

So, Kingsley had left supper to return to his cabin. Sometime between then and the ship running aground, he'd received a mortal injury. Had he encountered Miss Swan? Had he gone to *meet* Miss Swan? To what purpose? Nothing Henderson said supported such a theory, but he couldn't forget the blood staining the woman's gown.

Henderson cleared his throat, drawing Gavin's attention once more. The older man closed his eyes, and his voice roughened as he said, almost to himself, "If I'd known Kingsley's fate, I might have…"

Gavin frowned. "You might have…?"

Henderson looked up and his gaze met Gavin's. He appeared worn and weary in the yellow light of the lantern—from drink or sorrow, Gavin couldn't say. "I don't know," he said. "I suppose there was nothing to be done about the fog or the tide, but if we'd sailed earlier, we might have avoided both."

"If you'd sailed earlier—was that your intention?"

"Aye."

"What delayed you?"

"Kingsley. He decided to join us at the last moment, and we were forced to wait until his party arrived at the wharf. Isn't that a fine bit of irony?"

———

THE REMAINING MEMBERS of the crew had little to offer beyond what Gavin learned from Henderson.

The chief mate, a surly Irishman named Finnegan Doyle, reported that he'd been too preoccupied with the malfunctioning bilge pump and then with clearing the *Destiny* to notice anything out of the ordinary with Kingsley. Mr. Blackwood, the ship's carpenter-turned-cook, offered a similarly unhelpful report.

When he finished his questions and Miss Swan still had not awakened, Gavin found his cousin in the apartment she shared with Roddie.

"I'll not let you stand over the lady's bed," Wynne said when he asked her to accompany him to Miss Swan's room. "'Tis unseemly."

Gavin forced his jaw to relax. "Then tell me which room you've given the widow." If he couldn't talk to Miss Swan, perhaps he could learn more from Kingsley's wife.

"I'll not let you bully that poor woman, either." With a pointed look toward the still-dark street beyond her window, she added, "She's a new widow, and the sun's not even begun its climb yet. You can speak with her at a proper hour."

Gavin went next to Rowe's surgery, but the windows there were dark, too, and there was no answer to his knock. The blue-black ink of the night sky was only now beginning to yield to pink and orange.

Reluctantly, he admitted Wynne was right.

He retrieved his horse from the Feather's stables, intent on returning to the cove. It took him longer than he wished to mount, but devil take it, he was stiff. His every muscle ached from the previous day's exertions, and already he had dark bruises where he'd been battered against the rocks. He was grateful the Feather's grooms were too busy to witness his lack of grace, and when he finally found his seat, he turned the horse and rode back to the beach.

The tide had receded, and a pair of long-legged redshanks dug for mussels in the tide pool. By the time he reached the cove, the rising sun was throwing its first rays across the small beach, illuminating the *Destiny* where she lay on the sand. She'd been beached at an angle, a significant portion of the torn hull exposed for repair.

The shipwright's men had worked through the night by the light of the moon, and many remained. Beams were driven into the sand, and wide planks laid across them to form a makeshift quay. Gavin strode across the beach, stepping over flotsam that had washed ashore during the night. As he approached the ship's hull, he caught sight of John Nance directing the work from where he balanced atop a heavy timber.

"Nance," Gavin called, raising a hand in greeting. "A word?"

John Nance climbed from his loft, nimble despite

his years. The shipwright was a trim man of middling height, with shoulders broad enough to carry a ship's beam and hands like gnarled driftwood.

"Aye, Kimbrell," Nance said in his gravelly voice. "Quite a night's work," he said with a nod toward the ship. "I hear 'twas a near thing, getting 'er off the rocks. She's battered right enough, but she'll float again—which is more than many can say after such a scrape."

"I need to go aboard," Gavin said.

Nance's expression was grim. "Not today, ye don't. The hull's split in three places, and the deck's not safe to tread."

"There must be some way—"

Nance shook his head, his tone firm but not unkind. "We need to shore up the hull first and secure the deck. Then ye can go aboard."

"How long?"

Nance considered. "A week, per'aps more." Gavin's frustration was high, but he knew the shipwright spoke sense. He'd have to find his answers elsewhere. "You'll inform me when 'tis safe to board?"

"Aye," Nance replied. "The moment she's secure, you'll be the first to hear't."

"Nance," Gavin added as the man started to go, "set one of your men to guard her at night."

The shipwright gave him a curious tilt of his head, and Gavin could see him calculating the cost of such a measure. Before Nance could offer any argument, Gavin added, "Those who stand guard will be paid."

"Aye, Constable," Nance said with a grin. "The lads will appreciate the extra coin."

He left, and Gavin mentally tallied the cost to his own purse. He doubted the squire would permit the expense for Nance's men, but he couldn't allow any evidence to be removed before he'd had a chance to go aboard.

Turning to go, he was surprised to find Leo at his heels, kicking the sand. The boy bent and retrieved a shell. Pulling back his arm, he flung it in the direction of the rocks rising from the surf where the *Destiny* had run aground. The boulders closest to the shore resembled a tortoise, and it was hard to recall the angry sea of the day before. Another shell soon followed the first, then another.

The lad had enthusiasm, if not strength. Or accuracy, come to that, if he meant to aim for the rocks. His shells flew short and wide of the mark.

Without speaking, Gavin found a perfectly smooth, flat rock. He brushed sand from it and sent the stone skipping along the surface of the cove. It sank just short of the tortoise.

Leo's eyes widened. "Cor! How'd ye do that?"

"The trick is in the wrist," Gavin said, "and a fitty *lèch*."

"Huh?"

"A proper stone with a flat bottom," Gavin clarified, forgetting the lad was an incomer. "Here now, try this one."

He found a proper stone for skipping and handed it to the lad. Leo flung it with fervor, and the rock disappeared with a resounding, disappointing *plop!*

The boy gave a fierce scowl, and Gavin wondered if he'd ever been so young. Or so spindly. There didn't seem to be much to Leo but bones and the skin that held them.

Gavin had joined His Majesty's Royal Navy as a ship's boy much like Leo, but he'd been twelve to Leo's… nine? Ten? To be sure, he'd had a few years on the lad. Even so, Gavin's lieutenant had shown uncommon patience and grace with the young boy under his command—a kindness Gavin would never forget.

"'Tis a proper start," he said to Leo. "But you must move your arm like this." He demonstrated, amused but not encouraged when Leo imitated the motion with no grace at all. "Or you might try your hand at collecting mussels," he said, "if rock skipping is not to your liking."

"Doyle says I gots the strength of a flea and the"—Leo's expression twisted as he recalled his chief mate's words—"spindle-shanked manner of a new colt."

The boy's brow pitched low as he relayed his officer's less than favorable opinion, and Gavin chose his words carefully. "Aye, but the colt can grow to be a proper stallion in time."

Leo's brow lifted in surprise. "Do ye think that's 'is meaning?"

"Whether he means it or not, 'tis the truth."

Leo tried another rock, and another, with little success. As the lad tossed half the beach into the sea, Gavin returned his thoughts to the puzzle of Victor Kingsley. He handed another stone to the boy and said, "How long have you been employed aboard the *Destiny*?" The boy shrugged, and Gavin, eyeing his worn shoes and too-short sleeves, rephrased his question. "How many shirts have you worn since joining the crew?"

"Oh." The boy paused to think before saying decisively, "Two."

So, the lad had probably spent a couple of years, more or less, on the ship. "What are your duties?"

"Me duties? I does whate'er Doyle needs. Fetch things and run messages and the like."

"In the course of your duties yesterday," Gavin said, "did you encounter Mr. Kingsley?" Leo stopped throwing and considered the question with a squint. Gavin prompted him with, "Did you see him at supper, per'aps, or hear him below deck?"

Leo's expression cleared. "Aye, I heard 'im, I did. He was in 'is bunk when I went to tell Doyle 'bout the bilge."

That made sense. The captain had said Kingsley left supper to retrieve something from his cabin. Gavin found another skipping rock and handed it to Leo. "Was there anyone with him?" he asked.

"Oh, aye, 'e was with Miss Swan."

Gavin's stomach dropped, though he couldn't say why. He'd suspected Miss Swan of ill deeds as soon as he noticed her absence from the beach. Leo's statement shouldn't have come as a surprise, nor should it have caused such an uncomfortable queasiness. He would have pursued it with another question, but he was hailed by a man descending the cliff path at a rapid pace.

The newcomer was impeccably groomed, with dark hair that was shiny and slicked back with an excessive amount of pomade. He wore long sideburns angled halfway across his cheeks and carried a leather case on one shoulder. With his tailored suit and crisp collar, the man had clearly lost his way.

"Constable," the man said with a grin, "I was told I'd find you here. Percival Fairfax." He extended a hand and Gavin looked at it. "I represent Lloyd's," Fairfax added.

"Ah. You're the wreck agent," Gavin said. "You received Henderson's notification already?" He took the man's hand and found it damp and limp.

"Yes, yes, dreadful news about the *Destiny*. I've come to assess the loss. Were you present when she ran aground?"

Gavin replied that he and the others had arrived shortly thereafter, and Fairfax removed a notebook from his case. Gavin frowned to be on the other end of an investigator's inquiries, but he answered Fairfax's questions as best he could.

The man studied the underside of the *Destiny*'s hull. "Is that her?" he asked with a finger crooked toward Nance's dock.

It was a rather ridiculous question, Gavin thought, given the *Destiny* was the only wrecked ship lying about. "Aye," he said slowly.

"A significant loss then, but not a complete one," Fairfax said, shaking his head as he made a notation in his book. "Has anything been salvaged?"

"Cargo, d'you mean?"

"Yes. I assume your men have secured the area against wreckers?"

"We've ensured nothing has been taken from the wreckage."

"Good, good. The firm will be pleased to hear it."

"Nance, the shipwright, tells me 'twill be some days or more before she's safe to board—"

"Yes, that's often the way of it."

"—but it seems there isn't much cargo to be saved."

"Eh?"

"Captain Henderson showed me the manifest. The *Destiny* carried silks and wine but little else."

"You've spoken with the captain already?"

"I have," Gavin confirmed. "He's understandably dismayed over the incident."

"Of course, of course. What can you tell me of the weather conditions at the time of the wreck?"

With a sigh, Gavin answered the agent's questions as Leo continued flinging rocks into the surf. When Gavin thought to take his leave—surely, Miss Swan must have awakened by now—Charles Tate joined them. There were blue shadows beneath the man's eyes. He tipped his head in Fairfax's direction when the man introduced himself, then gazed regretfully at the battered hull of the *Destiny*.

Gavin waited until Fairfax left them before asking Tate what he knew of Kingsley's activities the previous day. Tate merely confirmed what Gavin had already learned from Henderson. Then Gavin said, "Now that Kingsley is gone, what becomes of his merchant venture?"

Tate studied a point over Gavin's shoulder for a long moment. When it seemed as if he wouldn't answer, he said, "Victor's enterprise will go to his heirs."

"Lady Philippa, I presume."

Tate's gaze narrowed as it returned to Gavin. "That's a matter best put to Victor's solicitor, Constable."

When he left, Gavin resolved to do just that.

HANNAH'S DIARY
12 OCTOBER 1819

Victor came again today. Each time he leaves Eventon, I feel the ache of our choices, and I wonder if this is what Mama experienced with Father. She, of course, had the benefit of marriage once they were found out, though I can't think she found any happiness in it.

I long for guidance. I long for my sister's embrace, but I cannot bring myself to tell Mari of my foolishness. She is clever and would never have found herself in such a situation. I must find my own strength.

CHAPTER 8

MARI WAS JOLTED awake by the blast from a coach horn and shouts below her window. Her eyes were scratchy, and she struggled from the depths of a nightmare in which Hannah was drowning, her face stark beneath the waves, and Mari could do nothing to save her.

She squinted against the cheery morning light streaming in around the lace-edged curtain and tried to place her surroundings.

She was at a coaching inn, that much was certain. Tucked up in a warm, dry room, covered with a warm, dry quilt that felt pleasantly heavy on her limbs. A wedge of golden sunlight stretched along the wood floor and up the creamy wall. Its amber warmth was a welcome change from the thick fog of the night before.

A vague memory surfaced of a tall man leaning over her. His form had blocked the light as he felt the pulse in her wrist with warm fingers. Perseus.

Constable Kimbrell, she corrected herself.

She tried to recall how she'd come to be at the inn. She suspected she'd fallen into the man's arms again. It was not her habit to faint or swoon, and yet she'd done so *twice*. She laid the blame for that on the pounding in her head. Lifting a hand to her temple, she felt gently round the tender knot that had formed beneath her hair.

The events of the previous day were vague in her mind, the edges blurred. She remembered searching the Kingsley cabin and finding Hannah's necklace. Then Victor Kingsley had found *her* and she'd run. Leo, the cabin boy, had nearly been washed overboard.

She recalled the timber that had knocked her from the ship's deck and into the sea. She'd been fortunate the constable was there, else she might never have surfaced again. She shoved herself up in the bed, wincing at the pain in her head, and studied the room.

It was modest but inviting, with a single window and braided rug. A fire popped in the small hearth to keep the morning chill at bay.

To her left, a sturdy chest of drawers stood against the wall with a pitcher and basin for washing. A round table and two chairs sat beneath the window with a jar of wildflowers and a small amber bottle. Laudanum, most likely, as she had a vague memory of an older gentleman—the surgeon, perhaps—poking at the bump on her head.

Mari checked beneath the quilt to find she wore only her shift. Her slippers had been stuffed with newspaper and set to dry before the fire, and a dressing gown that was not hers hung from a hook near the door. She might have found the room welcoming if not for the fact that her own gown was nowhere in sight.

And what, she wondered, had become of Leo? The poor thing had put on a brave show before the constable, but he was only a boy. He must have been terrified by all he'd endured the previous day.

Slowly, she swung her feet to the floor, and the room swam. With determination, she stood and crossed to the dresser where she opened the drawers one by one. Nothing. No gown, and the paper from Victor's appointment book was gone as well.

The *paper*. She recalled now cutting it from his book. What had it said? She'd taken the page for a reason, clearly, but no matter how she tried to recall what had been written there, the memory eluded her.

The door to her room opened and she spun, immediately regretting the motion. When her head cleared, she saw it was only a woman carrying a tray. The warm scents of toast and tea caused her mouth to water, and she realized she was famished.

"You're awake," the woman said. "Gavin will be pleased to hear it."

"Gavin?"

"Constable Kimbrell, that is." The woman introduced herself as Wynne Teague, proprietor and keeper of the Fin and Feather Inn. And cousin to the constable, she explained. The lady had cheerful curls the color of old copper, clear blue eyes and a rounded belly beneath her innkeeper's apron.

"Do you know where my things are?" Mari asked.

Mrs. Teague gave her a small smile of apology. "'Tis a question for the constable," she said.

Mari tucked her chin against a frown. She had a dim memory of the constable's intent gaze in the smuggler's cottage. It had felt… accusatory.

The woman bustled about, freshening the wildflowers on the table and drawing the curtains to admit more light. "I'll send up fresh water for the pitcher," she said. Then, taking the dressing gown from its hook, she added, "You'll be wanting this. Gavin waits in the corridor, and my cousin is nothing if not determined." And on that cryptic statement, she left.

Mari didn't have time to make sense of her

words before a knock came at the door.

"Miss Swan," a gruff voice called through the wood. "'Tis Constable Kimbrell."

Mari gasped, conscious of her state of undress, and hurried behind the screen.

———

GAVIN ENTERED MISS Swan's room and stopped. The lady stood before the privacy screen in one of his cousin's dressing gowns. The tapes were tied securely, but there was something altogether too intimate about the delicate lace at her throat and the sight of her bare pink toes peeping out from beneath the hem. She looked wholly incapable of stabbing a man to death.

He swallowed and reminded himself to remain objective. The truth was the truth, no matter how fetching its package. He placed his hat on a hook by the door and said, "You seem much improved today. To be sure, you're more sprightly than the last time I saw you."

"Constable," she said with a bit of coolness to her tone. "Where is Leo?"

"And a good day to you, Miss Swan. Leo is in the Feather's kitchen, being plied with biscuits, I presume." She relaxed a fraction, and he entered the room more fully.

"And my things?" She moved to stand between Gavin and the hearth, and the fire outlined her form through the dressing gown. He swallowed, though he didn't need the fire's light to know the shape of her. He recalled clearly how small she'd felt in his arms as he carried her to his horse, the ship's boy nipping at his heels.

"I've sent your gown to be laundered. You shall have it back shortly. Here," he said, crossing to the small table. "Drink your tea before it grows cold."

He poured a cup for her then held a chair, wincing only slightly at the movement. She eyed him uncertainly before her stomach made the decision for her with a low rumble. She sat, a faint blush staining her cheeks, and spread a napkin over her lap proper-like.

Gavin took the opposite chair and removed his pencil and notebook from his coat. "I have questions about what you saw and heard aboard the *Destiny*," he said.

She eyed him for an overlong moment before giving him a short nod. Her manners must have made themselves known, for she indicated the pot. "Would you like tea?"

"I prefer something a bit stronger," he said.

"At this hour?"

"Coffee, Miss Swan. I prefer coffee." She buttered a triangle of toast. He waited until she took a bite before saying, "What is the nature of your relationship with Victor Kingsley?"

She coughed and he nudged her tea closer. She took a sip and swallowed. "I beg your pardon, Constable. My relationship?"

"Aye."

"I have no *relationship* with Victor Kingsley." She kept her eyes fixed on her teacup so he waited, prompting her with his silence. Finally, she looked up. Her gaze met his, and she held it steady as she added, "He is my employer's husband. That is all."

Gavin made a notation in his notebook, though he knew her words to be a bold lie. He couldn't put his finger on *how* he knew she was being untruthful, but he would bet his horse on it.

"The ship's boy, Leo, saw you in conversation with Kingsley before the ship ran aground. What did you discuss?"

She tilted her head slightly. "I do not see how that is any of your concern."

"Then per'aps you might explain the blood staining your gown," he continued. "How did you come by that?"

"The blood—?" Her brow pitched low as if she tried to remember, then her expression cleared. "Why, I imagine it must be mine."

Another lie. He closed his eyes briefly. Despite Victor Kingsley's final plea—*find her*—and Miss

Swan's flight from the beach, he'd hoped for her sake she was innocent of any wrongdoing. Even when he saw the blood staining her sleeve, he'd thought there must be an explanation, but so far, she'd handed him nothing but falsehoods.

At his silence, she continued her defense, and he allowed her to go on. "Yes," she said with a nod, "the blood must be mine. You'll recall the ship I travelled on *ran aground*."

Her tone carried a bit of prim derision that nearly had his lips curving in response. Still, he must not forget that a man was dead. "I don't believe the blood is yours, Miss Swan."

She set the remains of her toast on the plate and wiped the corner of her mouth with her napkin. "How can you be certain, Constable?"

"I checked your wrist for wounds and found none."

"You checked my—when?"

"After you fainted."

"I did not faint."

"You did." When it appeared she might argue the matter further, he added, "Per'aps you were overset by Kingsley's death." He watched her for a reaction and was rewarded when her eyes widened in surprise. More pretense? He couldn't be certain.

"Victor is dead?" Her breath came more rapidly now, her chest rising and falling beneath the dressing gown. There was an increased energy to her, as if she wanted nothing more than to stand and pace the room. She remained seated, though, and lifted a slender hand to her throat. He wasn't certain whether the slight tremble in her fingers was genuine; if not, it was nicely done.

"He is."

"And I gather from your questions you believe I had something to do with his demise."

"Did you?"

She looked at him in confusion for a moment before responding. "Of course not!"

"Then I shall ask again: what was the nature of your relationship with your employer's husband?"

"Constable, the *nature* of your question is insulting."

"Apologies, Miss Swan, but I haven't the time to be overly concerned with delicate sensibilities."

"I would like you to leave," she said primly. "And I would like my things returned posthaste."

He made another notation, conscious of her watching his hand. When she leaned forward as if she might read his words, he closed the book with a snap and gave her a short nod. "You shall have your things again once your gown has been laundered."

Her eyes narrowed at his even tone. His Maid Marian was no fool. "Am I to be a prisoner then?" she asked, her chin tilted at a stubborn angle.

A quiet thing. That was how Henderson had described the lady. He must remember to doubt the captain's opinion in the future. "'Prisoner' is a bit strong, don't you think?"

"I can hardly go about in my nightclothes," she said, drawing his eye once more to the lace at her throat. "So no, I think the term is rather apt."

He considered her another moment across the table. Miss Swan had said nothing about Lady Philippa, which he found rather odd. "Your employer has inquired after you," he said slowly, pleased when her eyes widened the merest fraction. "My cousin informed her you'd suffered an injury."

"Lady Philippa?"

"Aye. You seem surprised."

"Yes—no, it's only... I thought she might wish to remain abed after such a harrowing night. Does she wish me to attend her?"

"I believe 'tis the expectation of a lady's companion, is it not?"

Miss Swan appeared to consider this. Perhaps she questioned the propriety of accepting a wage from the widow after killing the lady's husband. He was disappointed when she overwhelmed her conscience to say, "And that, sir, is precisely why I need my things. Lady Philippa desires my attendance, and it would be remiss of me to abandon her, especially in her time of need."

Gavin stood and reclaimed his hat. "You shall have your gown returned to you shortly," he repeated, "but I insist you remain in Newford until this matter is sorted."

She sank back against the chair, clearly displeased with his direction. She had a pair of dimples that appeared in her cheeks, even when she frowned. It was his experience that few ladies appreciated his forthright manner, and Miss Swan, it seemed, was no exception.

"How long do you anticipate this sorting will take?" she asked.

"I intend to see the matter resolved as expeditiously as possible."

"You are eager to find your coffee, I presume."

"I am eager to find the truth."

She snorted softly and he lifted a brow in question. "A constable eager for the truth?" she said. "That's rich."

"You've some prior experience with the constabulary, Miss Swan?"

"More than I would like to claim."

———

VICTOR WAS DEAD. Mari couldn't be sad for the news, but neither did it bring the elation she might have expected. He'd never been held to account for his treatment of Hannah, and in death, Victor became a *victim*, not the heartless seducer she knew him to be. It was all so unfair, and she wondered if she'd ever find justice for Hannah. More to the point, with Victor gone, would she ever find Hannah's child?

She paced the room after Constable Kimbrell left and cursed her stupidity. She'd allowed herself to be unsettled by the man's gruff manner and dark good looks. He may have resembled a Greek demi-god in appearance, but there was nothing heroic about a man who would question her on such feeble evidence, much less keep her clothing from her. She should have used the opportunity to gain more information.

How, precisely, had Victor died?

What had become of Hannah's necklace?

She swallowed as she recalled searching the man's pockets the night before. Had he been dead even then? She shivered to think it, but no. A memory flashed, and she saw again Victor's intent gaze, felt the grip of his hand closing about her wrist as she'd pulled it from his coat. Her heart pounded at the recollection.

So, Victor had not been dead then, but had he been *dying*? He'd been limp and cold when she first approached him, but she'd attributed that to his swim to shore. But, from the constable's questions and the copious notes he'd made in his little book, it was clear he believed Victor's death was *not* due to the wreck of the *Destiny*. Even more alarming, he suspected *Mari* of some foul deed.

She slowed her steps, which were making her dizzy in the small space. Her memory of the previous night was inconsistent, with images coming to her in fits and starts. Had she done something of which she'd no recollection? No, of course not.

But the constable must have some grounds for his theory. Despite the man's eager leap to assumptions about her relationship with Victor Kingsley, his eyes hinted at *some* intelligence. She couldn't believe he questioned her so pointedly because of a few spots of blood on her sleeve.

Without intending to, she recalled the constable's expression as he'd taken the chair across from hers. He'd winced at the motion, though he tried to hide it, and she saw then the abrasions along the top of his hand and the faint bruising on one side of his face. Had he earned his injuries in the sea? Had he earned them rescuing *her*?

She felt a bit of remorse for her tart manner, but she pushed it down. She couldn't feel any pity for the man when he asked such insulting questions. When he drew such hasty conclusions with little regard for the truth.

She needed to know what evidence the constable thought he had to implicate her in Victor's death. She could hardly discover what happened to Hannah and her child while swinging from the gallows.

Mari stopped her pacing altogether as a new question occurred to her. Did Victor's murderer know something about Hannah's death? Was that why Victor died? She imagined any number of scenarios, many which involved Victor Kingsley as blackmail victim, but none of them fit. If someone were using knowledge of Hannah's death to gain an advantage, then killing Victor would hardly suit their purposes, would it?

All of her questions led to one inescapable conclusion: she must speak with Gavin Kimbrell again. The realization caused her heart to jump anew, but the next time, she would not allow him to distract her, and she would be fully armed with all her clothes.

CHAPTER 9

GAVIN LET HIMSELF out of Miss Swan's room and closed the door behind him. Given all that had occurred over the past hours, it seemed wrong to feel any degree of excitement, to say nothing of the energetic tug of anticipation that pulled at him. A man was dead, after all, but Gavin had always enjoyed a clever puzzle. He couldn't deny the day held more promise than he was accustomed to having.

He hurried down the stairs, ignoring his aches and bruises. Though it was early still, the inn was alert with the sound of pots clanging in the kitchen. Morning sun came through the coffee room's front window, and Mr. Clifton's baker's cart could be heard rattling along the high street.

Newford was awake.

Wynne passed him with a stack of neatly folded linens. She stopped her progress to say, "Can I instruct the laundry maids to wash Miss Swan's gown now?"

Gavin replaced his hat on his head, intent on making his way to Rowe's surgery. "Not yet." He moved to the door, but then he recalled Miss Swan's words. She'd asked about her "things" not just her gown. He stopped and retraced his steps. "I imagine there must be other items with Miss Swan's gown—undergarments and the like?"

His cousin narrowed her gaze at him. "Aye," she said slowly. At his silence, she elaborated. "Her corset and petticoat. A tucker. Stockings and garters, o' course, and a pair of pockets." Then, with a sigh, she added, "I suppose you'll be wanting to see them?"

"I will."

"'Tis most irregular," she grumbled.

"And yet, you'll not deny your favorite cousin."

"I've never claimed any such thing."

"You don't need to when we both know't to be true."

Wynne looked toward the ceiling as if she might find her patience there, but she set aside her linens and led him to the Feather's laundry next to the stables. Bundles of drying herbs hung from the low beams, their fragrance mingling with the sharper scents of lye and damp linen. The hearth blazed beneath three large kettles, and Gavin removed his hat, his hairline damp despite the laundry's open windows.

In the center of the room, a pair of Wynne's laundry maids worked a bedsheet over the large wooden press. One of them, a stout woman Gavin knew as Mrs. Thatcher, wiped her hands on her apron and approached them.

"What can us do for ye, Mrs. Teague?"

"The constable has come for the lady's garments—the ones we set aside from the *Destiny*."

"Aye, they be just here," Mrs. Thatcher said, shuffling across the room to retrieve a wooden box. "I don't mind saying 'twill be a proper trial to remove the stains, now that they've set."

"To be sure," Wynne agreed, "but I've every confidence in you, Mrs. Thatcher. I've seen how well you manage the squire's gravy stains on my best supper linens."

Mrs. Thatcher pulled her shoulders back and smoothed her apron over her middle with a thick hand. "That man can't seem to find 'is mouth," she said with a chuckle. "But aye, Mrs. Teague, Lizzie an' us'll see't done. Ye've but to say the word."

Gavin tapped his hat against his thigh while they exchanged more words about stains and wrinkles, then Mrs. Thatcher left them to return to the press.

Finally, Wynne removed Miss Swan's blue gown from its box. Though soiled, it had been carefully folded into a neat square, and Gavin took it from her. She gave him a glower for his impatience, but he ignored it and lifted the garment. It was small, easily half his own width, and he knew a twinge of guilt for keeping it from the lady. He pressed his remorse down and set the gown aside to examine the rest of the box.

A scrap of lace-trimmed linen—the tucker, he presumed—lay beneath the gown. He ignored the cloth's intriguing scents of lemon and vanilla and cast it aside.

Next were Miss Swan's unmentionables. A lawn petticoat and a pair of cotton stockings, which he found ridiculously dainty for a murderess. A short corset with a line of embroidery along the top of the bosom. It had been stitched and shaped to fit Miss Swan's form, and he made a noble effort to think of anything *but* Miss Swan's form. His horse... Wynne's beef pie... the coffee he'd still to find this morning.

"Is that embarrassment staining your cheeks?" Wynne asked with irritating accuracy.

"'Tis devilish warm in here," Gavin complained.

Finally, he found what he'd been looking for: a set of pockets sewn onto a length of ribbon. He turned them out.

The first contained nothing but a coin and a simple hair comb, but the second held a slip of paper, folded and damp, and a handkerchief. He unfolded the latter. With a rose and vine embroidered in one corner, it was nicely made but otherwise unremarkable.

He set it aside before taking the paper gingerly between his thumb and forefinger. It was too damp to risk unfolding now, but soon, he might see what Miss Swan had written. Would he find a *billet-doux*, perhaps, or arrangements for a clandestine meeting with her husband's employer?

Wynne eyed him with reproach as he returned the pockets to her without the paper. "I'll not have anyone accusing the Feather of pilfering pockets, Gavin Kimbrell."

He took the gown from her as well then backed away with his spoils. "The lady will have her things returned," he said. *Probably.*

"Can I at least provide her with a set of clothes from the parish boxes?"

Gavin considered Miss Swan's talent for disappearing and shook his head. Victor Kingsley's death was the first matter of any import to fall to him. He had no intentions of losing the lady who'd roused his suspicions in such a curious manner.

"No lady ought to be left to sit about in her

dressing gown," Wynne pressed. "'Tis unconscionable."

Gavin snorted. "You speak as if I've chained her to the wall, Wynne. She's not a prisoner."

"I imagine Miss Swan might be of a different opinion," his cousin called after him.

———

GAVIN LEFT WYNNE'S scowl and strode along the high street to Rowe's whitewashed surgery. Pushing open the door, he entered to the heavy scents of camphor and alcohol. The surgery was lit by a row of windows in the front, the sills cluttered with herbs in pots of various sizes. Shelves along one wall held jars of specimens and ominous instruments that caused a shudder to dance along Gavin's neck.

"Rowe," Gavin called. A muffled reply came from the back of the surgery, and he passed a line of tidy cots to push through another door. He descended the back stairs to the cool cellar below.

Barnabas Rowe was a tall, lean man with dark, silvered hair. He'd attended Gavin's mother during Gavin's birth and had set more of his cousins' limbs than any of them could count. His cuffs were perpetually dark with ink, and Gavin wondered what Mrs. Thatcher would make of *those* stains.

The room glowed beneath the light of several lanterns and tallow candles, and the sounds of the street were muffled by the cellar's thick walls. Rowe stood beside a stone slab, atop which lay the colorless figure of Victor Kingsley. A sheet covered the body's lower half, and bruises and abrasions marred the exposed skin. Rowe looked up at Gavin's entrance and slid his spectacles up the bridge of his nose.

"Constable," he said, "your timing is excellent. I've just completed my examination."

"What have you learned?" Gavin said, setting Miss Swan's gown and paper aside.

"A few things of note." Rowe motioned for Gavin to take a place on the opposite side of the slab. "For one," he began, "the abrasions you see here and here"—he pointed to Kingsley's shoulder and temple—"appear to be injuries from his time in the sea. Rocks or flotsam or both. He's received a lump to the back of his head, as well, probably enough of a blow to render him unconscious. But the mortal wound was most definitely *not* sustained in the shipwreck, unless this man had the misfortune to impale himself upon a blade when the ship ran aground."

Rowe pulled the sheet lower to reveal a dark cut on the man's abdomen. The blood had been wiped away, and the wound's edges were smooth. It was a neat incision, approximately an inch in length. A small blade, then.

Gavin leaned in to study the wound further. It was shadowed with purple bruising and something more. "What d'you make of the darker places about the edges?" he asked, pointing.

Rowe bent low to study the skin. "'Tis nearly black—too dark to be bruising, I think."

"Could it have come from the knife?"

"Aye, 'tis possible, I suppose." Rowe rummaged about on a shelf and returned with the man's grey silk waistcoat. He unfolded it and Gavin held a lantern to better see the cut in the fabric.

"'Tis stained as well," he said.

"You've a good eye," Rowe said as he replaced the waistcoat on the shelf.

Gavin considered the body. It was a distressing fact that such a tidy, insignificant wound could bring about a man's death. "The size of the injury hardly seems enough to fell a man," he murmured.

"Aye, but the depth and angle suggest the knife penetrated the stomach or per'aps the spleen, and the mottling on the abdomen is consistent with what I've read of internal hemorrhage. 'Twill be my opinion for the jury that this was the fatal wound."

Gavin looked up. "The jury? You'll be convening an inquest then?"

"Aye, though Carew won't like it."

Gavin couldn't disagree. Certainly, the squire would not be pleased to have a suspicious death on his doorstep, but 'twas clear enough Kingsley's death had come at the hands of another. "I've already sent a note round to apprise Carew of the shipwreck," he said. "I'll notify him of the inquest as well. D'you have a jury in mind?"

It had been years since a coroner's inquest had been held in Newford, and never since Gavin's appointment to constable, but he'd studied enough accounts from other parishes to know how it was done. Rowe listed twelve men, and Gavin recorded their names in his book so he might deliver the summonses.

After he had his list, Rowe cleared his throat, the sound loud in the cellar.

"Is there something more?" Gavin asked.

"I understand from Tate that the widow would like to see her husband returned to Bath as soon as may be done. I haven't told him there's to be an inquest..."

"I've still to speak with Lady Philippa regarding last night's events," Gavin said. Charles Tate, in fact, had been stalwart in protecting the new widow from any unpleasantness. "When I do, I'll inform them both of the inquest."

"Excellent," Rowe said. "Now, what have you brought there?" He motioned to Miss Swan's folded gown. "D'you have something that will help with the inquest?"

"'Tis possible," Gavin said slowly. Rather than explaining, though, he asked a question of his own. "But first, can you tell anything from the wound about the person who did this to Kingsley? Was she—or he—tall or short? Slight or sturdy?"

Rowe shook his head. "'Tis hard to say, but you said 'she.' D'you have reason to believe the perpetrator is a female? The wife, perhaps? If you've already identified the guilty party, 'twill make the inquest all the easier."

Gavin opened his mouth then closed it again. He was certain, or very nearly so, that Miss Swan had inflicted the mortal injury on Victor Kingsley's person.

Despite her protests, he couldn't forget Kingsley's final words or Miss Swan's bloodied sleeve. Or her less-than-forthright answers to his questions. Had they had a lovers' quarrel? Had she defended herself against Kingsley's advances? He knew little enough of her character, but the latter picture was easier to countenance than one of Miss Swan as a murderous virago.

Rowe waited for his answer. An accusation of murder was serious business, and he must be sure.

"I'm not entirely certain," he admitted. Then, lifting Miss Swan's gown, he indicated the sleeve.

"But in your opinion, d'you think the wound is consistent with the stains here?"

Rowe took the gown and inspected the sleeve before unfolding the garment to its full length. He lifted it against his own longer frame and, holding the sleeve with his left hand, eyed the body on the slab.

"Most assuredly not," he said.

Gavin frowned. That was unexpected. "How can you be sure?"

"The angle of the wound suggests the blade was driven in thusly"—the doctor mimicked the action with a thrust of his right hand—"but the stains are on the left sleeve."

Gavin stilled as he considered Rowe's words. Then he thought of his encounter with Miss Swan earlier that morning, and he distinctly remembered she had buttered her toast with her left hand. The stain was on the wrong sleeve.

He took the gown back from Rowe and studied it some more, turning the sleeve one way then another as he imagined it on Miss Swan's arm. "There's a small amount of staining atop the wrist as well as on the inside," he said. "'Tis as if… as if the wearer placed her hand between Kingsley's coat and waistcoat. *After* he'd been stabbed."

Rowe's thick brows lifted behind his spectacles. "D'you know, I dare say you might be right."

What were you searching for, Miss Swan?

When he'd informed her of Kingsley's death, she'd certainly seemed surprised, but that didn't mean there wasn't something off about her. She acted as companion to Lady Philippa, but she was too… something. Too distinct… too original, perhaps, to simply fade into the background as companions were meant to do. That she wasn't being entirely truthful with him was clear, and he mustn't forget that.

He had many questions, more than he'd started his morning with, but one thing was certain: his Maid Marian was *not* a murderess.

HANNAH'S DIARY
17 OCTOBER 1819

This week, I made the acquaintance of Miss Thornton, a spinster who's let the cottage next door. Her kindness reminds me of Mama, and her company is a balm to my solitude.

Miss Thornton lost her one true love to the war in Spain and has resigned herself to her situation. I find inspiration in her quiet strength, though I regret the lie of my widowhood has her believing we are kindred spirits.

CHAPTER 10

GAVIN CONSIDERED HIS next steps as he returned to the Feather. He left Miss Swan's gown with Wynne with a curt, "You may launder it now."

"Thank you, my lord," she said with a mocking curtsy, which he ignored.

Besides releasing the lady's gown, he wished to speak with Lady Philippa to continue assembling the events leading up to Kingsley's death. He'd also interview the crew again. Someone must have seen or heard something, even if they didn't realize it. A reward, if it came to it, could be useful in loosening tongues, though he doubted the squire would approve the expense. And of course, the jurors needed to be summoned for the inquest. Twelve men scattered across the parish—it would take *hours*, but it must be done. For a bit of coin, he might persuade Matthew and Daniel to deliver the summonses.

But first, he must notify the squire of Rowe's inquest. It wasn't a task he anticipated with any eagerness, but it must be done. The man would not be pleased. He might even try to dissuade Rowe from his course. Gavin didn't think their magistrate was crooked so much as slightly bowed, but perhaps with some careful managing, Carew might be persuaded Kingsley's death was a matter which required their full attention and diligence.

As luck would have it, Carew hailed Gavin as he crossed the Feather's coffee room. "Kimbrell," Carew said. "Received your note about the *Destiny*. Dreadful business, shipwreck. You've a report?"

"Aye, sir."

Carew sent one of Wynne's barmaids for ale and the pipe stand, and they adjourned to the inn's private parlor. When they were seated one across from the other, Carew filled his pipe bowl and lit it. As he puffed steady rings of blue smoke, Gavin shared what he knew thus far of the grounding of the *Destiny*.

"An inquest!" Carew bellowed when Gavin relayed his discussion with Rowe. "Whatever for? The man died in a shipwreck. It's unfortunate, but there's no need for proceedings."

Gavin peered at Carew through the pipe smoke.

"Rowe believes Kingsley's death was *not* a casualty of the grounding. Our coroner is of the opinion that an inquest should be called."

"Then surely, it's a matter for the Admiralty. Crimes on the high seas and all that. Don't you have a contact in Falmouth?"

"Aye, my former lieutenant," Gavin agreed. "But with respect, sir, we don't know the crime occurred on the high seas. 'Tis entirely possible the deed was done while the *Destiny* foundered in Cornish waters or even as the man lay on our own beach. He was still alive when he came ashore."

"Blast it, man! Let the Admiralty sort it. The quarter sessions are in three weeks, and I'll not sully my report with nonsense from another jurisdiction."

Gavin pulled in a long breath and held it, thinking. He felt confident his former lieutenant, who was now a captain, would lend the Admiralty's aid upon a direct appeal, but he would rather not request a favor unnecessarily. He already owed Arthur Edwards too much as it was.

He released his breath to say, "I'll send word to Falmouth if you wish it, sir, but I doubt the Admiralty will act until Rowe's inquest confirms the manner of death. Even then, 'tis possible they won't have the resources to investigate properly. I understand they're still addressing treason allegations from the war."

Carew puffed long and audibly on his pipe before saying, "So, we're to be cursed with this inquest then. Very well. Whom has Rowe selected for his jury?"

Gavin hid his surprise at the relative ease of Carew's acceptance. He'd expected more of a debate. Blinking against the wreath of Carew's pipe smoke, he recited the names Rowe had given him. Carew nodded and hmmm'd at some and frowned at others.

Gavin's own grandfather and his cousin Merryn were among the jurors, as well as ten more landowners from the parish. It was an acceptable group, and Gavin was optimistic that once the jurors heard Rowe's findings, they'd agree with the surgeon's conclusion. They'd rule the manner of Kingsley's death was murder, and Carew wouldn't be able to dispute it. Gavin would dutifully notify the Admiralty, who would reply that they had neither the time nor the resources to address the case, and Gavin could get on with the business of investigating the matter more fully.

Carew stood and emptied his pipe at the hearth. Replacing his hat, he said, "Deliver your summonses posthaste, Constable."

"I thought to send Matthew and Daniel—"

"See to it personally. Let's have this inquest done with."

——

MARI NEARLY EMBRACED Mrs. Teague when the innkeeper arrived later with a pile of familiar, neatly folded garments. "Oh, thank you," she said, unable to temper her elation. She'd fully expected the constable to leave her sitting in her shift, but she wouldn't question her good fortune or his unexpected display of reason.

"The laundry maids had the devil of a time with the stains on your gown," Mrs. Teague said, "but I think you'll be pleased to see 'tis good as new."

"Please extend my compliments to them," Mari said as she shook out the gown and laid it across the bed. "Do you know what's become of the boy, Leo?"

"Aye, he's been properly fed and clothed. I think he's finished an entire beef pie by himself."

Mari smiled, relieved that Leo was being cared for, but there was still the matter of Doyle's punishment. Pulling the corset over her chemise, she asked, "And the *Destiny's* officer? Has Mr. Doyle asked after Leo?"

"That one's not asked for anything since he sent down for the gin bottle," Mrs. Teague said. Her expression softened a bit as she added, "You needn't worry about Leo. Well before the sun was fully risen, I hear he received lessons in being a boy."

Mari directed a questioning look at Mrs. Teague. "Dare I ask what that involves?"

"My cousin tutored him on the proper way to pitch a rock into the sea. 'Tis apparently required instruction in every boy's education."

"Your cousin…"

"Gavin, aye. He's not always the insensitive lout he pretends to be."

Mari held her opinion on that. Mrs. Teague was too kind to hear what Mari thought of her cousin. She donned her petticoat and stockings next. When she reached the pockets, she found her comb and a coin. Hannah's handkerchief was there, but the paper Mari had cut from Victor's appointment book was gone.

Mrs. Teague, who'd been watching her inventory the contents, said, "Before you cast aspersions on the Feather and my maids, you'd best speak with—"

"The constable," Mari said with resignation.

"Aye." Mrs. Teague quirked her lips in apology as she said, "He has your paper."

Mari ought to have known. She shoved her irritation aside. "It's no matter," she said easily. "I mean to speak with him as soon as possible anyway. I will simply inquire about my paper then."

"That may not be as soon as you'd like," Mrs. Teague said. At Mari's raised brow, she added, "Gavin's ridden out on some task for the magistrate.

From the sounds coming from my parlor earlier, the squire's some displeased about something."

The squire, as magistrate, would be the constable's superior. Mari couldn't help the smile that teased her lips to hear Constable Gavin Kimbrell was being served up a fair bit of justice. She hoped the magistrate had taken him to task for some petty infraction—not polishing his boots, perhaps, or failing to submit a report timely. Keeping a lady confined to her room with nothing but her shift and a borrowed dressing gown. *That* deserved nothing short of a ready dismissal.

"I can see this pleases you," Mrs. Teague said with a barely-concealed smile of her own.

"Your cousin has posed all manner of insulting questions," Mari said. "I'm pretty certain he kept my clothing from me and now, I find he's taken my paper. You'll understand if I don't feel any sorrow for his troubles." She ignored the twinge of conscience that reminded her he'd also saved her from the sea, and at great peril to himself.

"Gavin can be a bit high-handed," the innkeeper acknowledged as she held Mari's gown for her.

"A bit," Mari agreed wryly.

"You'll not find a truer heart, though."

Mari had to admire the lady's loyalty, even if it was misplaced. She tied the front laces of her gown. Then, with the application of an excessive number of pins, she arranged her dark hair in a simple style, though it would begin to fall soon enough. A final adjustment to the tucker, and she was pleased to be fully dressed once again. Or very nearly so. She eyed her bare hands. There'd been no time to retrieve her gloves or hat when the *Destiny* ran aground. For so long, she'd impressed upon her students that they must never go out without their gloves or bonnet, and it felt odd to have neither.

Mrs. Teague must have divined her thoughts, for she said, "My cousin-in-law, Keren, has set aside some of the nicer bonnets from our parish collection. You may choose one that suits you until you have your own things again. They're nothing as fashionable as what you may be used to in Bath, but with a bit of brushing, I'm certain you'll find one to be acceptable."

"That's very kind," Mari said.

"What will you do now?" Mrs. Teague asked.

Mari couldn't address the matter of her missing paper until the constable returned from his task, but wouldn't it seem odd if she didn't go to her employer? And until she'd been acquitted of any wrongdoing in the constable's eyes, *odd* was something she ought to avoid.

"Mrs. Teague," she said, "will you please direct me to Lady Philippa's room?"

HANNAH'S DIARY
28 NOVEMBER 1819

Winter is upon us. Oh, heavens, I sound gloomy, but I can't seem to lose the megrims. I've begun countless letters to Mari—real letters without the lies of my sparkling life in Bath. Each has landed in the fire before making it to the post, but putting the words to paper calms my mind, even if she never hears my thoughts.

My stomach quickens, a reminder of the tiny life within me. My regret seems to have no end, or mercy.

CHAPTER 11

GAVIN STRAIGHTENED HIS neckcloth and rapped twice on the door of room twelve, Lady Philippa Kingsley's room. He'd sent a note up earlier and had been assured the widow would receive him. Hushed voices came from inside before the maid—Beatrice—opened the door.

"Constable," she said. "Please come in. Lady Philippa has been expecting you."

The maid, a pretty girl with a soft smile and rounded cheeks, stepped back from the door and Gavin entered. Wynne had installed Lady Philippa in one of the Feather's best rooms. It was modest but comfortable, with velvet curtains on the windows and a low fire burning in the hearth.

Lady Philippa sat by the fire in a tall-backed chair, pale but composed in a simple gown of dyed black wool. A gown purchased from his cousin Morwenna's shop, he suspected, as it was finer than any the lady would have found in the parish boxes.

Charles Tate stood guard behind her, one hand atop the back of the chair. He, too, acknowledged Kingsley's death with a dark cravat and a crepe armband.

Gavin entered fully into the room before he spied Miss Swan at the window, hands folded before her. It didn't miss his notice that Mrs. Thatcher had been successful in removing the stains from her gown. Unlike the others, Miss Swan wore no obvious signs of mourning, though her blue gown was appropriately subdued.

There was a curious tension to the room, as if none of the occupants knew quite what they were meant to be doing. Grief, Gavin supposed, had a way of robbing the day of its routine.

"Lady Philippa, Miss Swan, Mr. Tate," Gavin said, greeting each in turn.

"Constable," Tate said, "what news have you brought?"

Gavin gave him a nod before addressing the lady directly. "My lady, 'tis my duty to inform you there will be an inquest into your husband's death."

"An inquest? What does that mean?"

Miss Swan remained by the window, but he could tell her attention had been caught by the way her dark brown eyes watched him intently. Gavin hesitated, momentarily distracted by her study of him, before continuing.

"The inquest is a brief legal proceeding to determine how your husband died. We'll convene a jury of men to hear the evidence—"

"Evidence?" she said, dabbing the corner of her eye with a handkerchief. "My husband died when the ship ran aground. That much should be clear, I think." She looked up at Tate. "Charles, I would like to return to Bath so Victor may have a proper burial."

"Of course," he said. "Constable, what can be done to resolve this matter swiftly and without any more upset to Lady Philippa than she's already suffered?"

Gavin clasped his hands behind his back. "Every effort will be made to do so, but there are inconsistencies that suggest Mr. Kingsley did not die from injuries he sustained in the wreck. The inquest is necessary to confirm the manner of death."

Lady Philippa paled, and Beatrice stepped forward with a vial of salts. "My lady," she whispered.

Lady Philippa waved the maid off. Then, collecting herself, she said more briskly, "Tea, if you please, Beatrice."

"Yes, my lady."

The maid went to the tea service, and Miss Swan accompanied her. As they quietly set about preparing cups of tea, Lady Philippa returned her attention to Gavin. "What inconsistencies?" she pressed.

Gavin thought Miss Swan might break, so tightly did she hold herself as she listened for his answer. She may not have done the deed herself, but she certainly had an interest in whatever fate had befallen Victor Kingsley.

"My lady," Gavin said, "can you think of any grievance your husband may have had with those aboard the *Destiny*? 'Twould seem he suffered a mortal wound from a blade of some sort."

A teacup rattled in its saucer, and Beatrice set it on the table with a clatter. "A blade!" she exclaimed. "You mean 'e was murdered?" Belatedly, she recalled her mistress and added, "Beggin' your pardon, my lady."

Tate removed his hand from the back of Lady Philippa's chair to rub a shaky thumb and forefinger along either side of his mouth where he might once have worn a mustache. "Stabbed, you say."

"My husband was a formidable man," Lady Philippa said, "but I can't imagine anyone aboard the *Destiny* wished him ill. Are you quite certain, Constable, that he didn't simply fall or injure himself when the ship ran aground?"

"I'm afraid not," he said.

"How long before this inquest is complete?"

"The magistrate has ordered it to take place as soon as may be done."

"And then I might take my husband home?"

Gavin shook his head regretfully. "The body will be released for burial, of course, but the inquest is only the first part of the investigation. If the jury rules the cause of death to be murder, then everyone who sailed aboard the *Destiny* will be required to remain in Newford until all inquiries are complete."

"I don't think so, Constable."

"Absolutely not."

Lady Philippa and Tate spoke at the same time, each equally opposed to the notion of remaining in Cornwall longer than necessary.

"It's simply out of the question," Tate added. His hand was steadier now, and he fisted it at his side as he added, "If it comes to it, I shall speak with your magistrate."

"You must do as you wish," Gavin said, though he really hoped he would not.

A man had been murdered by means most foul, but if Tate pressed the matter, Gavin feared Carew would release everyone involved. He'd have the devil of a time performing a proper investigation if he must spend his days chasing witnesses to the other end of England.

"Miss Swan," Lady Philippa called to her companion.

"Yes, my lady?"

"Have we any ink? If we're to remain here, there are letters I must write."

"I shall request writing supplies from the innkeeper. Mrs. Teague has been very hospitable." Gavin didn't miss the emphasis on her words or the implication that others had *not* been hospitable.

"Constable," Lady Philippa said, "see that my trunks are brought to the inn."

Gavin checked his irritation at the imperious command, but before he could respond, Tate interjected. "Lady Philippa," he said, "please allow me to go and retrieve your things. I must secure Kingsley's papers, at any rate—"

Gavin shook his head. "The *Destiny's* been careened. The shipwright and his men are working to repair it, but I can't permit anyone to board until the ship is secure again."

Tate's expression was one of displeasure. "And when do you suppose that might be?"

"'Tis hard to say," Gavin replied. "Some days or more. Per'aps a week. The damage to the hull was substantial—"

"A week! But that's absurd. Lady Philippa can't be without her things for such a length of time."

"My lady," Gavin said, directing his reply to the

widow herself. "'Tis a trying time, to be sure, but I'm confident the shipwright and his men will do all they can to restore the *Destiny* as soon as possible. I understand the ship and cargo were insured. Anything lost during the incident will be duly addressed through the wreck agent's report. In the meantime, I see you've already found Newford's dressmaker. Morwenna Williamson will be pleased to see you have everything you require during your stay."

The widow accepted her tea from Beatrice and gave him a silent nod, which he took as a dismissal. He bid them good-bye.

"Constable," Miss Swan called softly as he reached the door. "I shall accompany you." He lifted his brows in question, and she reminded him, "I've ink and paper to procure."

He held the door, trying not to notice how a lock of her hair had slid from its pins to brush her neck.

―――

MARI'S RELIEF AT escaping the close room was immediate. Since presenting herself to Lady Philippa that morning, her employer's manner had been more curt than usual. Mari assumed that could be attributed to the death of the lady's husband, but she couldn't help the sensation that Lady Philippa watched her. That she scrutinized Mari's actions.

Mari was certain Lady Philippa knew of her encounter with Victor, or perhaps her search of the Kingsley cabin. Her employer said nothing, though, and Mari felt no impulse to volunteer the information.

She waited for the constable to close the door behind him before saying, "Does the fact that I'm wearing my own gown again mean you have acquitted me of nefarious deeds?"

He cast her a sideways glance. "Nefarious?"

"It means vile."

"I'm aware of the word, Miss Swan. I will say only that I've cleared you of being directly responsible for Victor Kingsley's death."

She didn't mistake the distinction, but she indulged her curiosity. "On what grounds?"

"On the grounds that you butter your toast with the wrong hand."

Mari stopped. He took a few more steps down the corridor before turning back to face her. "You are an odd man, Constable."

He considered her for a long moment. Finally, he seemed to reach a decision. "The person who killed Victor Kingsley did so with his—or her—right hand," he said. "Thus far, you are the only person I can confidently say did *not* do the deed."

"Because I am left-handed. How… clever!" The constable lifted one brow in wry amusement for her assessment of his intellect. His capability was unexpected, as was her admiration, but his news was more welcome than he could know. Despite her arguments to herself, she'd not been able to shed the notion that she'd done Victor Kingsley some grave injury of which she had no memory. Not that he hadn't deserved it, but still, she was not a murderess.

"Thank you," Mari said, the words tight in her throat as they resumed walking toward the stairs.

"For what, Miss Swan? For being clever? That honor goes to the surgeon."

"Well, then, I thank you for seeing my things returned to me. Or rather, *most* of my things." The reminder that he still had her paper quickly dispelled any admiration she might have felt. Forcing an agreeable smile to her face, she said, "I believe you still have something of mine."

The constable pulled his head back, a frown darkening his countenance. "Your head still pains you?"

It took Mari a moment to work out the reason for his question. When she did, she bit out, "My apologies, Constable. That was meant to be a smile."

"Aye? Per'aps you should try again."

"Do you or do you not have anything of mine?"

"I suppose you mean this?" He withdrew a folded paper from his pocket and handed it to her.

"I regret to inform you 'tis no longer legible."

"You opened it?" she asked as she took the paper from him. His expression made her realize how foolish she was. He was a constable. Of course, he'd opened it.

She stopped walking and gingerly unfolded the page, dismayed to see he was right. The sea had done its damage, and the notes from Victor's appointment book were unreadable save for a few scant words. If only she could remember what had been written there.

"What was it?" he asked with a nod toward the page.

"Nothing." She resumed walking and he followed.

"An inventory of illicit goods?"

She cut her eyes to him but remained silent.

"A list of jewels to steal? A cipher that requires decoding or…" He snapped his fingers and added, "Arrangements for a secret rendezvous."

An unexpected rush of heat filled Mari's cheeks at that last one, but she said pertly, "It was merely an order for the butcher." She was pleased with how she kept the asperity from her voice.

"Ah. The butcher, of course. 'Tis a list of jewels—in cipher form—for the butcher to steal. The butcher with whom you're engaged in a very secret, very tawdry affair."

"Tawdry!"

"It means vulgar."

Mari huffed a laugh. "Are you always this absurd?"

"D'you mean to say I'm wrong?"

"You are wrong." Her memories were patchy, but in this, she was certain. "But since we're devising theories," she said, "I have a proposal."

"Aye…?"

"I would like to aid you in your investigation."

His frown was immediate. "No."

"No? But you haven't even heard my proposal."

"That wasn't it?"

She ignored him to say, "I am a lady's companion—for all practical purposes, I'm a *servant* in the Kingsley household."

They'd reached the stairs by now and he stopped. "Miss Swan, if I know one thing in all of this, 'tis that you are no more a lady's companion than I am."

She checked her scowl and began to descend, waiting until he walked abreast of her before continuing. "No one pays any mind to servants. I could listen, perhaps ask a question or two—"

"No," he repeated.

"Why not?"

"This is a serious business."

"Precisely. That is why you need an advantage."

When he remained silent, she added, "I suppose I could always ask a few questions on my own—"

"Why would you wish to?"

"A man has died," she said. "Certainly, that deserves all our efforts to see justice done."

"You are a poor liar, Miss Swan." He turned at the base of the stairs, and she hurried to catch him.

"Why do you not believe me?"

He stopped and folded his arms across his chest. She tried not to notice how the action strained the cloth of his coat over his shoulders.

"I don't know."

"I beg your pardon?" She'd lost the thread of their conversation.

"I don't know *why* I do not believe you." His frown deepened as if the admission pained him. "I simply know that I do not. Call it intuition, but I *believe* your version of the truth and mine are miles apart. And now, if you don't mind, I've an inquest to prepare for."

He turned on his heel and strode for the Feather's door. She didn't follow him, but she did call out, "Only consider it, Constable."

HANNAH'S DIARY
4 FEBRUARY 1820

I have a daughter, and she is perfect.

CHAPTER 12

THE MORNING OF the inquest arrived with more birdsong than it ought to have had for such a grave event, and a good portion of Newford's citizens gathered at the Feather to hear the proceeding. The inquest was to be held in the assembly rooms on the inn's upper floor, and extra chairs had been brought in for the occasion. Wynne and Roddie joined Gavin at the back of the room as the seats filled.

"'Tis a fair showing," Wynne said. Her expression was a bit sullen as she added, "I don't see what harm a few tables for refreshments would have done."

"Wynnie," her husband admonished softly from her other side. "The widow will not appreciate you peddling ale at her husband's inquest."

Gavin ignored their debate and marked jurors off his list as they began to arrive. His grandfather and Merryn were the first, and they took their seats at the front of the room. Three more came next, then Tate strode in with Lady Philippa on his arm and the maid, Beatrice, trailing them. The widow appeared drawn and pale as one might expect. Elegantly mournful.

Of Miss Swan, there was no sign. Curious, he thought, for a female who'd expressed an interest in finding justice for Victor Kingsley.

The room filled and the eager buzz of speculation hummed like spring bees. Or rather, speculation tinged with impatience, for it was nearly a quarter past the hour set for the inquest to begin, and two of the jurors had yet to arrive. Squire Carew, Gavin noted, was also absent.

As he frowned at his list, Daniel and Matthew entered with their usual exuberance. The pair were breathless when they reached Gavin's side.

"Hawke sends word he's taken ill," Daniel said.

"And Grenfell's over to Truro," Matthew added. "His wife says 'twas an urgent matter that couldn't be avoided."

Squire Carew arrived then, accompanied by a pair of gentlemen who were *not* on Gavin's list. Killigrew owned a small manor some miles west of Newford and Trewyck maintained an estate near Weirmouth. Both men were unexceptional members of the parish, but they were also known to share an occasional game of hazard with the squire.

Carew looked about until he spied Gavin then strode toward him. Gavin's suspicions climbed higher when the squire said, "Heard the jury may be short. Killigrew and Trewyck are prepared to stand in and do their duty."

Gavin frowned. How had Carew heard the jury would be short when he himself had only just learned of it? At the front of the room, Rowe consulted his watch. The inquest was already delayed, and there was nothing to be done now for the absent men. Carew led the new arrivals to join the rest of the jurors. Jaw tight, Gavin took his place along the back wall and crossed his arms.

Rowe was explaining the purpose of the inquest to those gathered when Miss Swan entered with a black silk shawl draped over one arm. She stopped short at seeing all the seats were taken.

"Did something keep you, Miss Swan?" Gavin whispered at her ear.

She didn't flinch as he'd expected but indicated the shawl on her arm. "Lady Philippa sent me to the dressmaker to purchase a few items." After a moment's hesitation, she took the place next to him. With effort, he tried to ignore the faint scent of lemon and vanilla that accompanied her. She put him in mind of warm lemon biscuits, though to be sure, her tartness overcame any sweetness.

Neither of them spoke, and Gavin wondered again at the nature of her role in the Kingsley household. Despite Miss Swan's wish to aid him in his investigation, she didn't seem terribly overset by her employer's new widowhood. In fact, her duties with regard to Lady Philippa seemed little more than an afterthought. She'd certainly been surprised when Gavin mentioned Lady Philippa during their initial interview, though he supposed with the events of the past days, there'd been plenty to distract a body. The trouble was, Miss Swan didn't seem the distractible sort.

The inquest began in earnest, and the room fell silent. Miss Swan's posture was attentive as she listened to Rowe explain the nature of Kingsley's wound. Once, when the surgeon turned to the jurors for questions, he thought Miss Swan might raise one of her own. She lifted a hand chest-high then brought it back down to her side.

Rowe called Gavin to testify to what he'd learned in his investigation, which was sadly very little thus far. The jurors' questions and Gavin's responses further emphasized the scarcity of the information he'd gained.

Juror: "Constable, have you identified any reason why someone would wish to harm the deceased?"

Gavin: "My initial interviews with the ship's crew and passengers have not revealed a motive as of yet. 'Tis early, though, and further investigation will—"

Juror: "Do you have evidence of a specific weapon used to inflict the wound found on Mr. Kingsley's body?"

Gavin: "The injury appears to have been inflicted by a small blade—"

Juror: "Do you have knowledge of a *specific* weapon, Constable?"

Gavin: "No. At this point, I do not. You'll understand the grounding of the *Destiny* and the current inaccessibility of the ship make such a determination difficult."

Juror: "Have you identified any witnesses to Mr. Kingsley's injury?"

Gavin: "In the course of my initial inquiries, no witnesses have come forward with direct knowledge of the offense."

Juror: "I imagine the *Destiny's* crew and

passengers were rather preoccupied with other matters at the time." (The other jurors and a few of the spectators chuckled softly at this, and Gavin ground his teeth.)

Juror: "Were there other injuries found on Mr. Kingsley's person that are, in fact, consistent with the grounding of the *Destiny* or with a body washed onto the rocks?"

Gavin: "Dr. Rowe and I observed bruising and abrasions that appear consistent with such events."

To his cousin's credit, Merryn tried to remind the jurors that an inquest was merely one part of the greater process.

Merryn: "To be sure, an inquest is a matter of expediency that allows only for the most cursory of inquiries. If 'tis determined the actions of another resulted in Mr. Kingsley's death, how confident are you that further investigation will reveal the person responsible?"

Gavin, with relief: "I remain fully confident that additional inquiry will reveal the truth."

Throughout his testimony, the two new jurors—Carew's jurors—asked few questions, and Gavin couldn't divine the direction of their thoughts. He was soon dismissed, and Rowe led the jurors to his surgery to view the body. It was the final step in the inquest before the men deliberated.

The spectators stood and whispered amongst themselves while they awaited the jurors' return. Gavin took his place at the back of the room again, but Miss Swan had gone. He searched the crowd and found her at Lady Philippa's side.

The widow wore her new silk shawl wrapped loosely about her. Charles Tate assisted her when it slipped, his hand brushing Lady Philippa's shoulder with unexpected familiarity. The motion was so swift, Gavin thought he must have mistaken it, but then he noticed the maid, Beatrice. Her head was down, but she watched Tate's hand with what could only be disapproval before resuming her study of the floor.

Opening his notebook, Gavin made a swift note to speak with Kingsley's man of affairs again.

"What do you write in your book?"

He closed it with a snap to find Miss Swan standing too close. "'Tis none of your concern."

"Have you learned something more about Victor's death?"

"Was your association with him of long

standing?" he asked.

She pulled her head back, eyes narrowed. "I thought you acquitted me of any wrongdoing."

"I believe I said you were not responsible for Kingsley's death, but that doesn't answer for why you refer to him in such familiar terms."

Her jaw tightened in an expression he was beginning to recognize. It brought out her dimples and spoke of irritation—with him or with herself, he wasn't certain. "I misspoke," she said evenly. "Have you learned anything more about *Mr. Kingsley's* death?"

He didn't answer her question but asked one of his own. "What do you know of Charles Tate?"

She gave Tate a considering look then returned her gaze to Gavin. She eyed him for a long moment, her dark eyes intent on his. Gavin's neckcloth had begun to feel too tight when she said, "If I share my observations of Charles Tate, will you tell me what you know?"

"'Tis a poor bargain, Miss Swan. How do I know your observations are worth my knowledge?"

"You're that confident in your knowledge?"

He wasn't, but there was no reason she needed to know it. "You're that confident in your observations?" he returned.

She shrugged carelessly and moved to stand beside him again, the wall at her back. They remained like that for some moments, and her silence nearly drove him mad. He opened and closed his mouth twice before she murmured, "Maddening, isn't it?"

"I beg your pardon?"

"The silence."

Silence. It was a strategy he employed with success himself, and now she was using it on him. With a sigh (and the merest smidge of admiration), he relented. "One question."

She tilted her head, listening, but remained facing the room.

"Tell me what you know of Charles Tate," he said, "and I will allow you one question." She looked at him then, her eyes bright with anticipation, and he hastened to add, "A very direct and specific question, Miss Swan. None of this 'what have you learned' business."

She gave him a short, barely perceptible nod before saying, "Charles Tate is engaged in a flirtation with Beatrice."

———

"WITH BEATRICE?" THE constable said in a low whisper. His surprise was gratifying. He stood close so they might not be overheard, and a trace of his scent teased her nose. It was faint but… masculine…

like soap made from warm salt and amber. It sent an unexpected fizziness spiraling through Mari's belly. She ignored the sensation and answered his question with a nod.

"Not with Lady Philippa?"

Mari felt her brows climb. "Heavens, no. Tate is pockets to let. He may have his own ideas in that direction, but Lady Philippa would never entertain the notion. Not when she has Kingsley." Frowning, she amended her words. "Or had, rather."

"How can you be certain of Tate's regard for Beatrice?"

Mari hesitated. Beatrice's tale wasn't hers to share, but if she meant to show the constable she could be useful to his investigation, then share she must. "Beatrice is in a family way," she said softly, a flustered warmth filling her cheeks. "She says the affair is one of long standing."

The constable's brows lifted. "Isn't she worried she'll lose her position?"

"Oddly, no, though when I first suspected her condition, I told her Lady Philippa wouldn't hesitate to turn her out, especially if Kingsley was the father."

"Kingsley? I thought you said it was Tate."

Mari waved his words aside. "It is. Beatrice informed me I was mistaken."

In fact, the maid had given her a shaky, watery

laugh when Mari asked if Victor had fathered her baby. "Mr. Kingsley?!" she said as if Mari had suggested the archbishop.

"Beatrice assures me," she told the constable, "Lady Philippa is aware of her condition and means to aid her in any way she can." She couldn't help but wonder how Hannah's fate might have been different if she'd had someone so willing to lend support.

"Will Tate acknowledge the babe, d'you think?"

Mari snorted in disgust. She couldn't help it. "Charles Tate is a climber," she said. "He's too concerned with appearances. He'll no more acknowledge a maid's child than he'll waltz about in a lady's gown."

"What makes you think Tate's short of funds? He appears prinked out well enough."

"*Appears* is the key," she murmured. "I gather he's a fondness for the gaming tables. Just last week, I overheard him ask Victor for another loan."

"Did Kingsley comply?"

"I don't know," she said with a shake of her head. "He said only that he'd think on it."

"Why did you assume Kingsley was the father?"

Mari opened her mouth then closed it again. She'd been surprised and not a little dismayed to be so mistaken in her assumption, but it had been an understandable error. *Because he's already left one young woman in such a condition*, she wanted to say but did not. Instead, she admonished the constable, "You've strayed from the original question. I have given you what I know of Charles Tate."

The hard line of his jaw tightened in irritation, and she was intrigued to see how fierce it made him appear. "Very well, Miss Swan," he relented. "What is your question?"

"What items were found on Victor Kingsley's person?" When his eyes narrowed in speculation, she reminded him, "Our bargain, Constable."

He sighed. "The usual items for a man of his station. A gold watch in his waistcoat. A ring on his left hand and a diamond pin in his cravat. His purse was also found."

"Was there anything in the purse?"

"That is another question, Miss Swan, but yes, he carried a few coins and banknotes."

"There was nothing else?"

"No. What, precisely, were you expecting?"

His gaze was intent, and she felt the heat of it. Mari swallowed and shook her head. She'd *seen* Victor pocket Hannah's necklace in the ship's hold. It was possibly lost to the sea, but now she wondered if he hadn't returned it to his cabin. There'd certainly been time enough to do so before the *Destiny* ran aground.

She must return to the ship. She wouldn't mind

having another look at Victor's appointment book, too, before it was packed away with the rest of his things. Perhaps his notes might rekindle her memory about the ruined paper she carried in her pocket.

"Miss Swan," Constable Kimbrell said. "I can't say I like your expression. 'Tis much too intent."

Mari relaxed her frown, but before he could challenge her further, the jury returned. As the gentlemen walked to the front of the room, those gathered for the proceeding found their seats again. One of the jurors—a man with the dark good looks of the Kimbrells—eyed the constable at the back of the room. His expression was tight as he gave the merest shake of his head.

Mari looked up to see Constable Kimbrell's jaw had hardened. Silence fell on the room when Rowe asked the jury if they'd reached a decision on the cause of Victor Kingsley's death.

"We have," the foreman said. "We rule it death by misadventure."

A murmur rose and fell among the spectators. The magistrate stood and shook the hands of the jurors while beside Mari, the constable stood rigid. He barely moved from his position near the wall, but the tension that flowed from him was palpable.

"Death by misadventure," she repeated slowly. "What does that mean?"

"It means," he said tightly, "the jury does not agree he was murdered."

Mari frowned as the import of his words settled on her brain. The jury had it wrong... again. She gripped her hands to still their shaking. In her mind, she was back in Drayton-Marsh with another jury's verdict and Constable Bragg's refusal to hear anything else: *The coroner's inquest has made their ruling.... I have neither the time nor the resources to ask endless questions about an affair that has already been decided.*

Blood rushed in her ears, drowning out the sounds of the crowd around her. Mari felt wooden, as though her joints no longer worked properly. Finally, she found her tongue. "I suppose your investigation has reached its end, Constable. You must be pleased to have the matter concluded so" — she searched her mind and found his word — "expeditiously."

When she looked up, she was startled to see the fierceness had returned to his gaze. He did not look pleased in the least. He appeared... determined, a fact which caused a curious warmth to begin at her center and spread to her fingertips.

"I am never pleased, Miss Swan, when questions remain unanswered." He left, and she considered his retreating form.

"Miss Swan." Mari turned to find Lady Philippa,

a somber expression settled upon her pale brow. "Now that this business is behind us, we shall be returning to Bath at once. I'll ask Tate to arrange a private coach. Please see what you can do to hurry the dressmaker along with whatever ready-mades she has on hand—there's no time for more than the essentials. I mean for us to depart at first light."

HANNAH'S DIARY
24 MARCH 1820

I've resolved to take in sewing to support my little family. I must make peace with my choices and build an honorable life for my daughter.

I will tell Victor that I cannot continue our association. He won't understand my decision, or perhaps he will. Either way, I must think of my daughter first. It's no less than Mama did for Mari and me.

CHAPTER 13

GAVIN LEFT THE Feather's assembly room and descended the stairs, uncaring how the banister shook with each heavy step. His anger climbed his throat, nearly choking him. How had he not seen the lengths Carew would go to hold his pristine record? As he strode across the flagstones toward the door, a thin voice called to him.

"Sir!"

"Aye," Gavin said gruffly, too incensed by the machinations he'd just witnessed to temper his tone. He spun to find Leo on his coat tails. The boy stumbled back a pace, eyes wide as if anticipating a blow.

Gavin drew a slow breath to calm himself. It was not his habit to go about terrifying young boys. "What is it, lad?"

"I only wanted to see if'n ye need me to fetch ye anyfin'?"

"No," Gavin said. Pushing through the door, he began walking. To his irritation, the boy scrambled to follow.

"I kin bring yer pipe, mebbe."

"I don't have a pipe."

"Then yer gin?" Leo looked about them before adding, "Where is't ye live, anyways?"

Gavin ignored the question and slid a glance toward his unexpected companion. "Where is your commanding officer? Shouldn't you be tending *him*?" He didn't recall the *Destiny's* chief mate among the inquest's spectators.

"Me wot?" Leo's brow furrowed like a fallow field before it smoothed again. "Ah, ye mean Doyle. He be too foxed to be givin' orders. Passed out like a rum doxy, 'e is."

"The captain then. Per'aps he has something that needs fetching."

"Cap'n is blue-deviled o'er the whole de—debockery—"

"Debacle?" It was an odd term to describe the *Destiny's* grounding.

"Aye, that."

The day had turned warm, and the sun had long since burned off the morning mist. Few walked along the high street as most of Newford had gathered for the inquest. Gavin passed the Feather's stables and was halfway to Rowe's surgery. He didn't know where he meant to go, only that he needed to move. His strides were long and impatient, but Leo was persistent. Much to Gavin's annoyance, the boy kept pace with him, taking three steps to Gavin's every one and dogging him like a buzzing midge.

"Mrs. Teague makes a bang-up tart—I could fetch ye one o' those. I've light fingers, I do, and she'd never—"

"No tarts," Gavin said, though the prospect was tempting. Then, with a scowl for the boy's proposed larceny, he added, "And you're not to take things that don't belong to you. 'Tis a sure way to find your feet dangling. So long as you're in Newford, if 'tis food you need, you've only to ask."

The boy gave a disbelieving snort, and Gavin replied with a quelling frown.

"A lass then," Leo persisted. He looked about the high street, frowning, and added, "Though… there don't seem to be many of'm 'bout this place. Leastways, none younger than ol' Bess what hawks fish on the docks. Did ye know she's near to sixty?"

"Leo, I don't need a lass, and if I did, I certainly wouldn't need you to fetch me one."

"Well, ye look as if ye need *somefin'*. Ye look… ye look like I feels sometimes."

"Aye? And how is that?"

"Like ye wanna give sommat a good lick."

"A *proper* lick," Gavin corrected. "You're in Cornwall, lad."

Leo made an energetic swing at the air and then another. Gavin watched from the side of his eye until he realized the boy was miming a punch. He shook his head. "Your technique is all wrong."

"Punchin's punchin'. 'Ow can there be a wrong way, so long as ye hit somefin'?"

"You have to keep your striking arm tight." At Leo's confused look, Gavin pulled his own arms in and demonstrated. "Keep your arm close, like this. Avoid drawing it back beyond your side. Fighting— 'tis as much about wits as brawn. Use your weight and your opponent's to your advantage."

Leo's expression was dubious, but he tried again, mimicking Gavin's motion. Sadly, his second attempt was more ungainly than the first and would leave the lad open to a proper drubbing. He was still swinging when footsteps sounded behind them.

"Gavin."

He stopped, unsurprised his cousin had found him. "Merryn," he said tightly.

"You're providing instruction in pugilism?" Merryn said with a raised brow for Leo's technique.

"No," Gavin said automatically. Then, "Someone ought to, though."

They walked several more paces without speaking before Merryn said, "We couldn't make them see reason. Grandfather and I... many of the other jurors... we argued that Rowe had it right. To be sure, there's something off about Kingsley's death."

Merryn's expression was full of apology. Gavin rubbed an impatient hand over the back of his neck as he said with a sigh, "I know 'twas Killigrew and Trewyck."

"They were unmovable. Were't not for their certitude, I think the others could have been brought around." After a pause, Merryn asked, "What will you do now?"

Gavin released a short breath as Leo jumped to hit—and miss—a low hanging sign board. What would he do? He felt much like the boy, swinging at air. Insignificant and ineffectual.

A theory had begun assembling in his thoughts, but now he was out of time. His investigation was at an end. With the jury's verdict, Carew would consider the matter closed, and Gavin would go back to mediating his neighbors' disputes.

At his side, Leo made another awkward punch. Fighting was as much about wits as brawn; perhaps Gavin needed more of both just now. Something foul had occurred aboard the *Destiny*, and he wasn't about to let the inquest's ruling, or Carew's part in it, put an end to things. What would he do? "I mean to find the truth," he replied.

———

LADY PHILIPPA MEANT to depart in the morning. There would be no time to search the *Destiny* for Hannah's necklace, much less learn what had happened to Victor. Mari didn't know where he'd gone after she left him in the *Destiny's* hold, but something—intuition, providence, instinct—*something* told her that in finding the answer to that question, she might finally know more of what had become of Hannah and her child. And though she was reluctant to admit it, Gavin Kimbrell seemed the most likely path to that end, but his witnesses would soon decamp.

She'd not seen the constable since the inquest ended, so she went in search of his cousin. She found Mrs. Teague directing a pair of serving girls in the Feather's coffee room as her husband poured ale behind the bar. The inquest's spectators filled the tables, and the steady hum of conversation rose and fell amid the sharper sounds of pewter and crockery. Delightful smells of roasted beef and warm pastry came from the kitchen, and Mari's stomach rumbled. It had been some time since she'd eaten, but this was a matter that couldn't wait.

"Mrs. Teague," Mari said when the lady passed her.

The innkeeper replied without looking up. "What can I do for you, Miss Swan?"

"Do you know where I might find the constable?"

Mrs. Teague handed her full tray to a passing maid and wiped her hands on her apron. "Aye," she said. "'Tis a grim mood that one's found. I suspect you'll find him walking it off somewhere."

The second maid approached, face flushed and hairline damp from her exertions. "Mum, the squire says the pie be 'avin' too many neeps and not enough beef."

As the innkeeper left to see to the squire's pie, Mari wondered where Gavin Kimbrell might go to walk off his 'grim mood.' She was surprised when his deep voice sounded directly behind her.

"Miss Swan." She turned with relief, which he eyed with an equal amount of suspicion. A crease pulled his brows together as he said, "D'you require some assistance?"

She stepped toward a corner away from the bustle, and he followed. They were far enough from the others that they might not be overheard, but still, she lowered her voice to say, "You said you are never pleased when questions go unanswered. Do you mean to pursue this matter?"

His jaw tightened. "Aye."

"Then you must do something." At the encouraging lift of his brows, she added, "Lady Philippa has asked Mr. Tate to secure a private coach. She means to return to Bath in the morning. If you intend to find your answers, you must act quickly." She stilled her hands and waited, willing him to see the urgency in the matter.

He eyed her for an overlong moment, and she feared she'd overplayed her hand. He confirmed it when he said, "Miss Swan, why do I have the feeling I'm being managed? And why d'you care so much? Justice for a dead man is a noble aim but 'tis not, I think, *your* aim."

Mari was saved from answering when Charles Tate appeared in the doorway behind Gavin. She leaned to one side to observe him as he spoke with Mr. Teague. There was an impatience to his manner. He was as eager to quit Newford as Lady Philippa. Tate looked up, his brow dipping when he saw Mari in conference with the constable. It occurred to her then how closely they stood to one another, and she took a tiny step back from the man.

"Tate is asking about the coach," she whispered as she continued to watch him over Gavin's shoulder. Tate finished his conversation with Mr. Teague and crossed the slate floor toward them. "Oh, he's coming this way," she added urgently.

Then, lifting her voice slightly, she said for Tate's benefit, "Constable, I thank you for your direction to the apothecary."

"Miss Swan. Kimbrell." Tate gave Mari a dismissive glance then, addressing the constable, he said, "Lady Philippa wishes to leave in the morning. I gather we're still not permitted to retrieve our things from the *Destiny*?"

"I'll speak with the shipwright to see what can be done," Gavin said. "In the event 'tis still unsafe to board, I will arrange for your belongings to be delivered to Bath if you'll leave your direction."

Mari pulled in a sharp breath of alarm, but she held it at a quelling glance from the constable. Tate tugged at his cuffs, his lips pressed flat. "I expect you'll see that it does not come to that," he said. And with that presumption, he spun and left them.

"Do you see?" Mari whispered as soon as Tate was beyond their hearing.

"You may set your mind at ease," he replied. "We've but one private coach in Newford, and 'tis unavailable for another day still. Unless Lady Philippa wishes to travel with the mail, she'll not leave in the morning."

Mari pulled her gaze sharply back to the constable. "Unavailable? Have you contrived some sort of problem?"

"I have."

"Oh!" she replied, surprised at his foresight but pleased, nonetheless. "That is good, but you can't delay the coach indefinitely—"

"I'll ask again, Miss Swan. Why do you care? Or, per'aps the more proper question is this: what were you searching for on Victor Kingsley's person as he lay dying?"

Mari flinched at his words, but she wouldn't feel sorry for her actions.

The constable's arms were crossed, his feet planted like the roots of an ancient oak. She suspected he was just as immovable. When she didn't respond, he sighed. "Are you aware that impeding a constable's lawful duty is a punishable offense?"

"Are all constables so eager to arrest lady's companions?"

"Are all lady's companions so irksome?"

Mari pulled her head back. "Irksome?"

"It means—"

"I know what it means."

He rubbed his forehead. When he lowered his hand, it was to say, "I am not your enemy, Miss Swan. I gather from your manner you've not had a favorable experience with the constabulary, but I can assure you I mean to investigate this matter to the fullest extent of my abilities. You may as well give me the truth of it now."

Mari swallowed and studied his features. His gaze remained steady on hers, despite her rude examination. It was earnest and determined. How had she not noticed the deep blue hue of his eyes? More importantly, could she trust him, or would he tell her to go back to her teaching post and forget her questions? Or worse, would he reveal her identity and ruin any chance she had of finding the truth?

The inquest had ruled Victor's death an accident. *Death by misadventure.* Constable Kimbrell could wash his hands of the whole business and return to whatever tasks normally filled his days. She must consider the fact that he was still asking questions a mark in his favor. He was *not* Constable Bragg, and the truth was, she needed his help. Mari made her decision.

"I will tell you, but you must do more than simply delay the coach. You must take measures to prevent anyone from leaving until this matter is resolved."

"Rest assured I will do what I can."

She waited, and when he didn't move, she said, "You wish me to tell you *now*?"

He lifted his brows in expectation. "D'you have a better time?"

"But shouldn't you—?" She motioned to the empty doorway where Tate had gone.

"'Tis already done, but 'twill take some hours for

my plan to work. *If* it works."

Mari couldn't help the narrowing of her eyes. "'Tis already done?" she mimicked. "Constable, why do I feel you've tricked me into an unnecessary bargain?"

"You made a *concession*, Miss Swan, not a bargain. I merely accepted your offer of information—an offer which was not contingent on any *quid pro quo*."

Mari considered their exchange, and she had to admit the truth of his words, though it pained her to do so. With grudging admiration for his argument, and a reminder not to underestimate his skills in the future, she said, "Very well. I yield the point, but I submit that we might *both* benefit from a mutual sharing of information. Perhaps I know more than either of us realize, but until I know what *you* know, we'll never… know." She hid a grimace for the way he had of turning her thoughts—and her tongue—to pudding.

He studied her much as she'd done him earlier. She grew warm beneath his regard until, with a relaxing of his jaw, he seemed to reach his own decision. "Per'aps," he conceded.

"No half measures," she insisted, to which he gave a reluctant nod. "Shall we consider ourselves at a truce?"

HANNAH'S DIARY
FINAL ENTRY, 5 APRIL 1820

I told Victor of my decision. He was at turns angry and determined to change my mind, and I'm ashamed to say my heart quickened to think he might end his betrothal. But I reminded him the contracts are signed, and it would be wrong to break a promise of such long standing. He needs the connections such a union will provide—connections I could never offer.

Though my heart is truly broken, I take comfort in doing what is right for myself and my daughter. Perhaps in time, Mari may know her niece. I'm lighter for my decision and hopeful for the first time in many months.

CHAPTER 14

"A TRUCE," GAVIN agreed, though he wondered if he'd come to regret it. But Miss Swan's expression had lost some of its guardedness, and he couldn't regret that. She was direct, when she wasn't trying to keep things from him, and he found he liked her for it. And there was some truth to her proposition—he'd be a fool to pass up the chance to learn what she knew.

"What is this plan of yours?" she said softly.

"I have summoned the cavalry, Miss Swan, or the Admiralty, as the case may be." She tilted her head at him, and he only hoped Carew's reaction was as mild. He doubted it would be. "Now," he said, "'tis your turn."

"You said we've time before you know if your plan will work?"

"Aye, some two hours or more, I expect."

She nodded. "My story may well take that long. Will you walk with me? Lady Philippa has sent me on an errand with the dressmaker, and I should have already seen to it."

He agreed and motioned for her to precede him. As they turned onto the high street in the direction of his cousin's shop, he wondered if their truce required him to offer his arm. Miss Swan clasped her hands loosely before her, though, settling the matter, and he fell into step beside her.

"Victor Kingsley has—or had—a necklace that did not belong to him. *That* is what I was searching for on his... on the beach." She gave him a curious look. "How did you know?"

"The stains on your sleeve," he said. "The pattern suggested you had placed your hand between two stained articles of clothing. A coat and waistcoat were the logical assumptions."

"Clever," she murmured, though she cast a pensive glance toward her hands. "When you first pointed out the blood on my sleeve, I thought he must have sustained an injury on the rocks. I didn't know he'd been stabbed."

"Tell me about this necklace," he said before she could dwell too long on that.

"It's a pendant—a ruby teardrop." At the lift of his brows, she hastened to assure him, "It's not a real ruby. The thing isn't but a bit of paste, really, but it has value to *me*."

"The necklace is yours?"

She shook her head and her hands tightened, one thumb worrying over the other. "Perhaps I ought to start at the beginning," she said.

"'Tis always a good place."

They'd reached Morwenna's shop, and she hesitated before the door. Casting a glance along the nearby shops, she said, "I ought to address my errand, in case anyone is observing our conversation."

He wondered if she used her task to delay her story, but he couldn't disagree with her logic. *Someone* had killed Victor Kingsley, and until the perpetrator was identified, it was best to act as normally as possible.

The interior of the shop was cool compared to the sunbaked cobbles outside, and his cousin stood at the counter assisting another customer. Gavin nodded in her direction and said softly to Miss Swan, "Morwenna can be trusted to be very… thorough… with your order if that is your aim."

"An added delay," she murmured. "A wise course, but how can you be certain the dressmaker will agree?"

"She's my cousin."

Miss Swan's brow quirked as she said, "Another

cousin, Constable? How do you ever arrest anyone if they're all related to you?"

Gavin didn't reveal his magistrate's aversion to paperwork or that he'd never, in fact, arrested anyone. They may have had a truce between them, but that was a confession for another day. Instead, he told her, "My responsibility extends across the entire parish, Miss Swan. They are not *all* related to me." Even to his own ears, his words sounded pompous and a little petulant, and she gave him a sideways glance. He cleared his throat. "Morwenna is nearly finished with her customer."

When the shop was empty, and Miss Swan had relayed her request to Morwenna, Gavin encouraged his cousin to "take as long as you need to complete the order."

She gave him an odd look to match such an odd request, but Miss Swan added her agreement. "I shall impress upon Lady Philippa that, even with ready-mades, a proper fit takes time."

"The lady is a bit more slender than average," Morwenna said slowly. "'Tis true the items require some alteration."

With Morwenna's assurances that it would take at least two days to complete Lady Philippa's order, Gavin followed Miss Swan from the shop. "The necklace," she said, resuming her tale, "belonged to my sister Hannah."

"How did Kingsley come to have it?"

She was quiet for several paces as if considering her words. Finally, she said, "I don't know how or why, only that the necklace was missing until I discovered it in Victor's cabin. When he found me with it, I hid in the ship's hold, but he followed me. There was a bit of a… a struggle, and I lost it."

"A struggle?"

She swallowed. "Victor pursued me and I shoved him." At his expression, she quickly added, "I did not *stab* him."

Gavin nodded, though he fisted his hands to think she'd been *pursued*. Had Kingsley meant to do her harm? Then he recalled Leo's report that Miss Swan had been with Kingsley in his cabin before the ship ran aground. "Your sister's necklace," he said, "*that's* why you were in Kingsley's cabin."

Too late, he realized his surprise might be unflattering. He was intrigued to see a bit of color staining her cheeks for his assumption. Whether it was from irritation or embarrassment, though, he couldn't say.

"Constable," she continued, "Victor Kingsley seduced my sister, and I have reason to believe he murdered her as well."

Gavin nearly missed a step at her words. Miss Swan's hands were gripped tightly before her, the knuckles white. "You'd best tell me more," he said.

"Do you believe me?" He didn't miss the slight note of surprise in her voice.

"I believe *you* believe what you're saying, and that is good enough for now. Tell me about your sister."

She smiled, and her dimples made an appearance. "Hannah and I were twins," she began, "but we were as different as two sisters could be, in looks and in temperament. Hannah had the fairest hair and pale blue eyes that gave her the look of an angel come to earth. She loved music and sewing, and she can—could—embroider the most perfect little flowers. I, on the other hand, prefer stories of Greek mythology. Hannah was always up for a party or a new gown—she loved to study the fashion plates— while I'm content to read or draw." She gave a little shrug of her shoulders. There was no apology in her words, only a statement of fact.

"Our mother died when we were young, and after our father's death, what funds he had left went to pay the money lenders. We had no prospects, but we were fortunate to find teaching posts at the school where we'd been students."

"D'you have no other family?" he asked. "No one who might have come to your aid?"

She shook her head. "No, but the headmistress had been a friend of our mother's, and I think she must have made some exception to hire us both, though she's never admitted as much. I've found enjoyment in the work, but Hannah… she always wished for more. You mustn't think any less of her for it," she hurried to add. "Her light was simply too bright to hide it in Drayton-Marsh."

"Some people are not meant for a quiet life in the country," Gavin said.

"That is true, just as I'm not meant for the bustle and excitement of Bath or London. But Hannah wanted so desperately to go. When the family of a former student asked her to chaperone their daughter for the Season, she leapt at the chance."

"And was Bath all she hoped it would be?"

"She seemed happy at first, or so her letters would have me believe. But over time, they came less and less frequently until they stopped altogether."

"When was that?"

"A few weeks before her death. I've since learned she'd been living just a short distance away in Eventon. I believe she was posting her letters through Victor to maintain the fiction that she was still in Bath, but when they parted ways, she wouldn't have had any way of sending them without me learning of her situation."

She drew a long breath before continuing. "I'm getting ahead of myself, though. My sister's diary was among her things. From reading it, I've been able to piece together some of what happened."

They'd reached the Feather once more, and he sought a way to prolong their walk so she could finish her story. "D'you need anything from the apothecary, Miss Swan, or the chandler, per'aps?"

"I—yes, I suppose I should inquire about more rose water for Lady Philippa."

"The apothecary is this way," he said with a nod.

When they continued past the inn, she resumed her story. "Hannah met Victor in Bath, but he was already betrothed to Lady Philippa. It had been arranged for some time—Victor's money for Lady Philippa's family connections. His betrothal didn't stop him from seducing my sister, though.

"When Hannah found she was in a family way, he put her up in a cottage in Eventon, under another name, without the benefit of her family or friends. My sister's diary is clear that she'd made peace with her situation. She even told Victor she wouldn't see him anymore. She meant to take in sewing so she might give her daughter a good and honorable life, but she never had the chance. She drowned in the river, and the coroner's inquest ruled her death a"—Miss Swan's voice caught, but she mastered it once again—"a suicide. My sister was buried at the cross-roads, Constable, with no marker, and I have no notion what has become of her daughter. Hannah's light is gone, and no one but me will ever recall how bright it was."

Gavin pulled in a long, slow breath then let it out. "I do not doubt your convictions, Miss Swan, but what makes you believe your sister's death was anything but what the jury said it was?"

She stopped walking, and he did as well. "My sister and I may have been different," she said, "but I know Hannah. She would never have taken her own life, and she would certainly not have left her child behind."

"Per'aps she sent the babe to live with a family somewhere?"

"I considered that, but she gave her baby my name. Marianne. Why would she do that only to abandon her to live with strangers?"

Gavin considered for one brief moment the horrible notion that Hannah Talbot had taken her infant daughter to the river with her, but he wouldn't speak the words aloud. He asked instead, "Can we ever truly know what's in another's heart?"

She frowned, and he got them walking again. He was surprised when she dipped her head in agreement, saying softly, "I have wondered the same thing many times. There is something about the word 'suicide' that causes those left behind to doubt their hearts and their own minds. I began to doubt, so I made a list. There are other things, Constable, that simply don't fit the circumstances."

They'd reached the apothecary, but he thought she could use a visit to the church instead. When he kept walking, she didn't argue.

"For one thing," she said, "there was no note. When a person seeks to end their own life, is there not often a note left to explain the reason? To say goodbye, if nothing else, and to ease their family's hearts for not seeing what should have been apparent?"

His heart twisted a little at her unwitting admission. If Hannah's death had, in fact, been at her own hand, then it was clear Miss Swan wanted—needed—her sister's absolution. She needed assurances and explanations that may never come.

"A note is often found," he said gently, "but not always." A dark look settled on her face, and he added, "D'you wish for my agreement or the truth?"

She puffed her cheeks with a sigh. "The truth, of course."

"D'you have a second point?"

"Yes. Hannah would never have been without her necklace. It's only a trinket—a memento our mother bought off the gypsies when they came through—but she gave one to each of us to match her own. As long as we had our pendants, she said, we would always be together. Our mother was buried with hers, but Hannah"—her voice broke again—"Hannah was not wearing her pendant when she was found."

"'Tis the necklace you found in Kingsley's cabin."

"Yes."

"How d'you know *he* didn't buy one off the gypsies as well?"

She cast him a look of ironic disbelief. "That's a coincidence that stretches credibility," she said, and he couldn't disagree. "At any rate, it doesn't signify. The clasp on Hannah's necklace never closed properly. The blacksmith tried to repair it, but the finish didn't match. The difference is unremarkable unless you're looking for it. The necklace Victor had—the clasp was broken again in the same place, with the same unmatched finish. I'm certain it was hers."

"D'you have yours?" Gavin asked.

She pulled a thin gold chain from beneath her linen tucker to show him. It was as she described, with a small tear-shaped ruby at the bottom. The stone sparkled as it spun in the light, and if she hadn't told him it was paste, he would have thought it a pretty jewel. But to be sure, it wasn't anything worth killing a body over.

"How d'you know your sister didn't give hers to Kingsley as a token?"

"I would not have put it past Hannah to offer a lock of her hair or a ribbon or some such—I found one of her handkerchiefs among Victor's things—but she would not have given away our mother's necklace. My sister may have lost her way," she said firmly, "but she did not become another person entirely."

Gavin understood intuition. He felt it often enough himself, so he didn't doubt her certainty, but it wasn't enough to lead him to a conclusion of murder. Not yet, anyway.

"Were there marks on your sister's body that were inconsistent with drowning?" At her frown of confusion, he clarified gently, "Any bruises about her neck, for example, or cuts that shouldn't have been there?"

"I—I didn't notice any. I didn't know to look."

"'Tis no matter," he said. "The coroner would have done so. Was there anything found at the scene to indicate another person had been present?"

"Constable Bragg didn't say."

"I'll write to Bragg and the coroner and request their reports."

She directed a long glance at him. "You would do that?"

"Aye. I have many more questions for you, Miss Swan, but there's no harm in reviewing what's been done already."

She smiled again, and her shoulders relaxed as if a great weight had been pulled from them. "Thank you," she whispered. The look she gave him made him uncomfortable, as if he'd done something great and wondrous when he'd only offered to post a few letters. Had she been so truly alone since her sister's death?

CHAPTER 15

GAVIN CLEARED HIS throat and sought to return Miss Swan to her story. "So, 'twas the necklace you were seeking from Kingsley. 'Tis possible it was simply lost when he landed in the sea." At the narrowing of her eyes, he added, "You must acknowledge the possibility."

"I know," she said. "I'm also not blind to the fact that Victor might have returned it to his cabin. There was certainly time enough to do so after our encounter in the ship's hold. Or..."

He directed a questioning gaze toward her, and she continued. "Or it might have been lost during Victor's encounter with the person who killed him. If I could find Hannah's necklace, we might know more of what occurred. At the very least, we might know *where* it occurred."

Gavin considered her words. It was a theory that couldn't be ignored, though the odds of finding such a small item within the *Destiny's* upturned interior were slim. He brought them back to the matter of her sister. "D'you have any reason to believe Tate or Lady Philippa knew your sister? Or that anyone in the household knew of Kingsley's affair with her?"

Miss Swan shook her head. "I've searched Lady Philippa's correspondence and listened at doors, but I've found nothing to indicate she was aware of her husband's association with my sister. Regarding Tate, though, I couldn't say. In my role as lady's companion, he's not been accessible to me."

Her words brought to mind still more questions. "How did you come to be in the Kingsley household?" Gavin asked. "More importantly, what is your name? I have to think Kingsley would have recognized you for Hannah's sister if you'd given your own name."

The color on her cheeks grew, and she gave him a weak smile. "It's Talbot," she said. "Mari Talbot. But you must continue to call me Miss Swan," she hurried to add. "I don't think Lady Philippa will look too kindly on the deception, and I'd like to maintain my post for as long as it's useful to do so."

He frowned but held his silence, waiting for her to continue. Twisting her hands one inside of the other, she said, "I went to Bath for answers, but I was unsure how to gain access to Victor's household. It was fortuitous, really, when I made the acquaintance of Lady Philippa's new companion, a young lady she'd engaged through an agency by the name of Mary Swan. Miss Swan—the other Miss Swan, rather—had not met her new employer yet, so… in exchange for a good portion of my savings, she gave me her name and her new post."

Gavin blinked. He couldn't approve of such a scheme and it must have showed, for she stopped and gave him an earnest expression. "Constable," she said, "do you have sisters?"

"No." When her brow furrowed at his curt reply, he sighed and added, "But I've female cousins who are like sisters to me. I'm not insensitive to your plight, but d'you think 'twas the best scheme, to attach yourself to the household of a man you believe to be a murderer?" The very notion that she'd done something so reckless caused a cold sweat to form at his temples, even as he admired her resourcefulness.

"Would you not have done the same for them?"

He rubbed a hand along the back of his neck. It was not in him to lie, no matter how much he wished to. "Aye," he said reluctantly. He would have done everything she had, and more, were he faced with the same dilemma. "I will keep your secrets," he said, "for *now*."

She smiled, and the dimple in her left cheek appeared. He firmed his jaw against it and got them walking again. Turning the conversation back to more immediate matters, he asked, "Why did Kingsley join the *Destiny*? Henderson said his arrival at the wharf was unexpected."

"It was," she said, nodding, "though I don't know the reason. One moment, we were preparing for Lady Eagerton's ball, and the next, Lady Philippa was calling for Beatrice to pack her trunks."

"It was Lady Philippa's decision to travel with the *Destiny*?"

"No, I believe she meant only to accompany Victor. I gathered at the time he wasn't pleased with his wife's insistence on joining him, but Lady Philippa can be a force when she wishes to be."

Gavin considered this, still unsure what might have prompted Kingsley's hasty change in plans. They were nearly at the church, and though he was pleased with his "truce" with Miss Swan—Miss *Talbot*—he was still no closer to discovering what had happened aboard the *Destiny*. Before their conversation, his tentative theory had begun to firm, but this new information about Hannah Talbot and her missing necklace didn't seem to have a place in it.

He stopped them outside the lychgate. As if

reading his thoughts, Miss Swan said, "I've told you my story, but I've not asked if you have a theory of your own. Do you?"

"That, Miss Swan, is for the walk back. Now," he said gruffly, "our church has some comfortable benches, though I'd avoid the fourth one on the left. It wobbles something dreadful." Not to mention, Matthew and Daniel had scratched something inappropriate in the wood during last week's sermon. With all that had happened in the past days, he'd not found the time to drag them back with the sanding block.

Miss Swan looked up at the church's tall square tower as if she only now realized where they stood. "I've not been to a church since Hannah died," she whispered.

"You don't have to go inside if you don't wish to, but I thought per'aps you could use a bit of comfort."

———

COMFORT? MARI CONSIDERED the constable's words. How long had it been since she'd felt any measure of ease in her soul? Her nose stung, and she blinked before she could embarrass either of them with tears. "Perhaps you're right," she murmured.

She looked at him—truly *looked*—and was struck by the softening that had appeared in his gaze. His face was still all masculine angles and hollows, his nose sharp and the line of his jaw sharper still, but there was a bright warmth in his blue eyes that wasn't usually there. At least, not when they'd been directed at her. It was the warm look of… a friend, perhaps. An ally, at the very least. And that was something she'd not had in quite some time.

She left him at the gate and entered the church, the heavy wooden door echoing behind her as it closed. As her eyes adjusted to the dimness, she breathed in the scents of damp stone and old wood. The church was sparsely adorned, its pews empty and worn smooth. Wooden crates piled high with linens and toys lined one wall, and pale light filtered through small, deeply set windows to throw diamonds onto the grey stone floor.

Her steps were soft but loud at the same time as she moved toward the front. She slid onto a bench and, after a moment's hesitation, closed her eyes. The stillness pressed on her from all sides, unbearably tight in its absoluteness, like water closing over her head.

Her heart gave a panicked little flutter, and her eyes flew open again. She forced herself to remain on the bench, though the urge to leave was there. If God had wished to comfort her, there were any number of ways He might have done so already.

Answers. *That* was what she needed.

Then she thought of Gavin. He'd said he would write to the coroner in Somerset and to Constable Bragg. He'd listened to her—had truly seemed to *hear* her, which was a remarkable thing after months of being silent and invisible to everyone around her. Perhaps, she allowed... just perhaps, the crossing of their paths had been by design. And now, Gavin had brought her to the church. For comfort.

Settling once more on the bench, Mari shut her eyes again and allowed the silence to close over her. She'd felt so many things in the past weeks and months. Anger and frustration, of course, but also an overwhelming disbelief at everything that had occurred. But beneath it all lay the sharp sting of guilt, for she'd failed her sister when Hannah needed her most. Regardless of the manner of Hannah's death, she'd not trusted Mari enough to confide her situation. They weren't close as sisters ought to be, but what had they ever had, if not each other?

Mari wondered again if Hannah's death had been swift, or if she'd had time to despair for her child. Where was little Marianne? Was she cared for? Loved?

Mari had gone to Hannah's home in Eventon after burying her sister, but no one there had any answers for her. The friend Hannah described in her diary, the spinster, had been away visiting relatives during Mari's visit and again when she'd passed through on her way to Bath. Vines had already begun to climb the walls of Hannah's cottage, and as the sun shone on Eventon and carriages rolled down its pretty lane, Mari had been struck with an overwhelming sorrow. Everything went on as if her sister had never lived.

Now, she looked up before her thoughts could overwhelm her heart. A soft, almost imperceptible breeze stirred the air, setting the light from a single iron candelabrum to dance and bringing with it the faint scent of… lavender. Mari's throat grew tight, and she imagined the weight of her sister's hand pressing her own. Her heart quickened, though she was certain it was a trick of her mind to imagine her sister's presence. But what a comfort, to think Hannah might still be welcomed in such a hallowed space.

The heaviness on her chest shifted until she was able to draw a full breath for the first time since learning of her sister's death. She pulled it in and exhaled slowly. Mari would discover what had happened to Hannah, and she would find her sister's child. Over the past weeks, she'd never lost that grim certainty, but now it was buoyed by the knowledge that she wasn't entirely alone in her endeavor. She thought of Gavin waiting for her outside, and she felt a tiny flicker of hope.

———

GAVIN CROSSED THE church's small graveyard while he waited for Miss Swan to emerge. The rows were tidy, the grass recently clipped to perfume the air. Crisp white headstones marked the places where souls had left this world for the next.

He considered Mari's sister, buried alone at the crossroads near her home. Whether her death had been at her own hand or not, she didn't deserve to be forsaken so completely. Surely, divine mercy must extend even to those deemed lost. He felt an uncomfortable sorrow, a hollowness behind his rib cage, though he'd never known the young woman. He could only imagine how Mari must feel.

He was paying his respects at his grandmother's grave when hooves sounded beyond the lychgate. Matthew and Daniel approached, and he crossed the grass to the low stone wall that bordered the high street.

"You found the Admiralty office?"

"Aye," Matthew said. He reached across the wall to extend a sealed letter to Gavin. "Captain Edwards sends his regards, as well as a reply to your letter and a separate missive for Carew. We're away to the squire's now."

Gavin stayed them with a hand when they would have ridden off. The horses snorted impatiently while he tore open the seal and unfolded the page. His former lieutenant's words were brief, the letters evenly scripted in the man's steady hand. In his missive, he provided an intriguing bit of intelligence on Captain Oliver Henderson in response to Gavin's inquiry.

> *Henderson seems to have trouble keeping his boats afloat. This is the second in four years that's foundered, though the first, I'm sorry to say, wasn't so fortunate as the Destiny. Twelve souls perished and the Mary Claire was a complete loss. Henderson, who'd been hired on as master, was acquitted of any wrongdoing, though there were a few rumblings of negligence. Those faded soon enough, though, when the insurance funds came through.*

Edwards went on to assure Gavin he would have the Admiralty's aid and urged him to follow his instincts, which had always been sound. Gavin finished the letter, relieved and pleased in equal measure with Edwards' reply, though he knew Carew would not be.

With a nod for Matthew and Daniel, he dismissed them. "Go," he said.

As his cousins turned their mounts to find the squire, Miss Swan emerged from the church. He was pleased to see her shoulders seemed a bit more steady. Not that they'd been *unsteady* before, but there was a renewed vitality to her, as if a light that had been missing was now returned to her features.

Gavin rarely missed a Sunday, though the task of attending church was one borne of habit rather than devotion. Their vicar's sermons weren't particularly original or enlightening, but there was always a measure of comfort to be found within the church's cool stone walls. If Miss Swan had found it too, then he was glad for it.

She smiled when she spied him at the wall, and his stomach gave an odd little twist. He couldn't recall seeing such an easy expression on her face. During their brief acquaintance, she'd always been a bit prickly.

He joined her, but before they could start back to the Feather, a cart pulled up at the church. At the reins sat an unfamiliar gentleman in a round hat with a plainly dressed lady at his side. He set the brake on his cart as Gavin approached the side.

Gavin introduced himself and Miss Swan and offered to provide direction if the man was lost. The newcomer was not lost. He gave his name as Cyril Harris, the new superintendent over at St. Lawrence, "and my lady wife, Mrs. Harris."

Gavin started. With the wreck and the inquest, he'd forgotten all about delivering the parish boxes. "My apologies for the delay," he said.

Harris shook his head. "Never mind it. We hear

Newford has enjoyed some excitement of late, so Mrs. Harris suggested we drive up and retrieve the boxes ourselves. Save you the journey."

Gavin gave them his thanks. "Let me summon the vicar, and we'll load them onto your cart." He turned toward the rectory behind the church but was stopped by the expression on Miss Swan's face. The line of her thin dark brows pulled low as she gave Harris a considering look.

———

MARI APPROACHED THE side of Harris's cart. Cyril Harris from St. Lawrence. *C Harris. St. L.* Her stomach tilted with excitement. Her mind's eye recalled the names written in Victor's hand as if she were back aboard the *Destiny* reading his appointment book again. St. L could be a place, rather than a person. Was it merely coincidence that this man—Cyril Harris—had come from a place called St. Lawrence?

"Is your home near Falmouth, sir?" she asked.

"Why, near enough, I suppose," Harris said. "The parish home at St. Lawrence is a small establishment just off the Falmouth road."

Mari nodded, though her heart jumped. "And are you acquainted with a man by the name of Victor Kingsley?" she asked.

Harris straightened, his eyes widening to give

him an owlish expression behind his round spectacles. "I've had some correspondence with the man," he said slowly. "How"—he paused, frowning—"how does he go on?"

"He's dead," Mari said. The man's wife gasped, and Mari knew a moment's regret for her indelicacy, but it soon passed. She had neither the time nor the patience to worry over such things. Gavin moved closer. His presence warmed her side, supporting her as firmly as his arm might have done had he offered it.

Harris rubbed a gloved fingertip along the point of his chin. "Dead, you say? I'm sorry to hear it. Were you well acquainted with him?"

"I'm in his wife's employ."

Harris tipped his chin soberly. "My condolences for your loss," he said, "and for the widow's."

"If I may ask," Gavin said, "what was the nature of your association with Kingsley?"

"He... our association was of a philanthropic nature. That is, he wished to make a donation."

Mari held a snort of disbelief. Victor Kingsley, a philanthropist? Beside her, Gavin said, "Kingsley wished to make a donation to a small parish home in Cornwall? Do you receive many contributions from outside the parish?"

Harris adjusted the reins looped around his hand. His wife's face was hidden by the brim of her bonnet as she looked on her husband. "Not many," Harris said, "but we do receive some."

"Did Kingsley have a prior connection to St. Lawrence?"

"I wouldn't know," Harris said. "I've only been in my position a short time. I'm sorry I can't be of more help, but if we might see to the boxes…"

CHAPTER 16

AFTER THE PARISH boxes were loaded and Harris had turned his cart back toward Falmouth and St. Lawrence, Gavin began a slow walk to the Feather with Miss Swan.

Mrs. Pentreath, one of Newford's matrons, gave them a curious glance as she bustled along the other side of the street, her cane thumping the cobbles. Gavin kept his hands clasped firmly behind him, lest she get ideas into her head about his squiring Miss Swan about. Or Miss Talbot, rather. Devil take it—*Mari*. That was better.

She'd revealed her full Christian name was Marianne, and he'd begun their acquaintance thinking of her as Maid Marian—a fact which caused him no little amusement. Still, he found he preferred the simpler, shorter name. *Mari*. It suited her.

He looked at her from the corner of his eye. She walked with her hands held together, her movements graceful if a little determined, and he wondered what she'd be doing now if not for this business with her sister. Did she have friends and acquaintances back home? A suitor? He usually enjoyed pondering questions, but this one caused him to swallow uncomfortably, so he turned his thoughts instead to other matters.

"What made you think to ask Harris if he knew Kingsley?" he said, pleased with the evenness of his voice. The revelation that Harris had been acquainted with their dead man still puzzled him. He wasn't certain how, or if, this new information might fit his theory, or if it meant his thoughts had been traveling the wrong path.

"His name was familiar," she said, "and now I recall seeing it in Victor's notes. The paper you found in my pocket"—she heaved a great sigh—"it was a page from Victor's appointment book. I'm afraid the bump on my head has dulled my recollection of what was on it, but when I heard the man's name, I recalled Victor had written *C Harris* in his book, with a reminder to pay the man one hundred pounds." She frowned, and Gavin wondered if she doubted Harris's story about a philanthropic donation, or if she was displeased by it. "Do you know anything of him?" she asked.

"Of Harris? Not much, I'm afraid. I knew from our vicar that a new superintendent had been placed at the parish home. He's only had the post for some two or three months, I believe." Her frown hadn't lessened, so he said, "'Tis possible Kingsley's business with the man was just what Harris said—a philanthropic matter."

She gave a delicate lady-snort to show what she thought of that. "You indicated you have a theory," she said, recalling him to their earlier conversation.

"Aye." He pulled in a long breath. "I believe Kingsley was stabbed in a dispute over the wreck."

"The wreck?" Mari pulled her head back to look at him. "But the timing suggests Victor was stabbed *before* then. Certainly, he never appeared on the quarter deck when everyone was summoned." Her eyes narrowed as she considered her words and the implications. "If he was stabbed over the wreck as you suggest, then the wreck must have been... planned."

"Just so."

She sucked in a startled breath, and Gavin explained his developing theory about the grounding of the *Destiny*. That her expression remained skeptical wasn't doing anything to bolster his confidence, but there were too many things that pointed to such a conclusion.

The broken mirror his cousins had found atop the cliffs, for one—it was clear evidence of a signal being sent that night. The signal might also explain the curious absence of wreckers on the scene. They hadn't come to plunder the grounded ship because they'd already had their payment for guiding Henderson to the beach ahead of the Devil's Teeth. In fact, in an ironical turn, the wreckers' actions may have been the only thing to *save* the ship, given the fog that evening and the strength of the tide.

The theory of a planned wreck also explained why Henderson hadn't put in at Falmouth as Kingsley wished. If the captain had already made arrangements to wreck near the Devil's Teeth, an unplanned stop in Falmouth would have thrown the scheme off.

His theory explained a number of other things, too. Henderson's hesitation at allowing Evans and Pengilley to board his ship so the salvage could begin, and why the *Destiny* sailed with such a small crew. Scuttling a ship was always a gamble, and Henderson, despite his apparent scheme, meant to spare as many as he could.

Gavin considered Captain Edwards' note from the Admiralty, still tucked in his coat. Had Henderson deliberately scuttled the *Mary Claire* as well? Or had he merely been inspired by it? Edwards' message suggested Henderson had been a hired master of the *Mary Claire*, not the owner. He wouldn't have gained anything directly from such a scheme. But the captain, by his own admission, had invested everything he had into acquiring the *Destiny*. An insurance scheme would have recovered his funds.

"Couldn't he simply have sold his ship?" Mari asked. "If he wished to retire, that seems an easier solution."

Gavin shook his head. "'Twould have been difficult if not impossible. Once the war ended, the Admiralty was left with a large fleet of unused ships. Much like His Majesty's sailors, the warships have been repurposed. They're being sold as private vessels, and there's little market for a retiring captain wishing to sell his ship."

What Gavin didn't understand, though, was the nature of the argument with Kingsley, if that indeed were the reason for the man's death. Had Kingsley discovered Henderson's plan, or had they devised it together?

He thought the latter the more likely circumstance. If the vessel had been lost, Henderson would have collected on his ship, and Kingsley would have been compensated for his cargo. Both men stood to gain from the scheme, so what had there been to argue over?

"You said you encountered Kingsley in the

hold," he said. "What did you see there?"

Mari considered him with a crease between her brows. "The hold was empty for the most part. There weren't but a few crates and bales lashed in the center." Her eyes widened as she realized the import of that. "The hold was nearly empty, but if Captain Henderson and Victor meant to claim the insurance funds, they would have to make it seem as if they carried more than they did."

"Aye," Gavin said. "They would need a false manifest and false bills of lading as well, but Henderson's papers seem consistent with the cargo you describe, at least in terms of volume." He recalled the manifest Henderson had shown him. The ink had been smudged in places, as if it hadn't dried properly. His heart raced as another piece of his theory fell into place.

"That was why Henderson took so long to leave the ship," he said slowly. "With a rescue at hand, he realized his scheme might not work. While the *Destiny* continued taking on water, he wrote out a proper copy of the manifest, knowing any false claims about the cargo would be disproved if the ship didn't sink."

"If your theory is correct, then there must be a false manifest somewhere."

"Aye. If Henderson hasn't destroyed it. He would be a fool not to."

"Would he have given it over to the Lloyd's agent?"

Gavin shook his head. "I don't think so. The ship didn't sink as planned, so there's no claim on the cargo. If there's no claim, there's no need to file the manifest with Fairfax."

"And there's no crime, I presume? Aside from Kingsley's death, that is."

"There's still the matter of the captain's willful endangerment of his crew and passengers, though I suspect any penalty for that would be minor in comparison to a charge of fraud."

Mari watched him, and Gavin knew a moment of doubt. The entire scheme was too implausible, and it still didn't explain Kingsley's death to his satisfaction. Was he mistaken in his theory?

If so, then why had the man from Lloyd's arrived so soon? Fairfax had appeared mere *hours* after the wreck. There'd hardly been time for the notification to reach him, much less for Fairfax to travel from Truro or wherever the company had posted him.

No, the wreck of the *Destiny* had been planned, and Fairfax knew about it.

That Newford's gigs succeeded in pulling the *Destiny* off the rocks before she sank was a turn no one had anticipated. He felt a smile starting, but it was too soon for giddiness.

———

MARI CONSIDERED ALL that Gavin had told her. His theory was a clever one, and she was impressed that he'd deduced it so readily. She didn't know how everything fit with her sister's death, but the pieces would come. One way or another, she'd find the truth.

She tilted her head, thinking. "If Victor and the captain argued, what do you think was the nature of their dispute?"

The line of Gavin's jaw shifted as he said, "Aye, 'tis a question I still haven't sorted."

"Whether he meant to retire or not, I can't imagine Captain Henderson would have been eager to destroy his own ship. Perhaps Victor was making him do it."

"'Tis possible, I suppose, but…"

"Yes?"

He studied her for a long moment then, lowering his voice, he said, "D'you think you might hold a bit prejudice toward Kingsley?"

Mari's frown was immediate—she couldn't help it. Was it prejudice to see Victor for the villain he was? No. It was practical and sensible. It was right. But Gavin's expression was not one of judgment but expectation. He didn't question her bitterness toward Victor, but he expected *her* to do so.

"You think I see a monster where there is none," she said.

"I do not excuse what Kingsley did to your sister. At the very least, he acted dishonorably, knowing he would not marry Hannah. He left her in an impossible situation. But"—Gavin hesitated, and Mari braced herself—"but in my experience, people are neither entirely good nor entirely bad. People are complicated and their motivations even more so. If I am to learn the truth of what happened, I must keep my mind open."

Mari opened her mouth to argue that people were not so complicated as he suggested. Then the example of her own sister halted her words. Hannah had made poor choices in her life, but at the heart of it all, she'd been a good person. She'd just been… complicated, as Gavin said.

She wished for a simpler world, where right was right and wrong was punished. But those, she knew, were the wishes of a child, of a girl lost in the clearly drawn world of Greek heroes. But even those heroes had flaws—gargantuan, epic flaws. How could she be so foolish?

Her eyes became hot with sudden, unshed tears. "I am becoming no better than Constable Bragg," she said softly. "So rigid in my thoughts that I fail to consider things properly. You are right, of course, though it's a difficult turn to make."

She paused to collect herself and Gavin looked ahead. Then, because she couldn't stop herself from asking, she said, "What role do you think any of this ship scuttling played in Hannah's death?"

Gavin clasped his hands behind his back. They'd reached the Feather's stable yard. From the hard line of his jaw, she was certain she would not like his next words. "None, that I can see, I'm afraid."

"Perhaps Hannah learned of the scheme?" Her desperation was clear even to her own ears.

"Did she say anything in her papers to give any indication she knew something she should not?"

Mari's jaw firmed in frustration. "No," she said with resignation. "Hannah was hopelessly in love with Victor. Her writings are absent any details as ordinary as his work."

Gently, he said, "Miss Swan—Mari—I don't know that you'll find the answers you seek aboard the *Destiny*."

———

GAVIN HELD THE door to the inn, and Mari passed through. He regretted being the one to put the slump back in her shoulders, but she ought to prepare herself for the truth. Hannah Talbot's death didn't have anything to do with Kingsley's. He was fairly certain of it.

They'd not gone more than half a dozen steps when Carew's gruff bellow called to him from the coffee room. Gavin took his leave of Mari with a nod, waiting until she ascended the stairs before going in search of the squire. If he were to receive a proper josing, he preferred not to have a pretty lass as witness.

"What's the meaning of this, Kimbrell?" The squire waved a letter as he spoke, and the paper crackled with the intensity of his irritation. Carew still wore his napkin tucked in his buttonhole, uncaring of the spectacle he made as several heads came up round the room.

Pengilley and Clifton, the baker, watched from their table in the far corner. Several of Gavin's cousins and a few cronies of his grandfather were witnesses as well, and Wynne, who'd been standing at the inn's desk, set her pen down gently and leaned forward to watch the unfolding scene.

Gavin wished the squire might have chosen a more private place for their discussion. He set his jaw. "You've received a letter from the Admiralty, I presume—"

"I've had a letter from the Admiralty," Carew said, deaf to Gavin's words. "They've decided to take an interest in our case, given the maritime nature of Kingsley's death. It has been *suggested* that I ought to bind over the passengers and crew until"—he read from the page—"'such time as all avenues of inquiry are fully explored.'"

It was clear that Carew read the Admiralty's *suggestion* for what it was—a subtly worded threat couched as well-intentioned advice. The Admiralty had no jurisdiction in the matter of Kingsley's death, but they could make the life of a local magistrate more difficult than it ought to be.

Carew tossed the letter toward his table, but it missed and fluttered to the Feather's slate floor. "What are you playing at, Kimbrell? The jury has made their ruling. This matter is finished."

Gavin pressed his lips before saying, "You did instruct me to contact my former lieutenant—"

"To take the case, not to prolong it, and certainly not to direct our efforts. I know you and I don't agree on this, just as I know you contacted the Admiralty for the specific purpose of going around me. You can't go about doing things to suit your own ends."

Gavin didn't mention his suspicions that Carew had swayed the jury to suit *his* ends. Instead, thinking on Captain Edwards' letter and Henderson's experience aboard the *Mary Claire*, he said, "Sir, I believe there are facts that, had they been known to the jury, would have altered their opinion."

Carew ignored his words. Plucking the napkin

from his coat and tossing it onto the table, he said, "I've been satisfied with your performance these past years, Kimbrell. Don't give me cause to rethink your appointment."

The Feather went unnaturally quiet and Gavin tucked his chin. "Duly noted, sir."

"Well, then. Let's get on with it. If you're to make more inquiries to please the Admiralty, then I must inform these people they cannot leave. Lady Philippa is Quality, and I can't say I'm pleased with the position in which you've placed me."

"Aye, sir."

"And I mean to attend these inquiries of yours."

Gavin puffed his cheeks with a sigh, but he could only nod. Duly and publicly chastised—he really should have expected nothing less—Gavin took the Feather's stairs with Carew close behind. But, he thought, his investigation wasn't ended yet, so that was something at least.

———

MARI LEFT GAVIN to his interview with Carew and returned to her room. Revealing her secrets—and Hannah's—had left her wrung out and spent, but still she had no answers.

I don't know that you'll find the answers you seek. She couldn't fault Gavin's words, or the gentle way in which he'd given them. But, coming so swiftly after her uplifting visit to the church, she was beginning to feel something like a clock's pendulum, up one moment only to fall the next.

Suddenly, she was more weary than she'd been in some time. She needed a respite from, well, everything. From Lady Philippa and Tate's urgency to leave Newford. From Gavin Kimbrell's gentle-but-precise probing of her heart. From too many questions without answers.

But most importantly, she needed a respite from her own thoughts.

She was not one to avoid difficult things, but a nap would not go amiss. Then, perhaps she'd take some supper from the Feather's kitchen. When she reached the upper landing, though, she found Beatrice in the hall outside her room.

"Miss Swan," the maid said. "Lady Philippa sent me to ask after your outing to the dressmaker. Did you have any success?"

The dressmaker. It had only been a matter of hours since Lady Philippa had sent Mari on her errand, but it seemed like days. Mari pushed open the door to her room, Beatrice following.

"Mrs. Williamson says it will take some time to complete the alterations," she said as she stoked the embers in the hearth back to life. She removed her bonnet and began to loosen the pins in her hair. "Is

Lady Philippa still determined to depart in the morning?"

"Oh, yes. There doesn't seem to be any reason to stay, does there?"

Mari swallowed and wondered if Gavin's plan would work before it was too late. Beatrice turned to pour water from the pitcher into the bowl, and Mari caught the slightest rounding of the maid's stomach beneath her apron.

"Beatrice," she said, settling onto the edge of the bed. "Have you given any thought to what you'll do?"

"Do, miss?" The maid's brows cinched together over her nose. Idly, she began aligning Mari's pins on the dresser.

Mari nodded at the maid's belly, hidden now by the fullness of her skirts. "When your condition can't be concealed any longer, that is."

"Oh," Beatrice said, her features relaxing into a smile. "Charles means to marry me."

"He does?" Mari said, with a bit more surprise than perhaps was flattering. "That is, I wasn't aware he'd offered marriage. You've my felicitations."

"He hasn't offered. Not yet, leastways, but I know he means to."

"Beatrice…" Mari began gently, but the maid stopped her words with a fierce scowl.

"I can tell you don't believe it, but he will," she

repeated with more force.

Mari could only nod in the face of such certainty. Poor Beatrice. Didn't she see Charles Tate for what he was? He certainly had the advantage. As Victor's man of affairs, he wasn't wealthy by any stretch, but he had some means and connections. Beatrice, though, was naught but a maid. Tate could save her or leave her, and no one would bring him to account for his actions. Lady Philippa's assurances aside, the maid would be ruined.

Would Beatrice, Mari wondered, be left to follow the same course as Hannah? She opened her mouth to… what? Warn her? It was rather too late for that, and she could see Beatrice wasn't of a mind to hear reason. She said only, "If there's anything I can do to help, you've only to ask."

Beatrice remained silent. She finished tidying the vanity, though there was no need for it, before leaving Mari to her thoughts.

Mari undressed and hung her gown so it wouldn't wrinkle. Then, wearing only her shift, she climbed between the sheets. A few moments' sleep was all she needed.

CHAPTER 17

MARI WOKE DISORIENTED. Her hair was damp against her scalp and the room had gone dark, though a bit of pale light still seeped round the edges of the curtain. She'd had another nightmare about water and drowning and Hannah. She tried to erase the images from her mind, but they were drawn in ink. Swinging her feet to the floor, she lit a candle and considered the day's events.

The inquest and the jury's ruling. Her truce with Gavin. Lady Philippa's decision to leave in the morning. Would Gavin's plan to keep everyone in Newford work? She recalled the magistrate's thundering voice as he called to Gavin from the inn's coffee room. He'd been displeased, but though she lingered in the corridor, she hadn't been able to make out his words. What if he convinced the constable to leave off his investigation? Would Gavin be so easy to sway?

He was not Constable Bragg, she reminded herself. His earnestness as they'd discussed the matter of Victor's death, as well as her sister's, seemed genuine. She could believe he wished to find answers almost as much as she did.

He'd called her Mari, a fact that had not gone overlooked. After being Miss Talbot for so long at Mrs. Sherwood's, and now Miss Swan, hearing her given name spoken in Gavin's rich voice, his tongue rolling gently over the R... it had been a balm to her ruffled emotions.

Her stomach rumbled, and she thought of the warm pastry smells coming from the Feather's kitchen earlier. She stood and washed. The water in the pitcher was cold, and it revived her somewhat. As she finished tying the laces on her gown, Beatrice arrived at her door to see if she needed wood sent up for the fire, which had gone out. How long had she slept?

"Do you know the time?" Mari asked.

"Nearly half six."

"So late?" She'd not meant to sleep through the afternoon.

"Early, do you mean?" At Mari's frown of confusion, Beatrice added, "Lady Philippa hasn't risen yet, of course, but—"

"Risen? Do you mean it's half six *in the morning*?"

"Well, yes." As if to add its agreement, a horn from the morning stage blared shrilly in the yard below Mari's window.

She couldn't recall a time in recent weeks when she'd found more than a handful of hours' respite, but she'd slept through the previous afternoon *and* the night? Panic rose. What had she missed? Spinning, she said, "Does Lady Philippa still mean to leave this morning?"

Beatrice took a step back from the abrupt question. With her brows low, she said, "You haven't heard then. The squire says as how we're all to remain in Newford. What do you think it means?"

Mari calmed herself with a slow breath. They were to remain in Newford. Gavin's plan had worked. "I think it means the constable hasn't finished asking his questions yet." Her pins were where Beatrice had left them, still arranged in a neat row next to the pitcher. She pulled a brush through her hair then began applying them as swiftly as she could.

"But Lady Philippa says the jury…"

Beatrice's words were lost as Mari considered the day ahead. She imagined Gavin would speak with Captain Henderson about his insurance theory. Perhaps the *Destiny's* first mate, Doyle, had been aware of the scheme, and they mustn't forget Charles

Tate. Surely, he knew more of Victor's dealings than he'd revealed so far.

It was too early to seek out the constable, but Beatrice left her with a promise to have breakfast sent up from the Feather's kitchen. Mari paced her room as she waited, but when the tray arrived, she found she couldn't eat. Despite the cloud-like texture of the Feather's muffin, it was dry as sand in her mouth. She washed it down with a swallow of tea, shoved the tray aside, then left.

She hesitated as she passed Doyle's room. When would Gavin speak with the man? Had he already done so? They'd seen little of the surly Irishman since arriving at the Feather. She'd been grateful for his absence for Leo's sake, but she couldn't imagine Doyle would be a cooperative witness. She leaned closer, putting her ear to the wood. There were no sounds coming from the room. He must still be abed.

"Wot're ye doing?"

Mari straightened abruptly as Leo eyed her from the end of the hall. "Shhh," she said softly. He gave her a suspicious squint, which she couldn't fault, lurking as she'd been outside his employer's room. She tried a smile, but his squint only narrowed. With a sigh, she whispered, "Do you know if Mr. Doyle is inside?"

"Aye," Leo said as he rapped on the door. "Mr. Doyle!" he called. "Miss Swan's 'ere to see ye."

Mari tried to shush him again, but the boy was having none of it. He knocked again, more loudly this time, and the door swung open beneath his fist. Frowning, Leo sauntered in as Mari tried to call him back. Footsteps sounded on the stairs, and Gavin arrived at the top with Squire Carew.

"Wot the bleedin' 'ell?" Leo said from inside Doyle's room, and Mari returned her attention to the boy. That was when she spied the form of Finnegan Doyle laid out on the wooden floor. Gavin had seen him, too. He and Carew rushed past her to enter, and Mari gripped the side of the door frame before following them.

The curtains were drawn, the room dim. Doyle's face was pale, his eyes wide as he stared at nothing.

"Gavin," Mari murmured, drawing his attention to the desk. A gin bottle sat next to an empty vial of laudanum. Beneath the vial lay a folded half-sheet. A jar of ink and a sharpened quill completed the scene, the ink from the quill still shiny where it had dripped onto the desk. Mari nudged the laudanum aside and opened the paper with her fingertip to read the words written across its surface. *I'm sorry. I see no earthly remedy for my sins.*

"Leo," Gavin said, turning to the boy. "When was the last time you saw your employer?"

Leo's eyes were wide as he stared at the scene. "Wot?"

"When did you last see Doyle?"

Mari settled her hands on the boy's shoulders. They were tense and bony, but he relaxed a bit beneath her touch. She pulled him closer. "Last night," he said, his voice thin and high. "'E was in 'is chair, right 'ere, sleepin' off 'is gin."

"You're certain he was asleep?"

Leo nodded then, frowning, shook his head. "Aye… no. Aw, bleedin—"

"Mind the lady, lad," Gavin said gently.

Leo looked up at Mari with an apology. "Sorry, miss." She gave him a tremulous smile in reply.

"Is this his usual bottle?" Gavin asked.

Leo bent forward to study the brown glass. "Aye."

Mrs. Teague passed the open doorway at that moment and, seeing the dead man laid out on her floor, pressed a hand to her mouth. Then her gaze landed on Leo who stood, chin tucked, studying his employer's prone form.

"Mrs. Teague," Mari said with a nod toward the boy, "do you require any assistance in the kitchen?"

Dropping her hand from her mouth, the innkeeper said with admirable calm, "Aye, Leo, Peggy's just pulling a fresh batch of tarts from the oven. Someone will need to taste them to be sure they're fit to serve."

Leo pulled his gaze from Doyle and cast it

toward Gavin, who gave him a nod of dismissal. The boy didn't need any further persuasion, and Mrs. Teague closed the door behind them as they went.

"Constable," Carew said when they'd gone, "you can't tell me *this* death is not exactly what it appears. The man left a note of remorse, after all."

"The note's a bit cryptic," Mari said. "Which sins are we to assume he's apologizing *for*?"

Carew eyed Mari as if just noticing her presence for the first time. "Why, for killing Kingsley."

Gavin stood and faced the magistrate. "So, now you believe Kingsley's death was murder after all?"

Carew scowled and crossed his arms over his chest. "Juries mistake the facts all the time, but what are we left to believe with a note like that?"

Mari could sense Gavin's frustration. It was in the line of his jaw and the sigh she suspected lay just beneath the surface. He held it and used his pen knife to lift the edge of Doyle's sailor's coat. He emptied the man's pockets, and they saw Doyle carried the usual items for a man of his rank and class—a watch, unremarkable in its design, a small knife, a pipe and tobacco pouch. There were a few sketches, which Gavin hastily hid, but not before she caught a glimpse of what was clearly not intended for the eyes of genteel ladies' companions.

But tucked inside the last pocket was a thick

folded paper. It crinkled as Gavin pulled it free and unfolded the pages. Mari peered over his shoulder to read.

SHIP'S MANIFEST
Vessel: Destiny
Captain: Oliver Henderson
Port of Departure: Bristol
Port of Arrival: London

Next, was the heading "Cargo." The inventory listed beneath it was extensive and included a description, along with the quantity and weight of each item. There were bolts of silk and crates of wine, figs and oranges. Ceramics and upholstery. Clocks and machinery for the London printers. The volume was far greater than what Mari had seen in the *Destiny's* hold.

She drew an excited breath. "You were right about the insurance scheme," she whispered.

"Aye, but wrong about the perpetrator."

———

"SCHEME?" CAREW SAID. "What scheme?" Gavin pulled his attention from Mari's admiring gaze and gave it to Carew. The magistrate had been a constant shadow at his elbow since their encounter the previous afternoon. Their knock at Doyle's door last evening had gone unanswered, but they'd spoken with the rest of the crew again, as well as Lady Philippa and Tate, to inform them of the Admiralty's order.

To no one's surprise, none of them were pleased with the direction. Even the maid, Beatrice, having just returned from Miss Swan's room, gave a little squeak of distress to learn they were to remain in Newford. No one had produced any new insights, and though Gavin had explained his theory to the squire, he'd sensed the man's growing boredom with the details.

"'Tis the matter I explained last evening," he reminded him now. "My theory that Henderson and Kingsley meant to scuttle the *Destiny* and collect the insurance funds."

"Ah, yes. And you believe Kingsley was killed over this insurance business," Carew said. Pulling his pipe from his pocket, he filled it, uncaring that there was a lady present.

"I thought per'aps Kingsley and *Henderson* had argued over it, but now, with the manifest in Doyle's possession..."

"It's clear enough to see what happened," Carew said. After lighting his pipe, he sent a wreath of blue smoke sailing toward the ceiling before saying, "Kingsley and Doyle devised the insurance scheme—it would have been easy enough for the chief mate to alter the ship's course a bit with no one the wiser. They argued over the matter—perhaps Kingsley refused to pay or altered the terms of their arrangement. Doyle killed Kingsley, then in a fit of remorse over the whole business, he took his own life."

The squire's logic made an odd sort of sense, but Gavin found it convenient that Carew used one murder, which he'd previously refused to acknowledge, to explain yet another death. "Or," he said, "Henderson found out about the scheme and has been removing the men he views as a threat to his ship, and his retirement."

He considered the scene before them, hands on his hips. Doyle's note lay open on the table, the script thicker in places where the man's pen had pressed more firmly. He studied the loops and strokes, but they weren't giving up anything. His eye then took in Doyle's body and the sunlight coming round the curtain before his gaze caught on an uneven place in the floor. The corner of one plank was slightly higher than the others. Gavin pushed at it with the toe of his boot, and the wood yielded slightly. Kneeling, he used his pen knife to pry at the board.

Mari stood behind him, and he felt her presence as solidly as if she'd laid a hand on his shoulder. He forced his attention to his task and soon, he lifted the plank to reveal a small cavity between the floor joists. Inside, lay a pearl-handled quill knife with dried blood still on the blade. Ink stained the small hilt, and he realized with a start of satisfaction that the ink must have been the source of the dark edges of Victor Kingsley's wound.

"That's Victor's quill knife," Mari said with surprise. "I recall it from his desk."

"Ah!" Carew said. "There you have it. A confession and the weapon."

Gavin looked to Carew and stood. "Why would Doyle go to the trouble to hide the weapon he used to kill Kingsley, only to apologize for the act in his note? It doesn't fit."

Carew drew more deeply on his pipe. "It fits perfectly," he argued. "He meant to hide his actions all along, but he couldn't overcome his guilt. We can consider the matter solved, and these people can be on their way."

"You don't find it the least bit curious that the ink on his note is dry, but the quill is not? His note was written earlier than the scene would have us believe."

Carew closed his eyes, one hand squeezing his temples. When he opened them again, it was with a sigh. "You're seeking questions where there are none, Kimbrell."

"Per'aps," Gavin conceded, though he wasn't convinced. "But I suggest we keep what we've seen to ourselves until we're certain. In the meantime, I've more questions for Henderson and Tate."

"Of course, you do. Sort this matter," Carew said, "and do it quickly. I'm going shooting with Trewyck."

"Aye, sir."

Carew left them and Gavin was not sorry for it. His magistrate's tolerance for the inquiry aspect of investigative work was low, and it had been reached.

Mari's expression was considering as she said, "You don't believe Doyle's death was a suicide."

"No."

"If Doyle obtained the weapon that killed Victor, then reason follows that he knew who the perpetrator was. He may have even threatened to reveal what he knew." Her eyes widened as the logical conclusion occurred to her. "He was blackmailing the person, and he lost his life for it."

"Aye. If 'tis true that Doyle didn't kill Victor, then the murderer is still out there."

"Do you think it's Henderson?" she said.

"To be sure, I've more questions for him," Gavin replied.

But though the pieces were beginning to come together, his intuition was at odds with his reason.

Henderson, as the person with the most to gain from the insurance scheme, was the logical culprit, but the image of the aging captain as ruthless murderer didn't fit Gavin's experience with the man. But then, neither could he imagine any of the rest of the ship's crew or passengers in such a role. Doyle's hot temperament had been the most aligned with the task of murder, but like Gavin had told Mari, he didn't believe in such clear lines between good and bad.

Mari nibbled her thumb, her shoulders rounded with frustration. With a sigh, she said, "There's still nothing to connect any of this with—"

Her voice broke, but Gavin knew the rest. There was nothing to connect any of this with what had happened to her sister or her sister's child.

"What will you do if you find your niece?" he asked gently.

"When, Constable. *When* I find my niece."

"When," he agreed. "It will be difficult to raise a child as an unmarried lady. Have you considered how 'twill affect your standing, or that of your niece? Of the hardships you'll encounter?"

"I have considered it," she said. "I want nothing more than to raise her as my own, but I recognize the difficulties of such a course. I will have to be content to know she's safe and loved by a family, but I would like to meet her, just once."

Mari's eyes were sad, and he knew an overwhelming urge to see them bright again. Crossing his arms, he said, "You could marry."

She started at his words but said only, "What sort of man would marry a woman just so she might raise another's child? That sounds like a poor bargain to me."

Gavin disagreed. He lifted a hand to her, to what purpose, he didn't know. Before he could offer any comfort, though, a creak sounded in the hall outside Doyle's room. He strode to the door and opened it to find Henderson on the other side, hand poised to knock.

"Is it true?" the captain asked. "Leo says Doyle's dead." His gaze caught then on the figure of his chief mate, still laid out on the floorboards. He paled, his cheeks stark against his dark beard. Gavin didn't think that sort of reaction could be contrived.

"Captain," he said. "Why don't you come inside. I have more questions to put to you."

Henderson looked as if he might refuse, then he surprised Gavin with a heavy sigh. Entering, he crossed to the window and stood with his back to the light, arms crossed. His avoidance of Doyle's prone form was clear, though whether that was on account of guilt or dismay, Gavin didn't know.

"If you wish to know if I killed Doyle," Henderson said, "then the answer is no."

"Thank you for the confirmation, but there's no need. He left a note," Gavin said, to which the captain frowned.

"A note?" Henderson shook his head. "No, Doyle wouldn't take his own life. He was too arrogant. He lacked the… introspection… needed for such an act."

Gavin didn't think a man who'd staged a murder as a suicide would call such suicide into question. That, combined with Henderson's immediate physical reaction to the man's death, eased Gavin's thoughts on Henderson's guilt, at least where Doyle was concerned. But if he'd not killed the man, then who had?

Mari must have agreed with his assessment, for she said softly, "Captain Henderson, I'm sorry for the loss of your colleague."

Henderson nodded. "What is it you wish to know?"

Gavin asked the man if he'd seen anything unusual prior to Doyle's death or if his chief mate had confided anything to him.

"Like what?"

"D'you think Doyle was involved in a scheme to scuttle the *Destiny*?" Gavin watched Henderson and was rewarded when the older man's gaze darted to a point over Gavin's shoulder. A visible pulse beat at his temple.

"Why would you think such a thing?"

Gavin ignored the question to say, "The manifest you showed me the first time we spoke—who wrote it?"

"The manifest? I did. I prepare all of them."

"Even the false one we found on Doyle?"

Henderson dropped his arms. "The false—if you found such a thing on Doyle, then it stands to reason it was his."

"I recognized the script," Gavin said. "'Twas written in the same hand as the one you showed me."

Henderson stared for a long moment before he said, "Even if there were such a scheme, the ship didn't sink, and the cargo wasn't lost. I imagine any penalty would be slight—"

"Ah, but you're wrong," Gavin replied as something Mari had said the day before struck him. *There's no crime, aside from Kingsley's death.* Warming to his idea, he added, "The jury has ruled the cause of Kingsley's death to be misadventure. In short, twelve men are of the opinion that he died as a result of injuries sustained in the grounding of the *Destiny*."

Henderson grew paler by degrees, and Gavin knew the moment Mari sorted his words. She gave a little gasp, her eyes wide. "If Victor's death was due to the wreck," she said slowly, "and if you prove that Captain Henderson caused the wreck… Well, I imagine you might arrest him for… what, precisely?"

"Manslaughter at the very least, with a penalty of transportation. Far worse than what he might receive for scuttling his own ship. That is, unless the captain knows some reason I ought to look more closely at other causes for Kingsley's death?"

It was a gamble—he didn't know if there was anything more Henderson might tell him, but he had to try.

The captain shook his head. "I can't be transported."

"I don't want you to be," Gavin said. "Your daughter's children need you."

The man began to pace, his shadow crossing the window once, twice, before he said, "I went below to check the bilge pump. I heard an argument coming from the Kingsley cabin."

"This was the night of the grounding?"

"Aye."

"Whose argument?"

"Kingsley's and… his wife's."

"Why didn't you say anything before?" Belatedly, Gavin wondered if his strategy had misfired. Was Henderson fabricating tales to save his own skin?

"I didn't see any point to ruining a lady's good

name over something that may have been nothing more than a quarrel between husband and wife."

"Why tell me now?" Gavin said. "What makes you think their 'quarrel' is worth my time?"

"Kingsley said he'd see her hang. If that doesn't inspire wifely ire, I don't know what does."

Mari's eyes were bright after Henderson left. "Lady Philippa," she said with meaning. "You have to talk to her again."

"You were unaware of Kingsley's argument with his wife?"

"I was unaware," she confirmed. "The pair weren't especially warm toward one another, but I never heard them raise their voices. Surely, Henderson's account must be significant."

"Aye, *if* he's being truthful, then I have to agree."

"Why would he not—oh, I see." Then, as if she meant to bolster his esteem, she added, "It was very cleverly done, though."

Her admiration, accompanied by a dimple as it was, warmed him clear through.

CHAPTER 18

ROWE WAS SUMMONED to tend the grim scene in Doyle's room. The surgeon estimated the man's death had occurred around the inquest, or possibly earlier, which made the wet ink on his quill all the more suspicious.

Given the captain's latest revelation, Gavin had more questions for Lady Philippa, but Wynne informed him the lady had gone out. Tate wasn't in his room, either, and he couldn't talk to Fairfax—with no lost ship, there'd been little reason for the agent to remain in Newford.

If the *Destiny's* passengers weren't giving up their secrets, then perhaps the ship would. He needed to speak with the shipwright and find out how soon he could go aboard. There were answers somewhere, he was certain. Gavin turned from

Tate's door where his knock had gone unanswered to find Mari watching him from her doorway. His stomach tightened in that pleasantly uncomfortable way it did whenever she looked at him.

"You're going to the ship, aren't you?" she said.

How could she know that when he'd only just decided it for himself? Were his thoughts so transparent? "How d'you—?"

"It's the only witness you've not yet interviewed. I would like to come." He shook his head, and she pressed the matter. "I know my way around the *Destiny*. I can show you the hold and the Kingsley cabin."

Gavin felt certain he could find his way around a ship without assistance. Before he could say as much, he considered Mari's dark eyes. She gazed up at him in the flickering light of the hall sconces. Her smooth hair had long since begun to slip from its pins, and a thick lock of it caressed her shoulder. He wondered if it were as soft as it appeared, if it would cascade over his hand like cool spring water. His heart gave a tremendous thump, and it struck him suddenly how dangerous this matter had become. Two people had been murdered, and Mari didn't seem to have a care for herself.

He cleared his throat. "The *Destiny* isn't righted yet," he reminded her.

"Then we should find out when she will be."

Stepping closer, he said, "And *you* should have a concern for your safety. Two men have been murdered. If that doesn't make you reconsider your involvement in this matter, then consider your reputation at the very least."

She left her doorway and crossed the hall. "I can join you under the guise of securing Lady Philippa's things. She is my employer, after all."

"It won't serve for us to be seen so much in one another's company—"

"Constable, my sister is dead and buried and my infant niece is missing. What others think of me is the least of my concerns."

Gavin swallowed. There was a light in her eyes that would not be banked. If he didn't allow her to accompany him, he had little doubt she'd go on her own. No, it would be better if she came with him, but there was no sense ruining herself in the process. With a sigh, he said, "'Twould be best to take one of Wynne's maids with us."

"You'll let me come?"

"Aye."

Gavin left her and descended the Feather's wide stairs. Wynne had thrown the windows open in the coffee room to admit a warm breeze, and it brought with it the faint brine of the sea. He strode toward the kitchen behind his cousin's office.

The smell of hot pastry made his mouth water as

he pushed open the door. Wynne was at the scarred wooden table kneading a round of dough, her face flushed from the heat of the oven. Her movements caused her rounded belly to stretch the cloth of her apron. It never ceased to amaze him that his tart-tongued cousin had a talent for making the most delicious sweets.

Leo sat opposite her, his legs swinging as he chewed one of Wynne's raspberry tarts. The sole of one shoe was nearly separated from the upper to reveal dirty toes beneath. At least he wasn't hungry. Judging from the crumbs on his plate, the lad would have a sore belly before long.

"Wynne," Gavin said, "Miss Swan and I mean to go to the cove. I need to borrow one of your maids to stand as chaperone."

Wynne's brow lifted as she kneaded, and he could see her calculating the number of minutes he'd spent in Mari's company. She'd probably had her nose pressed against the window as Gavin and Mari walked from Morwenna's to the church and back again. Now, he ignored her considering look and waited while she rinsed her hands at the pump.

"'Tis a wise course," she said, surprising him with her easy agreement. "Peggy can join you."

"You're the best of cousins," he said, to which she replied with an energetic, wet flick of her hand.

He brushed water from his face then his gaze

settled on Leo, who was grinning at their antics. The lad wiped crumbs from his cheeks with the back of his hand, and Gavin wondered what he was thinking now that his commanding officer was dead.

Clearing his throat, he said, "Leo, how much longer do you have in your apprenticeship with Doyle?"

The boy wrinkled his nose. "Me wot?"

"Your contract with Doyle." By Gavin's calculation, if Leo had served two years already, he still had five more at least. Gavin wondered if someone with the Admiralty might help him place the lad on another vessel to serve out the rest of his term. Leo shrugged and took another tart. "Doyle never says nuffin' about that."

Gavin tried another approach. "How did you come to be with Doyle? Did he give your parents any papers for your employment?"

"Nah," Leo said, his mouth full. Raspberry stained his fingers and both cheeks. "I ain't never had a da, and me mam's dead. Doyle bought me from me uncle."

"He bought you," Gavin said slowly as unease twisted through him. "How much did your uncle receive for your services?"

"A whole bottle," Leo said. "Doyle always says I be a square deal. Why do you think 'e says that when bottles be round?"

Before Gavin could think of a proper response to that, Wynne slid another tart onto Leo's plate. Pulling Gavin aside, she kept her voice low. "What's to become of him?"

Gavin shook his head. "I don't know. He doesn't yet realize he's a ship's boy without a ship. Or a master, for that matter."

Wynne's husband Roddie carried in an armful of wood for the fire. As he stacked it in the wood box, Wynne said with a note of pleading, "You can't return him to his uncle—he'll only sell him again. And the workhouse is no place for a growing boy, either. He needs a steady diet."

"Of sweets?" Gavin said with a pointed glance toward the boy's plate.

Roddie straightened. "Haven't you learned by now?" he said with a pat of his stomach. "Plying a man with sweets is how she shows her love."

Wynne swatted her husband who, despite his wife's sweets, hadn't gone to fat. He caught her hand with a grin and held it a moment longer than necessary. And Wynne, to Gavin's never-ending amazement, allowed it. Marriage and impending motherhood had softened her rougher edges, it seemed.

He considered Leo's raspberry-stained face for a moment longer before saying to Wynne, "Have you given any thought to taking on more help?"

Her eyebrow arched in question.

He gave her rounded belly a significant glance and received a glare for it. He'd long been impervious to her glares, so he added, for better or worse, "You'll be far busier soon, given the extra ballast in your bow."

Gavin didn't miss Roddie's resigned head-shake, but to his surprise, Wynne didn't punch him in the nose.

———

MARI RETURNED TO her room to re-pin her hair and collect her bonnet. She paused, though, when the paper from Victor's appointment book caught her eye from the small table. She still puzzled over the encounter with Mr. Harris from Falmouth. He and his lady appeared pleasant enough, kind and unassuming, but they certainly hadn't seemed the sort to associate with Victor and Lady Philippa's class. She couldn't imagine how they might have come to know one another.

Smoothing the paper on the table, she tried again to read what had been written there. *C Harris* and *St. L*, she now recalled from Victor's book, but those pieces didn't help her fill in the rest of the blurred and faded words. She squeezed her eyes shut. She thought he'd written her name on the page, but there was something else she was missing.

With a short groan of frustration, she cast the paper aside. She didn't want Gavin to leave without her. He was pacing at the bottom of the stairs when she descended. He looked up, and the intensity of his expression made her pause her steps. It was a look she'd grown accustomed to seeing on him, but with another murder now to solve, she could well understand his seriousness. More than once, though, since landing on his beach, she'd detected a bit of humor in his eyes and a dry wit, and she wondered what his smile would look like.

He came to meet her at the last step, and her added height put them on level with one another. "D'you wish to walk or drive?" he asked.

His question surprised her, as she'd come to learn he was the sort of man who followed his own lead. That he sought her opinion made something flutter in her midsection. "Is it far?" she asked.

"A mile per'aps. We'll have to take the last stretch from the cliff to the beach on foot, but there's a linney where we can leave the cart if we drive."

Mari eyed the crisp blue sky beyond the Feather's open window. The weather was fine for walking, but she was impatient to reach the ship and see what more they might learn. "We should drive."

With a nod, he led her outside as Peggy, one of Mrs. Teague's maids, fell into step behind them. A cart waited in the inn yard, the horse having already been hitched to it, and Mari looked at Gavin with surprise. With an apologetic clearing of his throat, he said, "I thought you might wish to drive. 'Tis what I would have chosen."

As he handed her up onto the narrow bench, she said, "Are we so very alike then, Constable?"

He considered her question for an overlong moment before saying, "Per'aps more than is good for either of us."

She gave a surprised laugh and was delighted to see his lips twitch in reply. The cart was small, with only room for two on the bench. As Gavin settled Peggy on a seat at the back, Mari adjusted her skirts to make room for him.

The wheels rattled over the cobbles as they set off, the noise affording a bit of privacy for any conversation they might make regarding the investigation. Gavin drove them past Newford's small harbor and up a gradually sloping rise. Soon, they were driving along the edge of a cliff with blooming wildflowers on one side and the frothing sea far below on the other.

Gavin cleared his throat, and Mari glanced at him beyond the brim of her borrowed straw bonnet. "I've been remiss in not asking," he said, "but are you recovered from your injuries?"

"I believe so. My head doesn't ache still."

"You said your injury caused some difficulty with your memory…?"

"There are a few details that remain muddled, as if my mind reaches but doesn't quite grasp the memory fully."

He nodded. "I asked Dr. Rowe about it. He said 'tis not uncommon in the case of such an injury to suffer some loss of memory, but he believes all will right itself soon enough."

"I—thank you," she said.

"For what?"

"For inquiring with the surgeon on my behalf." That he'd troubled himself to do so, and now asked after her welfare, caused a twisty sort of warmth to expand in her chest.

Of course, that could simply have been his proximity to her on the bench. With Gavin's arm and shoulder lightly brushing her side, she was very aware of him. Her father, when he'd lived, had been a man of modest proportions. She'd not seen him often—he'd spent much of his time in town, but he'd certainly not had the same height or breadth of shoulder as the constable.

"And you?" she said. "Are you fully recovered?" She couldn't forget his stiff movements from the morning after the *Destiny's* grounding, though his bruises had faded to a shade of pale yellow.

He slid a glance toward her from the corner of

his eye. She thought he would feign confusion at the question or offer some sort of denial, but he gave her a short nod.

They rode in silence for a minute or more. From somewhere nearby, a sea bird called to its mate. The air was clear, and Mari imagined she could see halfway across the Channel from their high prospect. She cast about for something more to say.

"Do you enjoy your work as constable?" she asked. Inwardly, she cringed at the dullness of her question.

He replied with an equally dull, "Aye." Then with a sigh, he added, "There are times, though, when I'm not certain 'tis the post for me."

His words surprised her and it must have shown, for his brow lifted at her expression.

"What is it you dislike?" she asked.

A long moment passed before he replied. "I enjoy puzzles," he clarified, "and sorting problems. We do have some in Newford, though rarely do they reach the level of a crime. 'Tis only that sometimes, it doesn't seem as if my efforts accomplish much. I've been thinking of removing to Truro."

She thought on that a moment. "Have you considered perhaps you're *too* successful in the role?"

He snorted. "'Tis a thing—to be *too* successful?"

Warming to her argument, Mari angled herself toward him. "I mean only that your efforts may be responsible for the lack of problems to… to sort."

His expression was kind but skeptical as he said, "I doubt 'tis my efforts so much as the disposition of my neighbors, but I thank you for the sentiment."

Gavin, who'd seemed nothing but confident in her experience, wore his resignation like a cloak. So much so, that she felt compelled to say, "It takes many grains of sand to make a beach. Small changes may feel insignificant, but you *are* making a difference."

He took his gaze from the horse to look at her. "How can you be certain? We don't know one another very well."

"The fact that you question your significance tells me enough." He seemed uncomfortable with her observations, so she let that be an end to it.

They rode on for several more paces before he spoke again. "And you? D'you like being a school mistress?"

"I do."

"And when you're not teaching or playing at lady's companion? What pastimes d'you enjoy?"

Mari considered his question. Her former life felt so far removed that she wasn't sure she'd ever get it back, but she answered anyway. "Drawing and painting. Reading." With a lift of her shoulder, she added, "I prepare illustrations, from the classics mostly, though I've done other subjects as well."

"Illustrations? For books, d'you mean?"

"Yes. I have a publisher in London who accepts many of my pieces. Or I *had* a publisher. It's been some time since we've corresponded."

"You must be talented."

Mari shrugged, unaccustomed to the praise but enjoying the novelty of it, nonetheless. Gavin was quiet for several turns of the cart's wheels, and she wondered if he'd brought his thoughts back to the investigation. When he opened and closed his mouth, she angled herself to face him more fully.

"What?" she asked. "Did you think of something regarding Victor?"

He shook his head. "No, I only—" He stopped, and she thought she detected a ruddy tinge on the top of his cheeks. Was the constable *blushing*?

"What is it?" she repeated.

They'd come to a straight stretch and he flicked the reins. The horse picked up speed before he said, "I merely wondered what it might have been like, had we met in the usual way of things."

Mari's mouth fell open. She couldn't help it. His words were far from what she'd expected him to say.

"My apologies," he murmured. "I didn't mean to cause you any discomfort."

"What"—she paused to lick lips that had gone dry—"what do you mean by the 'usual way'?"

"Outside the church, I suppose, or if we'd been introduced during one of the monthly assemblies." He cut his eyes to her before saying, "D'you enjoy dancing, Miss Swan?"

"When I have the time for it. Mrs. Sherwood—she's my employer where I teach back in Somerset—she often holds dances for the girls. The boys from the neighboring school attend, and everyone practices their steps."

"Sherwood, you say?"

There was a bit of laughter in his tone and she nodded. "Yes. Mrs. Arnetta Sherwood. Do you know her?"

"No." He cleared his throat and added, "'Tis only that, when I first spied you aboard the *Destiny* and then again on the beach, I imagined you as the maid Marian—from the stories of Robin Hood and his merry men. 'Tis fitting that your employer would be Mrs. Sherwood."

"Maid Marian?" she said on a surprised laugh. "Now you've piqued my interest. In what way did I remind you of such an intrepid lady?"

"There's a strength to you. I could sense even then that you were brave and determined—a valiant figure, to be sure."

Mari didn't know what to say to that. She'd never been likened to a heroine before. Of the Talbot sisters, Hannah had always garnered the admiration of others. Not that Mari had minded—she didn't enjoy being at the center of things. Her sister, though, had a manner about her that drew people in. Hannah had been charming and vivacious and irresistible while Mari had simply been… present. A fixture. An accessory. Always welcome but never needed. To hear the constable compare her to Maid Marian… it was enough to make her heart give an extra thump.

"It's a lovely sentiment," she said. "I don't think of myself that way, but I thank you all the same." She swallowed once before admitting, "I thought you rather resembled Perseus."

He pulled his head back to look at her. "Perseus? He's the one with little wings on his sandals?"

She huffed a laugh at his description. "Yes, but he was also incredibly courageous in his defeat of the sea monster."

"Courageous?"

She nodded.

"*Incredibly* courageous?"

"Fabulously."

He held his gaze fixed on the path ahead, but she thought she detected a hitch at the corner of his mouth. He shifted a little on the seat next to her before saying, "If we'd chanced to meet at the assembly and I asked for a place on your card, would you have granted it?"

A sudden heat filled Mari's cheeks as she tried to imagine dancing a set with Gavin Kimbrell. The man was gruff, his demeanor wry and sharp. He hardly seemed the sort to gallop down the line, but she thought she might have enjoyed partnering with him. She nodded in answer to his question then posed one of her own. "What would we have spoken of, do you think, without this grim business to occupy our conversation?"

"The weather, probably."

"And the dreadful state of the punch," she added.

"Not if the assembly is held at the Feather. Wynne would never serve watered punch."

"No," she said, laughing. "Based on my short acquaintance with your cousin, I would have to agree."

"If I manage not to tread on your toes during our imaginary set, I might invite you to walk with me after church. Or per'aps we'd take a drive."

"I would like that, and I—I would wear my best bonnet," she finished, enjoying their game. How long had it been since she'd simply… laughed? Since she'd had a conversation with another person for the mere pleasure of it?

"And I would be sure to offer my compliments."

"Even if it were the ugliest thing you'd ever seen? What if it had birds on the brim or… or fish?"

"Even if it had fish." He smiled, and Mari's breath caught at the way the act transformed his face. His smile was open and guileless, and it reached his eyes. It lacked his sharp wit and irony, and she felt special for having seen it.

It didn't escape her that Gavin spoke of courtship. The notion caused a flock of nervous swallows to dip low in her stomach. Not because she hadn't considered marriage for herself, but because she had. Many times in the last weeks, in fact. When she found her niece, a husband and a respectable marriage would solve everything rather nicely. She could keep her niece with her—she'd no longer be an unwed female raising a child of questionable parentage.

But now, with Gavin's arm brushing hers with every bump of the cart, she found the idea of such a practical marriage distasteful, for reasons she wasn't ready to explore just yet.

CHAPTER 19

GAVIN SECURED THE horse and cart in the smuggler's linney and escorted Mari and Peggy down the narrow path. They arrived on the beach of the small cove to find Charles Tate pacing the sand as Nance's men labored over the hull of the wrecked ship.

Leaning toward Mari, Gavin said, "Unless you wish your employer to know the extent of your interest in this matter, I suggest you allow me to ask the questions."

Her nose wrinkled to indicate what she thought of his suggestion, but then to his surprise, she said, "You are right, of course."

"Though it pains you to say it."

"Though it pains me," she agreed.

When Tate spied them, he pivoted, his shoes kicking up sand in his haste to reach them.

"Constable," Tate said, pulling a cheroot from his mouth and indicating Nance's men. "You must tell these men to stand down so I can collect my things. It's bad enough they've been tossed about, but I'll not leave them to molder and rot."

Gavin rubbed the back of his neck. "If Nance says 'tis still unsafe to board, then 'tis unsafe."

Belatedly, Tate acknowledged Mari. "Miss Swan," he said, "you've made an unnecessary trip if you hoped to go aboard."

To Mari's credit, she didn't hesitate before giving Tate a demure nod. "It would seem so, Mr. Tate. As I told the constable on the drive, I should like to see Lady Philippa's trunks secured as soon as possible." Her acting skills were admirable and a trifle alarming, but then, Gavin didn't suppose she'd have gotten as far as she had in Kingsley's household without some talent for misdirection.

Tate returned his attention to Gavin and continued to press his argument. "I've left important papers aboard the ship that must be retrieved."

"What sort of papers?"

"What—? Why, the usual. Contracts and correspondence and the like. Until Victor's affairs are sorted, it's up to me to see that everything continues to operate smoothly."

"D'you know what sort of cargo the *Destiny* was transporting?" Gavin dropped the question without so much as a warning, curious to see how Tate might react. While he was confident in Henderson's role in the insurance scheme, he wasn't so sure about Tate's.

The man's frown intensified as he said, "What has that to do with anything?"

"In your role as Kingsley's man of affairs, you must have been involved in purchasing goods from his suppliers and organizing them for transport."

"Yes, of course."

"And the insurance? Did you manage that as well?"

"No," Tate said with an irritated grimace. "Victor always preferred to handle that himself. His relationship with Lloyds was one of long standing."

"Was there anything unusual about this particular voyage?"

Tate eyed him with suspicion. "Unusual?"

"There are indications the cargo may not have matched the manifest. Per'aps there was some sort of scheme afoot. Were you aware of anything irregular?"

Tate tossed his cheroot to the sand. "No," he said, releasing a stream of smoke. "But it wouldn't surprise me to hear it. Victor was bold as brass and always pushing the limits."

"Per'aps we'll know more once the ship is cleared," Gavin said. He considered revealing what he'd learned from Henderson or all they'd discovered in Doyle's room, but he wasn't ready to show his full hand just yet. Not until he had a look at what lay aboard the *Destiny*.

After Tate left them, Gavin excused himself from Mari and Peggy and went in search of Nance. He found the shipwright inspecting a newly tarred section of the hull, the pungent scent of pine pitch heavy in the air.

Nance stood when Gavin approached and wiped his hands with a soiled rag. "Constable."

"She's still unsafe to board?"

"Aye, but it won't be much longer now. We'll have 'er righted and on the water again by day's end tomorrow. She won't be fit for passengers yet, but she'll float."

"Have you told this to anyone else?"

Nance gave him a grin with one missing tooth. "I said ye'd be the first to know when she's ready to board," he said, "but I won't be able to 'old 'em off for long. Incomers be bleddy impatient."

"Have others come besides Tate?"

"Who *hasn't* come, be the more proper question." The shipwright's brow drew low as he recited the list. "First, there be Blackwood, the carpenter—he's come for his tools—and Henderson, after his log. A gen'leman's gen'leman be here not an hour agone, hot for cravats, and now that man, Tate, looking to retrieve his trunks. I s'pose the young lady be seekin' something, too?" he said with a nod for Mari, who waited near the water's edge with Peggy. Tom Hatch, a braw carpenter on Nance's crew, had joined them. Tom spoke, and the three of them laughed.

"Aye," Gavin said. A wave rolled over the sand near Mari's feet. She lifted her hem and danced back a step to avoid wetting her slippers. Turning his gaze back to Nance, he said, "You still have someone watching the ship, don't you?"

"Aye. Tom Hatch be stayin' the nights," Nance said with a nod in the carpenter's direction. Gavin approved even as he caught his scowl over the man's familiar manner.

"Tell him I'll return tomorrow night," he said. And though he'd probably regret it, he added, "I expect Miss Swan will accompany me."

———

GAVIN JOINED MARI at the water's edge. Tom had resumed his work, and Peggy, who was proving an inattentive chaperone, quickly moved off to flirt with Nance's son.

Mari was fetching with the strings of her bonnet blowing behind her and a bit of color in her cheeks. Before he could forget their purpose and pretend he'd invited her for their imaginary pleasure drive, he made a study of the sea.

"You made the acquaintance of Tom Hatch," he said.

Mari leaned toward him to whisper, although no one could overhear them. "Yes," she said, "and I think he has an eye for pretty maids. He seems rather taken with Peggy."

Gavin returned his gaze to Mari, pleased to see she was not dismayed in the least by the direction of Tom's eye. "Does he?"

"Yes, but that's not all. Mr. Hatch said it's no wonder the *Destiny's* bilge pump stopped working, as there was a piece of pipe wedged in it." She tilted her head at Gavin with an expression of such smug satisfaction that he chuckled.

"Nicely done," he said, though her words only confirmed what he already suspected: they'd learn more once they could get a proper look at the ship. He told her of his conversation with Nance, and of his plan to return to the ship the next evening. He'd wait until dark when no one was about to impede his investigation. As he'd expected, she insisted on joining him.

"We're close to the truth," she said.

"I feel it, too."

Folding her hands before her, she faced the sea. She'd barely glanced at it on their drive above the cliff, and he'd thought her uncomfortable with heights. Now, he wondered if it was the sea that discomposed her. It would have been understandable, given her recent ordeal.

"'Tis the sea that unsettles you?"

Her eyes pulled to his in surprise. "No, I—what makes you think me unsettled?"

"D'you mean aside from the fact that you've gone stiff as a ship's mast while you watch the waves?"

With a visible effort, her shoulders lowered a bit. "I'm not the fearless maid Marian you think me," she said.

"I don't believe Marian was fearless, but brave. 'Tis a far better thing."

She tilted her head as if she weren't quite certain of him before returning her gaze to the water. When he thought she wouldn't say more, she admitted, "I have dreams." Her words were so soft they were nearly lost to the waves. Gavin remained silent, and at length she added, "I dream of my sister's drowning, and I feel helpless to stop it. Her terror is my own. I can't… I can't get it out of my heart."

Gavin checked his frown. The terror she described, the helplessness, it was something he knew well, though for different reasons. Several beats passed before he said, "You have more courage than you credit yourself with."

"I don't know if I'll ever be able to enjoy the water like I once did."

Gavin considered her for a moment before saying, "D'you swim?"

"No. I never learned."

Gavin's certainty grew and he gave her a nod. "Learn to swim," he said. "'Tis only a matter of buoyancy."

She laughed. "Is that all there is to it? Buoyancy?"

"Per'aps there's a bit more required, but learning the skill will give you confidence. No one can master the sea, to be sure, but you'll feel less at the mercy of the water if circumstances require you to face it again."

"That's rather philosophical of you, Constable." She was quiet for a long moment before she said, "Have you ever had to master a fear?"

"To be sure," he said, "everyone has fears."

"Yes, but you're..." She eyed his form, her glance quick but admiring enough to cause his insides to tighten, as if he'd taken the cart too swiftly over a hill.

"Aye?" he prompted.

"You're... you. I doubt you've ever known a moment of fear in your life."

"'Tis not so hard to believe," he said. She thought him fearless? What a thumping pile of—

"Tell me then. What fears plague *your* dreams?"

———

MARI WAITED AS Gavin held his hat in one hand, the wind ruffling his hair. "Everyone has fears," he repeated.

She gave a dramatic sigh. "It's as I thought. Advice is easy to dispense when you've not had to heed it yourself." She meant her words as a jest, something to lighten the moment, but Gavin didn't reply. She watched his profile as a muscle ticked in his jaw.

Perhaps her question had been too personal. She ought not to have asked it, but there was something about their shared endeavor that made their association seem closer than it was. He fixed his gaze on a tortoise-shaped boulder in the water, and she wondered if he didn't answer because he couldn't or… because he could.

"I'm sorry," she said. "I should not have—"

He interrupted with a soft clearing of his throat. With a glance behind them to ensure they weren't heard, he said, "As a lad, I was not very accomplished at… reading."

Mari nearly laughed, certain he was having her on. Reading was not something to be *feared*, not in the way a person might fear the sea or heights or any number of mortal dangers. But his expression was serious, a bit of color staining his cheeks and ears, so she said gently, "Many people do not read."

"No," he said, his voice low despite the noise of the sea and the hammers behind them. "It wasn't that I didn't receive instruction or that I didn't wish to read. I was *unable* to do so. 'Twas as if something were broken"—he tapped his head once—"for me to be so incapable of a task that came readily to others. I would have sooner braved a thousand seas than be called to read aloud."

Mari tilted her head, considering him. "I—I'm not sure I understand," she said. "A person is not broken simply because they cannot read."

He turned away from her, frustration evident in the line of his shoulder. Lifting a rock from the sand, he sent it skipping far across the cove before returning to her side.

"'Tis not an easy thing to explain, and harder still to understand, I imagine."

"I will try if you will."

He nodded and with a breath that lifted his chest, he said, "Despite all the learning I received with my cousins, reading and writing was a chore I avoided whenever I could. I couldn't sound out the words properly, and I devised all manner of ways to hide my ignorance. If one of my cousins read first, I memorized their words and simply repeated them when it became my turn. And if I was called to read first, I challenged Gryffyn or Jory until one of them had no choice but to take my place or appear lacking themselves. I was a proper bully."

Mari considered the tall, straight form of the man beside her and tried to imagine him as a frightened boy, too embarrassed to reveal the truth. The image wouldn't come. "Your cousins don't seem to resent you for it," she said. "You share an enviable ease with one another."

"Aye. 'Tis a reflection of their dispositions rather than my own, but that wasn't an end to it. When I was eight, I convinced my father I was too old for a governess because I lived in terror my secret would come out. I didn't think it through, though, to see that once he dismissed my governess, he'd set a tutor on me." Shaking his head, he made a scoffing sound. "I went from the soup to the fire."

He tapped his hat against his leg, keeping his gaze forward as he spoke. "The tutor, and the two or three that came after, accused me of laziness. And my parents, who were unaware of my troubles, insisted the tutor must try harder. But the words simply would not come together as they ought. 'Twas as if they played tricks on me."

He cut her a glance, and Mari drew a slow, considering breath. In her years at Mrs. Sherwood's school, she'd never heard of tricky words or anything like what Gavin described, but to hear his account, to know the proud man he'd grown to be, she could imagine what a torture his lessons must have been for him. How the simple act of reading, something she'd always taken pleasure in, must have made his life a misery.

Then she recalled, from nowhere in particular, a boy who'd lived near her childhood home. Anson Wilder had been bright and clever and quick at games, but she'd overheard several children from the village mocking his laziness in the schoolroom. Had he suffered a similar affliction to what the constable described?

Her heart twisted for the boy Gavin had been, but he'd clearly overcome his problem. How many times had she seen him writing in his book?

"What did you do?" she whispered.

He shrugged one shoulder, the motion causing his arm to brush against her own. The sensation was not unpleasant. "I ran away to sea."

Mari turned a look of surprise on him. "That seems… extreme."

"It was, but it was the only solution I could devise at the age of twelve. I stowed away on a ship of the line sailing out of Falmouth."

Mari held a gasp. "That would have been during the worst of the fighting with France. Your family must have been terrified for you."

"They were," he said with a grimace. "My mother still frets when she's had more than a few days without my company. 'Tis my greatest regret, the worry I caused them."

"But you came through the war unscathed."

He nodded. "I was a ship's boy much like Leo, though I had the good fortune to advance in time. 'Twas how I met Lieutenant Edwards—Captain Edwards now."

"Your contact at the Admiralty."

"Aye, but to add to my misery, he insisted all the ship's boys receive book learning."

"Oh, no."

"'Tis what I thought, but Edwards has a brother with a similar affliction. Just when I was certain he'd wash his hands of me and leave me at the next port, he realized my trouble. He made me read aloud to him and write everything, even the simplest of instructions. Eventually, I found a way to see the letters differently, to finally see patterns in the words. To be sure, I don't always put the letters in the right order, but I can make sense of them now."

"You were fortunate your lieutenant was so persistent." Then with sudden realization, she said, "It's why you write everything in your journal." It was also, she suspected, why he closed his book whenever anyone drew near.

He tucked his chin in a curt admission.

They stood motionless for a time until she asked,

"Does your family know?"

He shook his head, and she absorbed the import of his revealing such a closely-held secret to her. It couldn't have been an easy thing to do.

"I stand by my earlier words," she said. "A person is not broken simply because they do not read. Your determination to overcome what must have seemed insurmountable only increases my admiration."

"Your admiration?"

Mari felt a blush climb her throat for such plain speaking, but she nodded. He remained silent as they looked out over the sea, though she detected from the corner of her eye the merest hint of a smile upon his face. Her own lips began to curve in response until he spoke again.

"And the swimming…?" he said.

It was a sharp reminder of what had led to his confession. Gripping her hands together, she considered what he expected of her.

Learn to swim.

No lady of her acquaintance *swam*. But he'd confided his fear—a secret he'd not even told his family—so that she might confront hers. Perhaps she could. "I shall give it some thought when I return to Somerset."

The reminder that one day she must return to Mrs. Sherwood's was a sobering one. Her life would never be as it once had been, not with Hannah gone from it. Not with everything that had happened since she'd joined the Kingsley household, and certainly not since she'd met Gavin Kimbrell.

He must have been pondering something of equal weight as he fell quiet, hands clasping the brim of his hat behind him.

———

ON THE DRIVE back to Newford, Gavin made plans with Mari for their return to the ship the following night. Taking the cart along the cliff road would draw too much attention, and it would be dangerous, even with the moon to light their way. They arranged instead that Mari would walk the short distance with Peggy, and Gavin would join them there.

As he drove and planned, though, his heart was numb, as if it had been pulled from a rough sea and wrung out on the sand. He didn't know why he'd confided his troubles to her. He'd certainly had no plans to do so. They were a secret he held close inside, a fact of his life his own family didn't know.

There'd been no need to tell them. With Edwards' help, he'd solved his problem, inasmuch as it could be solved, and rarely did he think on it now. It was merely another part of him, like his dark hair or the tiny scar on the back of his hand.

But with Mari, he *wanted* her to know. He might pretend he'd made his confession for her, to help her fight her own fears and know she wasn't alone in them, but the truth was, he'd done it for himself. He wanted her to know him.

As soon as the words were spoken, though, he'd felt intense regret, certain he'd made a mistake. He imagined the shift in her thoughts, the subtle recalculation of what she knew about him. To be sure, she would think him less capable now that she knew the truth.

But her gaze hadn't wavered from his, even as she spoke of admiration. It remained steady, and his heart had lifted, until the reminder that she would return to Drayton-Marsh.

CHAPTER 20

THE NEXT EVENING, Mari paced her room, waiting for the time when she and Gavin had agreed to meet at the ship. Soon, it would be dark.

She went to the window, but the only activity in the inn yard was the arrival of the mail coach. She craned her neck to see the market clock down the street—and puffed a sigh of impatience. There was nearly an hour to go still.

She dropped her curtain and checked her hair once more in the small mirror beside her bed. Though a pleasant appearance wasn't required for the evening's endeavor, she was vain enough to wish her hair might obey the pins, just once. It was a futile wish.

With nothing to do but wait, she considered ways she might pass the time. Collecting her bonnet, she strode to the door and went down the Feather's wide stairs. The coffee room was noisy with passengers from the mail coach eager for their supper, and Peggy carried a laden tray to a table in the corner. The maid hadn't offered any argument when given another chance to see Tom Hatch. Still, Mari felt a pinch of guilt for taking her from her duties.

Through the window near the Feather's entry, she watched as Leo swept the street outside Morwenna Williamson's shop. He stood aside as a couple passed, grinning when the gentleman handed him a coin. Mari was relieved he no longer had to suffer Doyle's threats, but her heart twisted for him, nonetheless. She knew what it was like to have no family. Even before learning of Hannah's death, she'd been on her own for some time, with only her sister's irregular letters to remind her she was not alone in the world.

She checked the time once more on the inn's clock. There were still some thirty minutes or more before she and Peggy needed to go. She left the Feather and, lifting her hem, crossed the darkening high street toward the dressmaker's. Leo looked up, his grin returning when he spied her.

"I can't talk, Miss Swan, I've 'portant business to tend." His motions with the broom were more earnest than effective, the bristles doing little more than pushing the dirt about.

"I can see that," Mari said. "I won't keep you. I just wanted to see how you're getting on."

He shrugged. "Awright, I s'pose." He paused in his sweeping and looked up. "Did ye know Newford ain't never 'ad a crossing sweep?"

Mari blinked. "I didn't know that." She'd encountered sweepers in the more heavily trafficked areas of Bath, but there seemed little need for the occupation in the relatively clean and unpopulated hamlet of Newford. Still, she could see how it pleased Leo to have a task to perform. "It's fortune-ate, indeed, that Newford has you now," she said.

"Aye. Mrs. Teague lent me 'er broom, *an'* she says I can keep me wages."

Another couple approached Leo's crossing, and Mari moved aside as he hurried to sweep the way for them. She thought to take her leave of him and return to the Feather, but she hesitated when a familiar figure emerged from the inn. Charles Tate. He looked around once—rather furtively, she thought—before turning onto the high street.

She stepped into the shadows of the darkened shop behind her as Tate passed the chandler. He neared the dressmaker's shop, and Mari angled herself as if to study the window display. When he passed the harbor and kept walking, she knew he was bound for the cove where the *Destiny* lay. Tate meant to board the ship.

"Leo," she said. "Do you know where I might find the constable?"

"Aye, I saw 'im at the post office. Ye want me to fetch 'im?"

The post office was at the other end of the high street, but Tate's figure was getting smaller. Precious seconds passed while she considered what to do. She could wait for Gavin—during which time, Tate might remove who knew what from the *Destiny*—or she could follow him and observe his actions. It was nearly dark, and Gavin would come behind them soon.

"There's no need to fetch him," she said to Leo, "but please let Peggy know I've gone ahead to the cove."

Leo frowned at this. "A gentry mort walkin' alone?"

It was his words, and Tate's disappearing figure, that firmed Mari's resolve. She *was* a "gentry mort walking alone"—and had been for some time. She could do this.

Mari left Leo and walked toward the harbor. The sky's edge still held the remnants of the day, but a full moon had begun its ascent. She followed the cliff road above the sea, watchful for any sign of Tate ahead.

———

GAVIN LEFT THE post office with a pair of letters: one from Kingsley's solicitor and another from the coroner in Somerset. He hurried back to the Feather and raced up the stairs to Mari's room. There was time yet before they were supposed to meet at the cove, but his news couldn't wait. His knock, though, went unanswered, and he checked his impatience.

The coroner must have responded to Gavin's letter as soon as he'd received it. In his reply, the man worried over the case of Hannah Talbot. On a second review, everything had appeared just as it seemed, he said, until he made the additional inquiries Gavin suggested. The coroner had been certain nothing would come of them, but then he learned Miss Talbot had a visitor shortly before her death. A cousin, it seemed, which the coroner found curious as he'd been given to believe the deceased had no relations other than her sister.

His description of Hannah Talbot's relation, as provided by Eventon's innkeeper, was unremarkable on its own, but Gavin knew the individual well enough. A lacquered coach bearing a lady of obvious breeding had arrived at the innkeeper's establishment the morning of Hannah's death. The lady's coachman inquired after directions to Hannah's cottage, and despite the innkeeper's offer of hospitality, had swiftly continued on.

Lady Philippa. Gavin was certain of it.

Had she viewed Hannah as a rival for Kingsley's affections? It seemed the most likely explanation, though he had trouble wrapping his thoughts around the notion of the elegant lady ruffling herself to the point of murder.

Had Tate accompanied her? The man was forever trailing the lady about, despite his association with the maid—perhaps he fancied himself her champion and had done the deed himself.

Regardless, Mari would have her answers soon. The thrill that fizzed through him—that he might help her find some measure of peace at last—had him pacing outside her room longer than was proper.

When the minutes passed and still she didn't appear, he couldn't delay any longer. Striding to the end of the hall, he rapped quickly at Lady Philippa's door. She answered his knock herself, scowling when Gavin entered without an invitation. A quick glance confirmed they were alone.

"Constable," Lady Philippa said.

With one pale hand pressed to her throat, she appeared fragile in her dyed-blacks. The flickering light of the lamp cast her in soft shadows, adding to the impression of vague elegance that clung to the lady. Gavin now knew it was an illusion, but he needed clear and certain proof. A confession would not go amiss, either.

"Tell me about Hannah Talbot," he said, pleased when the lady's eyes widened a fraction.

She recovered quickly, though. Closing the door, she went to the desk where she'd been writing a letter and sank onto the chair. "I'm afraid I don't know anyone by that name."

"I think you do," he said. "There are witnesses who saw you in Eventon."

The lady blinked. "Eventon… Oh, you must mean my husband's mistress. Constable, this is an unseemly topic to bring to his widow."

"You're aware of Kingsley's association with Miss Talbot then?"

With a tremulous smile, Lady Philippa said, "I'm afraid I had forgotten her name, but yes, I was aware. My husband didn't bother to keep his liaisons a secret. I admit I may have passed through Eventon on occasion, but that doesn't mean I ever met the woman."

"It must have angered you, to share your husband's affections with another."

"Why would it? She was nothing to him, but I was his wife."

"You speak of her in the past tense."

"She's dead, is she not?"

"I never said as much."

She gave him a pitying smile before saying, "Constable, I can't imagine why you're asking about that woman. Perhaps the notion of uncovering some sordid tale about my poor husband adds a bit of excitement to what must be a very dull existence in this colorless little hamlet, but if you continue to make insulting implications, I will make sure everyone knows what an incompetent constable Newford has in you. I'll see you ruined so thoroughly even your friends at the Admiralty won't acknowledge you."

Gavin tucked his chin and swallowed his irritation. Her threat gave him pause, but it was her slight toward his home that really stung. It was unsporting. Newford might have moved at a slower pace than Truro or Bath or any number of other towns and villages, but he would not stand for anyone to call it *colorless*.

He stood taller and crossed his arms. "Your marriage to Kingsley came shortly after Miss Talbot's death. He'd meant to end your engagement, hadn't he?"

Lady Philippa's expression remained still, but her color increased. It began at her throat and rose to stain her cheeks as she said, "You're mistaken. Victor knew precisely what he stood to gain from our match."

"And you knew what you stood to lose. The match would have benefited both of you—your family connections in exchange for his money. Did he love her?" Gavin pressed. "Is that why you—"

"Did he *love* her?" Lady Philippa repeated. Her voice increased in pitch as she said, "You know nothing of our world. There is no place for such driveling sentiment."

"And yet, he kept her handkerchief as a token of her affections."

"It didn't matter how he felt about her. Victor *needed* my connections, no matter that he was too stupid to see it."

Gavin considered the hard edges in the woman's voice—they were directed at her husband as much as Hannah Talbot. Suddenly, he wondered if Mari had been right all along, and Kingsley's death *was* connected to that of her sister. Had Lady Philippa murdered her husband over the matter of Hannah Talbot? Or had Tate done the deed for her? Gavin wouldn't be surprised to find one or both of them had done in Victor Kingsley. Doyle, even, if he'd witnessed their actions.

The pieces were beginning to come together, and they were far more connected to Hannah Talbot than he'd ever thought.

"Did you kill your husband, my lady?"

"I will not continue to be insulted by a *constable*. I insist that you leave or I will send for the magistrate." Lady Philippa resumed writing her letter as if Gavin weren't there.

He disregarded her threat to say, "What did Finnegan Doyle know of your actions? Was he blackmailing you?" Lady Philippa remained silent, so Gavin pushed harder. "I have Kingsley's quill knife—the one that was used to kill him—and I imagine I'll find more evidence aboard the *Destiny*."

The lady ignored him, and Gavin knew a moment of uncertainty until his gaze landed on the missive she was writing. The ink was thicker in places where she'd hesitated, perhaps distracted by his questions. The loops were tight, though not without refinement, and there was the merest irregularity in the slant of her strokes. After a lifetime of studying letters and words for patterns, Gavin saw what he needed to. Her script bore an odd similarity to that of the *Destiny's* chief mate, though it was decidedly more feminine.

"It was you who wrote the note," he said, pleased when her hand stilled over the page. "Where did you acquire the laudanum?" he asked. He didn't recall seeing any in her room on his previous visits, and the lady hadn't brought a reticule with her from the ship. He supposed she might have carried it on her person, though now they'd never know.

When she remained silent, he said, "Lady Philippa Kingsley, I am arresting you for the murder of Finnegan Doyle."

She threw her pen down, and it left a splotch of

ink on the paper. "That is absurd. I will see you ruined for this."

"You've said as much. Now, do you come willingly," Gavin said, "or do I use the manacles? It will make an entertaining account for the papers."

Lady Philippa glanced toward the door, but whether she sought escape or rescue, he couldn't say. Seeing neither, she said, "Do not even think to lay a finger on me."

Gavin allowed her the fiction that he was hers to command. He did try to help her stand, though, a courtesy for which he received a vicious swat.

"Where is Tate?" he said. When she remained stubbornly silent, Gavin tried again. "What role did he play in Doyle's death?"

Lady Philippa's eye turned shrewd. "I told him not to do it."

Gavin scoffed. He was beginning to recognize the cunning in her gaze whenever she handed him another fiction. "I have a feeling his story will be vastly different from yours, my lady."

The moon was high by the time Gavin secured Lady Philippa in Newford's gaol, which, in truth, was little more than a closet above the apothecary's shop. It had a sturdy lock on it, though, and the window was high enough to prevent escape.

He left her with a lantern and returned to the Feather, where he was met by Leo in the inn yard.

"Constable," the boy said, blowing out a breath of such obvious relief that a heavy unease started in Gavin's stomach.

"Leo."

"Miss Swan—"

"Aye?"

"She's gone to the cove, though I tol' her a gentry mort ought not be walkin' alone."

Walking alone? Where was Peggy? Gavin strode with purpose into the inn. Before he could ask Wynne where her maid was, he heard Peggy's high laughter coming from the coffee room. He spun back to Leo.

"What about Beatrice—did Miss Swan take Lady Philippa's maid with her, per'aps?"

"That's wot I'm tryin' to tell ye," Leo said with an exasperated sigh. "She didn't take *any* maid."

Gavin's unease bloomed into cold dread. She'd gone to the ship to meet him, and he had a notion that was where he'd find Tate as well. He hurried for the door then was struck with a thought and went for the stairs instead. Leo followed at his heels, quiet for once.

When Gavin reached Lady Philippa's room again, he entered without knocking. It was empty, just as he'd left it. No Beatrice. She'd not been there earlier, either, when he'd questioned her employer.

The last time he'd seen the maid, she'd been

coming from Mari's room. He'd not thought anything of it at the time—as a lady's maid, her actions were even more invisible than those of a lady's companion.

He went to Mari's room and, after a quick rap that went unanswered, he opened the door, uncaring as it hit the plaster behind. The room was tidy, the bed neatly made, and Mari's few belongings were aligned atop the chest of drawers. The small table beneath the window held a jar of flowers. The first time Gavin had questioned Mari, there'd also been a vial of laudanum, left by Rowe for Mari's head. As he suspected, it was gone.

Beatrice must have taken it. Now, she was gone as well as Tate, and Mari had left for the ship. Alone. Gavin hurried from her room, Leo close behind.

"Ye're goin' to the cove, ain't ye? D'ye need me to fetch ye anyfin'?"

"Aye, Leo. Fetch Mr. Teague. Tell him to bring as many of my cousins as he can find."

CHAPTER 21

MARI HURRIED ALONG the cliff road as Tate kept a rapid pace ahead of her. The way was bare, with few trees to shield her, but he seemed intent on his destination and didn't look back. When he arrived at the path to the beach, he made straight for the cove. She waited, ducking behind a thick hawthorn, to give him time to descend. Behind her, the cliff path remained empty with no sign yet of Gavin.

The *Destiny* was righted as Nance had said it would be, with ropes mooring the vessel to the dock. Its masts were bare, lit only by the moon as they stabbed the night sky. She couldn't see Tom Hatch from her vantage point, but there were barrels and tall stacks of timber blocking her view.

She searched the beach for Tate. She couldn't find him, but then a spot of light began to move along the deck of the ship. He'd gone aboard. He was impatient to retrieve his papers, but what if his urgency was for another reason?

She chewed her lip as she considered as many explanations as she could devise. Perhaps he meant to uncover Victor's murderer for himself, or maybe he'd left behind a valuable of some sort, but none of her imagined scenarios eased her mind.

Then a second lamp appeared near the cabins at the stern, and Mari sucked in her breath. Was it Tom Hatch? Or had the first light belonged to the guard? Her panic eased to think Tom was on the matter, until she realized the lights were moving in opposite directions. Tom was going the wrong way. He didn't know Tate was aboard.

If there was any evidence on the ship, she and Gavin must find it before Tate or anyone else did. She needed to alert Tom to Tate's presence. Stepping out from behind the scrub, she used the moonlight to pick her way down to the beach. She rounded the barrels, holding her breath against the strong odors of tar and fish coming from them until she stood on the *Destiny's* makeshift dock.

The ropes mooring the vessel creaked with the motion of the sea. The tide was flowing out. It lapped at the ship's hull and pulled water from the nearby cave. A sturdy plank had been laid across to the quarter deck. Mari's stomach swooped in distress at the thought of crossing it, but she couldn't discern any other way aboard. Keeping her gaze from the dark water swirling below, she grimaced and placed one slippered foot in front of the other until she made the ship's deck.

Once there, she found a sturdy hammer left by one of Nance's men and picked it up. The weight was comforting in her palm as she moved along the deck, though she didn't know for what purpose she might use the tool. She moved toward the stern and passed through the companionway, the soles of her slippers quiet on the steps as she kept her eyes alert for any sign of Tom or Tate.

The ship's interior smelled of salt and damp, and everything that hadn't been bolted down was unsettled from the *Destiny* being laid on its side. Though furnishings had been righted by Nance's men, little was in its proper place. Floorboards were warped and glass lanterns lay broken. It would be some time before the *Destiny* was returned to sailing shape.

She reached the passenger cabins, where the door to Tate's berth stood open, but the room was dark. There was no sign of either man. She paused and glanced about, using the moonlight coming through the hatch to gain her bearings. All was quiet, save the gentle slap of the waves against the side of the ship. Had Tate left?

She turned to retrace her steps to the quarter deck then stopped. The Kingsley cabin—and Victor's appointment book—were just ahead. It wouldn't take but a moment's time to retrieve it. She pressed her ear to the door and listened. Nothing.

Entering the suite, she made her way quietly through the salon until she stood at the threshold of the dressing room. Kingsley's chamber lay to her right, Lady Philippa's to the left. The vessel rocked gently in the current, and moonlight through a high window glinted on Lady Philippa's silver-handled hairbrush where it lay on the dressing room carpet. That was when she saw Hannah's pendant. It winked at her from where it had caught the edge of the upended chest of drawers.

Mari seized it in a rush of satisfaction, holding the thin chain tight in her hand. Victor *had* returned it to his cabin after all—

A faint thump came from the lady's chamber. Her pulse jumped, and the hair on the back of her neck lifted. Carefully, she tucked her sister's necklace in one of her pockets and adjusted her grip on the hammer. Something wasn't right.

She began a slow retreat from the dressing room. As she passed the open door to Lady Philippa's chamber, she spied an unnaturally pale Charles Tate slumped at the desk. Blood ran from a wound on his head and—heavens!—his wrists were tied to the chair. Who had done this to him?

He looked up, his hair disheveled and his eyes unfocused in the pale light until they caught and held on something beyond Mari's shoulder.

Spinning, Mari found Beatrice behind her. The maid's cap was slightly askew, and there was an increased color to her pretty cheeks. She gave a brief curtsy as she said, "Miss Swan."

Mari lowered the hammer. "Beatrice. You gave me a fright."

"I'm sorry."

Beatrice worried a pale shawl in her hands. Dimly, Mari recalled it was the same wrap Lady Philippa had worn the night of the *Destiny's* grounding, but her thoughts were on leaving the ship before Tate's attacker returned. "We must hurry to help Mr.…" she began, but then the moonlight caught the shawl, and she saw it was stained with what looked like blood.

The room was close, and she felt a trifle faint. Lady Philippa's shawl was stained with blood—Victor's, she was certain—and Charles Tate sat injured and tied to a chair. Nothing was as it should be. Bringing her attention back to Beatrice, she said evenly, "Mr. Tate is injured. He needs the surgeon."

"You were right," Beatrice said. "He was never going to marry me. Oh, Miss Swan, I have been so terribly foolish."

Tate's head fell forward a bit and he moaned.

"Beatrice," Mari said with some urgency. "I was mistaken. He *will* marry you, I'm certain of it, but first we need to help him."

"Why did you have to come to the ship? You've been nice to me, rather like a friend. I *liked* you."

The maid's regretful tone sent new alarm through Mari. "We can still be friends," she said.

"Not anymore." Beatrice eyed the shawl in her hands as if she'd forgotten she carried it. Her nose wrinkled with distaste to see the blood staining the edges. "Lady Philippa says we'll lose all our friends and acquaintances if they ever find out."

Mari considered the maid as pieces began to slowly settle into place. Victor's surprise on seeing Mari with Hannah's necklace, then his pursuit through the hold. He'd been angry at first—*Does my wife know she employs a thief?* But then he seemed… desperate. *Miss Swan, I must speak with you.*

She'd thought his surprised reaction a clever deception on his part, but now she saw it for what it was. The truth.

He hadn't known the necklace was in his cabin. It was Lady Philippa who'd had it all along. Victor had been as struck by its presence as Mari. Had Lady Philippa killed Hannah? Most certainly, she'd killed her husband. Mari's heart raced to think she might—*finally*—have her answers.

"Lady Philippa should never have been so careless," she said slowly with a nod for the stained shawl.

Beatrice shook her head. "The blood will never come out."

"You know she killed her husband. What she did was wrong, Beatrice, but you don't have to help her. We can go now and tell the constable—"

The maid shook her head. "He said he would see her hang. She only did what she had to do."

"Why do you think Mr. Kingsley would have said such a thing?"

Mari held her breath, waiting for Beatrice to confirm what she suspected. The maid remained stubbornly quiet, though, until she said simply, "I'm sorry." Then, turning, she left the cabin.

Mari started to follow, but a moan behind her halted her steps. Tate. He stirred again, his eyes catching hers. Mari glanced toward the door where Beatrice had fled, torn between helping Tate and finding answers. Admittedly, the debate took longer than it should have. At the end of her inner argument, though, she strode into Lady Philippa's chamber and knelt at Tate's side.

Beatrice had used strips of linen to bind his wrists. Mari worked the knots, frustrated when they only tightened beneath her impatient fingers. She was eager to escape the ship and find Gavin.

"She doesn't mean to let us live," Tate slurred as he fought to remain conscious.

Mari kept her gaze fixed on her task, though his words caused her fingers to stumble. "Beatrice? Or Lady Philippa?"

"Either. Both. Does it matter? Beatrice will do whatever Philippa tells her to do."

Mari swallowed at his grim assessment, relieved when the final knot came loose. Tate's color was still off, and blood continued to run from a gash near his temple. She wrapped one of the linen strips around his head, hopeful it was enough to staunch the bleeding.

As she tied off her makeshift bandage, a low thud sounded in the corridor outside the cabin. She hurried from the room and into the salon to find the cabin door closed, barred from the other side. Beatrice had locked them in.

The crash of breaking glass came to her from beyond the door. With a frown, Mari pressed her ear against the door but jumped back when an unmistakable smell reached her. Smoke. It was coming through the gap below the door.

The corridor beyond the cabin was on fire.

"Help!" she called, hopeful that Tom Hatch or Gavin might hear her. She pushed harder on the door but it held fast. There was no escape that way, and no answers to her shouts. Dragging cushions from the settee, she pressed them against the door to stop the smoke then raced through the cabin. There had to be another way out. She looked up, down, searching for a hatch to any of the other decks, but there wasn't one. The cabin had windows, of course, for light, but they were high on the wall and too small to climb through.

The salon door was the only exit.

Tate coughed and tried to stand, though he quickly fell back onto the bed. The smoke was getting thicker, despite the cushions.

Mari pushed and pulled the chest of drawers until it was beneath one of the windows. Then, dragging a chair to it, she climbed atop the chest. Using her hammer, she broke the glass, calling and waving her hand through the opening. The window faced the sea, though, rather than the beach. No one would hear her, much less see her hand.

Dispirited and more than a little terrified, she climbed down from the chest. Was this how she would die? She was certain fire would be just as horrific as drowning, though she'd not like to test either option.

Then, as the fire in the companionway grew louder, she thought of the gun port in her tiny cabin. From the outside of the ship, it was easy to see the even row of square openings that had once been used for cannon. They were evenly spaced and ran the length of the ship, even at the stern where the Kingsley suite was situated. The port in Mari's cabin had a cover, a hinged wooden hatch to guard against the elements, but walnut paneling covered the walls in the Kingsley cabin. Any matching gun port would be hidden behind the wood.

She spun and asked Tate, "Where's the hatch?" His eyes fluttered once before closing again. The smoke was thicker now, and Mari's eyes burned as the hull of the ship creaked and moaned. She stumbled a bit as the vessel swayed, and she realized with growing horror that it was moving.

Beatrice had cut them loose from the dock.

They'd gone from a bad situation to a disastrous one. She and Tate needed to leave the ship *now*.

She eyed the cabin's outer wall and tried to imagine the distance to her own berth. Then, picturing the outside of the ship, she took her hammer's claw to the wood. The paneling came off in long planks that she thrust aside, one after the other. Finally, when she thought she must have been mistaken about the gun port, she found it just above the Kingsleys' copper bathing tub. Using her hammer once more, she pried the hatch open.

The smoke in the cabin swirled as it rushed for the new opening. Mari took in a welcome breath of salty air, though her heart dropped to see they were already some fifty yards or more from shore.

"Tate," she called. "We must go."

She looked down to the sea below the hatch. The water swirled, reflecting moonlight and the orange glow from the ship's fire. To be sure, it was deep. Deep enough for a vessel the size of the *Destiny*. Certainly, deep enough for a body to drown.

Her palms were damp as she gripped a piece of paneling. *'Tis only a matter of buoyancy.*

Those had been Gavin's words. She hoped they weren't her last thought.

———

GAVIN RACED ALONG the road above the cliffs, losing his hat to the wind. When he reached the point overlooking the cove, the sight below was enough to stop his breath.

The *Destiny* was loose from her mooring, and the outgoing tide had pulled her from the shore. The vessel was nearly at the place where she'd run aground and was making straight for the Devil's Teeth. Gavin's chest felt impossibly tight. Was Mari aboard?

He jumped from his horse and tied the reins loosely in the linney before skidding down the path to the cove, his boots slipping on the gravel in his haste. The beach was empty. She was on the ship. Gavin ran an impatient hand through his hair and paced the sand, helpless as the vessel drifted farther on the tide.

Think! He needed the gigs. He spun, intent on finding the pilots when a glimmer from the *Destiny's* quarter deck flickered.

Fire.

"Mari!" Gavin shouted, though he knew she wouldn't hear him. His heart hammered a frantic pace and his throat burned with terror for her, but he refused to allow emotion to cloud his thoughts. There was no time to send for the gigs. He strode into the sea, heedless of the cold, frothing waves.

The water rose quickly, but before it passed his waist, a figure appeared some yards away, stumbling in the waves in his haste to reach the sand. Charles Tate. The man dragged himself onto the shore and collapsed.

"Tate!" Gavin called, splashing toward him. If he'd harmed Mari—

"Gavin."

His heart faltered. Mari's voice was soft beneath the sound of the sea, and he wondered if he imagined it. His eyes raked the darkened water, and there she was, walking out of the surf not more than a dozen yards from him.

He raced to help her, tripping once in the waves. She clutched a wooden plank to her, and water streamed down her cheeks and pressed her hair to her head. She was pale, her chest rising and falling with her breaths, but her eyes were wide and bright in the light of the full moon as he took in her beautiful face. He slowly peeled her fingers from the wood so he might hold her hands.

"I died a thousand times over," he said in a voice that was rough and not his own.

"I think I did, too," she said around the chattering of her teeth.

"My brave Maid Marian," he whispered. Then, because he couldn't help himself, he released her hands to cradle her face. Bending, he pressed a hard, fervent kiss to her cold lips. She froze for a tiny second before clutching the lapels of his coat. He'd never felt anything so wondrous as the pressure of her hands against his chest or the smooth curve of her mouth beneath his own. She tasted as she smelled, like lemon and warm vanilla, and his heart ached with the weight of his emotions. He might have prolonged the moment, despite their cold and wet surroundings, if she'd not pulled away to whisper urgently, "Beatrice."

He stared at her, uncomprehending. "Aye?"

She indicated a place beyond Gavin's shoulder, and he turned to see the maid hurrying from the shadows among the barrels and timbers. "Lady Philippa killed Victor," Mari said, drawing him back to her, "and Beatrice has been helping her." She paused, her fists tight on his coat as she added, "Gavin, I believe she killed Hannah, too."

"I know," he said. "She's under lock and key in Newford's gaol."

Reluctantly, he left Mari's side in pursuit of Beatrice as Teague arrived with Gavin's cousins on the path above. The maid's pace was hampered by the shadows and shifting sand. She stumbled and tried to run when she spied Gavin behind her, but seeing his cousins descending the path ahead, she stopped. Gavin couldn't tell if her tears were genuine, but she sagged in defeat. He wished she might kick up more of a fuss so he could use the manacles, but she went with him willingly.

CHAPTER 22

MARI PACED THE Feather's private parlor, waiting for Gavin. It was late. Or early, depending on one's perspective. Morning would arrive soon, but she'd never found her bed. There were too many buzzing questions for her to ever have fallen asleep.

Mr. Teague had roused one of the inn's maids to provide her with dry clothing as soon as they returned from the cove, and now she wore a borrowed gown and too-large half boots. The hem was a trifle long, and she held the skirts in one hand to keep herself from tripping. Beyond the parlor, the inn was quiet, the last guest having long since retired. A fire burned hotly in the hearth but still she was cold, inside and out.

Gavin had gone to see Beatrice properly secured in the cell with Lady Philippa. Tomorrow, the pair of them would be conveyed to the larger gaol in Truro, there being but one tiny cell in Newford.

Tom Hatch had been found among the timber stacks at the *Destiny's* dock, unconscious but breathing. A short, wide plank lay beside him, presumably the device Beatrice had used to thump him over the head. He'd since awakened, regretful for how easily his attention had been caught by the pretty maid's flirtation. He and Charles Tate now lay in Dr. Rowe's infirmary with matching headaches.

Gavin had Lady Philippa's blood-stained wrap from Beatrice, along with Mari's assertion that it was the same wrap she'd worn to supper their last night aboard the ship. Gavin was certain Lady Philippa would craft some explanation for the stained garment, but he'd assured Mari that too many of his cousins were aware of it now for the magistrate to ignore the implications.

So, Lady Philippa would likely stand trial for killing Victor as well as for her part in the murder of Finnegan Doyle. As far as they'd been able to determine, Beatrice had been the one to put Mari's laudanum in Doyle's gin, but Lady Philippa had given the direction and written the note.

But neither Victor nor Doyle were Mari's primary concern, though she couldn't like the manner in which either man had met his demise. Her thoughts remained on Hannah, where they'd been these past months. The first time she'd found her sister's necklace in the Kingsley cabin, she assumed it had been placed there by Victor, but Lady Philippa's things had been stored in the chest of drawers as well. She'd assumed Victor had it because that fit the story she'd built in her mind.

Now, with shame and irritation toward herself, she admitted how blind she'd been. It was Lady Philippa who'd killed Hannah and Lady Philippa who knew what had become of baby Marianne.

The door to the parlor opened and Gavin strode through. She rushed to his side. "Has she said anything more?" she asked.

He shook his head, his eyes tired and hair mussed. Neither of them had said anything about that kiss. There'd been far more pressing matters at hand, but that didn't stop Mari's neck from heating at the thought of it. Even now, she felt a tingle along the edge of her mouth, and she pressed her lips against it so she might think properly.

"Neither Beatrice nor Lady Philippa are saying anything at this point," Gavin said. He eyed her for a long moment, his blue eyes intent on hers. Then, with a sigh, he said, "You wish to speak with her, don't you?"

"I must," she said. "I need to ask her why."

He opened his mouth as if he might argue then closed it again.

"And I need to… I need to see her eyes," Mari whispered. She couldn't explain why, but she needed to look into the eyes of the person who'd taken her sister from her.

Rubbing a hand along the back of his neck, he surprised her with a nod. "'Tis what I would want as well." Then, gently, he added, "But you know she may never admit to what she's done. She's aware of her husband's relationship with Hannah, but she maintains she never met your sister."

"But she had Hannah's necklace."

"A circumstance easily explained. She'll claim her husband must have taken it, and without Kingsley alive to refute her…"

He was right, of course. Mari wanted to scream her frustration aloud. Gavin paced the length of the parlor, his strides long and purposeful. When he looked up, his eyes were more alert, and a smile tugged at the corner of his mouth.

"What?" she said.

"She still believes you're Mari Swan," he said slowly.

"You think we can use that to our advantage?"

"When she learns you're Hannah's sister, she might just be startled into betraying herself." His expression sobered, and he added, "But only if you're absolutely certain you wish to face her."

"I am absolutely certain," Mari said with feeling.

Then, reaching for the thin chain at her neck, she pulled her pendant free of the borrowed gown and allowed the ruby to settle atop the bodice. "It's time the lady knows the truth of her companion."

Gavin's smile grew. He tipped his head at her, and she felt his admiration clear to her toes.

———

THERE WAS AN energy to Mari that vibrated from her as they left the Feather. Gavin couldn't fault her for wishing to confront Hannah's murderer. Without this chance, she might never accept the loss of her sister, but he also wondered what toll such an encounter would take. He'd witnessed death and loss in his years at sea, but never the loss of one so dear as a sibling.

Had he been wrong to encourage the encounter? Mari was silent as they walked, though her grip on his arm was tight. Her profile showed nothing but determination, though, and he knew this was the only way forward for her.

The shop windows along the high street were dark as he led them to the apothecary, but the edge of the horizon showed a tinge of pink. Morning would be upon them soon. A steep, wooden staircase behind the building led up to the gaol, where a heavy wooden door marked the entrance.

When they stood at the bottom of the stairs, he asked again, "You're certain?" She frowned as if he'd taken leave of his senses, so he added, "You do not have to do it if—"

"I'm certain."

Gavin studied her for a moment longer as if he might divine her thoughts. When that didn't work, he said, "What are you thinking? You've had a harrowing ordeal tonight."

"I'm thinking it needs to end," she said softly. "All of it."

"It will," Gavin promised. He turned to ascend the stairs, but she stopped him with a hand on his sleeve. She paused as if to collect herself before speaking again.

"Tonight, I had a choice," she said. "When Charles Tate sat bleeding, I had a choice between helping an injured man or following Beatrice for answers."

"You're a kind and compassionate person," he said. "You chose correctly."

"Not immediately," she admitted. When he would have offered reassurances, she hurried to add, "I hesitated, and I don't like that it was even a question for me. I don't like that this has become my life."

"It will end," he repeated, desperately hoping he spoke the truth. They ascended the stairs and, retrieving the key from his pocket, Gavin inserted it into the lock. He entered first, assuring himself all was well before allowing Mari to follow.

——

MARI FOLLOWED GAVIN inside the gaol. The cell where the ladies were held was small and spartan with a bare window cut high in the stone wall. Too high and too narrow for an escape, it afforded only the slimmest view of the night sky, while a single lamp hung from a hook in the ceiling. Its dim flame cast long shadows in the confined space.

Opposite the door, Lady Philippa and Beatrice sat atop two small stools. The maid slumped against the wall of the cell, but Lady Philippa sat tall and rigid, as if she entertained guests in her drawing room. When she spied Mari behind Gavin her brow creased in confusion.

"Miss Swan," she said. "Has Tate sent you?"

"No," Mari said simply. Her eyes went to Beatrice who studied the stone floor with a marked interest. That she'd not confessed all her night's deeds to her employer was clear.

"Tell him to hurry and sort this matter," Lady Philippa continued. "I wish to have done with it." Her lip curled as she took in the cell's thin straw mattress and tin bucket. The room was cool and held the faint scents of herbs from the apothecary below. In Mari's opinion, it was far more agreeable than either inmate deserved.

Mari's borrowed half boots scraped softly on the bare stone floor as she advanced into the room. Behind her, Gavin remained quiet, but his presence was a comforting weight at her back. Clearing her throat, she said, "I don't know how much longer you'll have Mr. Tate's admiration, or his support, now that your deeds are being revealed. At any rate, I think it's safe to say his association with Beatrice is at an end."

Lady Philippa's brow furrowed in confusion as she stared at her maid. Beatrice closed her eyes and whispered, "He was never going to marry me."

"What have you done?" Lady Philippa hissed. Beatrice only moaned and pressed herself more firmly against the wall.

Mari stepped beneath the lamp, drawing Lady Philippa's attention with a hand on the chain at her neck. She knew the moment the light hit the ruby, for Lady Philippa's eyes widened before sharpening in accusation.

"You've been helping yourself to my things, I see. I always thought there was something a bit off about you. Now, it's clear you're nothing but a thief."

Satisfaction, hot and heady, rushed through Mari

at the lady's unwitting admission. "Do you mean this?" she said as she lifted the pendant. The glass caught the light to throw tiny prisms along the stone wall. "You're mistaken," she said. "This one belongs to me. It was a gift from my mother. My sister wore one just like it, but sadly, the clasp on hers is broken."

Mari waited a beat for the truth to make itself known. When it did, Lady Philippa stood abruptly, knocking the stool over in her haste. Her face turned ugly as she glared at Mari, and Beatrice looked between them in confusion.

"You're Miss Talbot's sister," the maid said with surprise.

"Be quiet!" Lady Philippa said.

"But—"

"Not a word, Beatrice."

"Hannah's clasp has always been a bit tricky," Mari said. "Did it break when my sister fought you?"

Lady Philippa's jaw tightened until Mari thought it might shatter. The other woman turned away from Mari's gaze and stared through the tiny window to the sky.

"Why did you kill her?" Mari pressed.

"Kill her? She fell!" Beatrice said. Then, spinning toward Lady Philippa, she said, "You told me she fell."

"Not another word, Beatrice," Lady Philippa said, "unless you wish to hang."

The maid's face blanched bone-white, and Gavin stepped into the light. "Don't listen to her, Beatrice," he said. "Revealing what you know may be the only way to avoid such a fate. As it stands, you'll both be charged in the murders of Kingsley, Doyle and Miss Talbot, but I suspect you played a less active role in the deeds than your employer. Per'aps we can persuade the judge that transportation is a more fitting punishment."

Beatrice looked between Lady Philippa and Gavin, uncertain. "Tell us what became of Miss Talbot's child," he pressed.

Mari held her breath as Beatrice stared at them. "What child?"

"My sister's daughter," Mari said. "My niece isn't but a few months of age."

"There was no child," Beatrice whispered.

———

GAVIN STOOD WITH Mari inside the Feather's entry. Her dark eyes were unreadable as she looked up at him, and tension filled her frame. He wanted nothing more than to wrap an arm about her shoulders and draw her to him. He did not, though, and said instead, "I'm sorry you didn't find answers to all your questions, but we know enough now to charge Lady Philippa with your sister's death."

"That is a comfort, to know she won't get away with what she's done." Her brows came together as she added, "What will become of Beatrice if she cooperates? Can she truly escape the noose?"

"'Tis difficult to say for certain. She risks transportation at the very least."

"But her child…"

"I believe the judge can be persuaded to delay her sentence, at least until after the child is born."

"That is good, I suppose. So many lives have been ruined by Lady Philippa's actions, and now, that of another innocent child."

The entry was shadowed, with intermittent pools of light where the sconces had been turned low. Despite all that Beatrice had done, Mari's eyes were bright with compassion for the maid's babe, and Gavin knew an overwhelming urge to kiss her again. That moment on the beach had been all too swift, a spontaneous reaction to the heady combination of terror and relief that had rushed through him, one after the other. He checked his impulse, though. Their next kiss ought to be one of deliberation and intent, given rather than taken, and accompanied by words neither of them were prepared yet to speak.

He settled for taking her hand in his. Her bare

fingers were slender and cool, and she curled them readily into his palm. Lifting her hand to his chest, he held her there, allowing their fingers to tangle as his emotions of the past hours—terror for her safety, excitement for their discoveries and sorrow for her unanswered questions—pressed against his ribs.

They stood like that for a long moment until he said, "Try to sleep."

"I don't know if I can." Her words were muffled by the darkness.

Reluctantly, he dropped her hand and stepped back. His skin tingled where her fingers had been. He cleared his throat, the sound loud in the silence. "Nevertheless, morning will be here sooner than we'd like, and the magistrate will require our statements."

And, though he didn't say as much, his night hadn't ended. He meant to see what more he could learn from Beatrice.

CHAPTER 23

LATE THE NEXT morning, Mari settled herself in the Feather's private parlor as Dr. Rowe and Squire Carew took their seats across from her. Gavin hadn't arrived yet, and she checked the clock above the mantel. It was well past the time when he should have been there.

The squire spent some minutes preparing his pipe, and when Mari thought he meant to begin his questions without the constable, Gavin finally arrived.

"Apologies for the delay," he said to Carew's scowl as he took the chair next to Mari.

Over the course of the next two hours, Mrs. Teague entered no less than three times with pots of tea and coffee and trays of muffins. Mari suspected the innkeeper's diligence was as much an effort to overhear their discussion as it was to extend the inn's hospitality, but she couldn't fault her curiosity. The combined matters of the *Destiny's* grounding and the murders of Hannah Talbot, Victor Kingsley and Finnegan Doyle were a tale fit for the pages of a Minerva Press novel, though Mari wished her life had a bit less color to it.

At Gavin's prompting, she explained her months-long search for the truth about her sister's death, including her suspicions of Victor's role in it. She maintained Hannah's fiction that she'd been a young widow, and to his credit, Gavin didn't dispute her.

"You say you found Lady Philippa's blood-stained wrap aboard the ship?" Carew said.

"Yes. It was the shawl Lady Philippa wore the night of the *Destiny's* grounding—the night Victor Kingsley was murdered."

"And the significance of the ruby necklace?"

"I initially found it in the Kingsley dressing room and assumed Mr. Kingsley had taken it from my sister, but it was Lady Philippa who had it all along. When Victor saw me with it, he must have drawn his own conclusions about his wife's role in Hannah's death."

Gavin cleared his throat. "The maid confirms it. Kingsley confronted Lady Philippa just before the ship ran aground. He meant to go to the authorities, no matter that she was his wife. He said he'd see her hang, and she stabbed him in a fit of panic to keep her secret. This was the argument Henderson overheard."

Carew frowned around his pipe. Turning to Mari, he said, "And you've been posing as a retainer in the Kingsley household all this time?"

"Yes, I—"

"That's highly irregular, Miss Swan. Er, Miss Talbot, rather."

Mari frowned, but Gavin redirected the magistrate back to the matter at hand. "Sir," he said, "If I might continue with the events aboard the *Destiny*, the maid has decided 'tis in her interest to speak as witness against her employer."

Carew motioned for him to proceed.

"Beatrice reports that after Kingsley was stabbed, he fell and hit his head, and Rowe's examination confirmed this." The surgeon nodded his agreement and Gavin continued. "I wasn't certain how Kingsley came to be in the sea until I recalled Miss Swan's clever escape from the ship."

Gavin paused to glance at Mari, and she felt her cheeks heat at his admiration. He held her gaze for a moment longer as he went on with his tale. "I surmised that Lady Philippa and the maid must have disposed of Kingsley's unconscious form through the gun port in the maid's cabin, and the maid has since confirmed that theory."

Carew lowered his pipe. "The gun port?"

"Aye. The main deck was too far to carry Kingsley, and it would have required them to negotiate the companionway. Any member of the crew might have seen them. With the gun port, they had only to drag him a short distance to the maid's berth, open the port cover and hoist him through the opening. If not for the *Destiny's* grounding, he probably would have drowned before succumbing to his wound. As it was, the tide brought him ashore where he died on our beach."

The magistrate's countenance darkened. "An unfortunate bit of timing, that."

"When the ladies returned to Kingsley's cabin, the knife Lady Philippa had used was gone." To Mari, he added, "They suspected at first that you might have taken it—"

"Me?" she asked in surprise, until she recalled Lady Philippa's scrutiny.

"Aye, but only until Lady Philippa received Doyle's demand for payment. The chief mate had gone below deck—presumably to see to the bilge pump—and saw what they were about. When he found the knife, he kept it for his blackmail scheme."

"And when Lady Philippa didn't want to pay, she killed him, too," Mari said.

"Aye, she sent Beatrice to retrieve your laudanum. I imagine you wouldn't have thought anything of her presence in your room."

"No," Mari said. "Beatrice frequently came with requests from Lady Philippa, and I never took the laudanum, so I didn't realize it was missing."

Gavin nodded. "The maid claims she didn't know what Lady Philippa intended with it—your employer said only that she had a headache. This was before the inquest, when there was still a possibility that Kingsley's death might have been ruled a murder." Gavin cleared his throat, and Mari didn't miss the firm shift of his jaw. Carew, though, ignored his constable's irritation and waved a hand for Gavin to go on.

"She only meant to put an end to Doyle's blackmail attempts, but when it seemed inquiries into her husband's death would continue despite the jury's ruling, she saw an opportunity. No one had discovered Doyle yet, so she wrote the note to shift the blame for Kingsley onto him and sent Beatrice in later to set the scene. I suspect involving Beatrice in her schemes was just another way to ensure the maid's silence. She wasn't able to find the knife, though, because Doyle had already hidden it in the floor."

"And what of the ship's manifest?" Carew said. "Why did Doyle have a copy?"

"The *Destiny's* chief mate had a penchant for seizing opportunity at every turn. 'Tis probable he deduced Henderson's scheme and took the false manifest for himself before the ship ran aground."

"What will become of Henderson?" Mari asked. "And Fairfax?"

"I expect their penalties will be minor as no one was injured in the wreck itself. Given Henderson's actions, Lloyd's cancelled their contract on the ship. They won't be paying for the captain's lost vessel, and that's punishment enough, I suppose."

The surgeon leaned forward, elbows on the table, and said, "And Tate—is he innocent in all of this?"

"In the matter of Kingsley's death, but not in the insurance scheme, according to Henderson."

"What did he stand to gain from it? He didn't own the ship or the cargo."

"Tate had heard of the *Mary Claire* and was intrigued by the notion of a large insurance payment. Henderson, by the way, maintains his story that the *Mary Claire* was truly an accident. At any rate, Tate persuaded the captain into the scheme with the *Destiny*, which wasn't too difficult as Henderson wishes to see his daughter's children settled.

"Tate had pursued Lady Philippa before and after her marriage, but he'd never had enough blunt or standing to tempt her. Added to that, 'twould seem he was perpetually on the wrong side of the cards. I suspect that once the insurance funds were paid, he meant to direct them into his own accounts. As there was no insurance claim, we'll probably never know what he intended."

"So, Kingsley was not a party to it?"

Gavin shook his head. "Henderson says the man was unaware of the scheme. 'Tis why the captain was so surprised when Kingsley arrived at the wharf in Bristol."

"Why *did* he join the voyage?" Carew said. "By all accounts, he wasn't meant to be on the ship. It sounds like the worst case I've ever heard of a man being in the wrong place at the wrong time."

Gavin appeared to consider his words for a long moment. "I'm not certain," he said, his gaze catching on Mari's.

But suddenly, she knew precisely why Victor had boarded the *Destiny*.

———

"WE NEED TO go to Falmouth," Mari said as soon as Rowe and Carew left. She stood and began to pace the room, her energy fairly bouncing from the walls.

Peggy appeared in the open doorway to the parlor. She carried an empty tray, probably to clear the tea things from the table, but at the fierce expression on Mari's face, she left them once again.

"I know why Victor was on the *Destiny*," Mari continued. "I finally remembered what struck me about his note. He didn't write *my* name in his book, he wrote *Marianne*. No one has called me that in years—not since my mother was alive. Victor wrote *his daughter's* name on the same page as his note about C Harris and St. Lawrence. He was looking for Marianne. I can't believe I didn't realize it sooner." She strode for the door as if she meant to walk all the way to Falmouth. When Gavin didn't follow, she hesitated. "I'm sorry. I have to go."

"You don't," Gavin said slowly.

She turned to face him, nodding as if she understood. "Of course, I do not require you to accompany me. You've already helped me so much already."

"And I mean to continue to do so, for as long as you need me," he said, irritated that she would say such a thing. "But you don't have to go to Falmouth. I've asked the Harrises to come here."

"Here? They're coming here? When?"

Gavin checked the clock. "Any moment, I imagine. 'Twas the reason I was delayed this morning. I went to Falmouth after I left you last night."

Mari came away from the door and sat abruptly. "I don't understand."

"Something had been bothering me for some time, as well. You said your sister gave her daughter your name. Marianne. That's the name Kingsley said to me on the beach. He spoke your name, 'Miss Swan,' and said, 'Find Marianne.' I thought he was telling me to find *you*, but he was—"

"Oh, Gavin," she interrupted as she jumped up again. "Do the Harrises have her?"

Gavin stood and crossed to her. Her dark eyes remained fixed on him, unblinking, as he said, "They do. I asked Matthew and Daniel to watch the road and alert me when they're near. I didn't tell you sooner because I wished to wait until…"

"Until you were certain they would come."

He nodded.

"Do you think they might not?"

"I've impressed upon them your good intentions where your niece is concerned, though they are understandably reluctant to reveal her location. They've been protecting her for some time."

"Protecting her? What do you mean?"

Gavin explained what he'd learned early that morning. "Harris has received inquiries from no less than three men searching for a baby girl delivered to a foundling home in Cornwall. It was only when Kingsley sent funds for Marianne's care that Harris knew which of the men he could trust."

"One hundred pounds," Mari said. "It wasn't a

philanthropic donation but funds to care for his daughter. But who else would have been looking for her?"

"Lady Philippa, I presume. You may have noticed last night, Beatrice was the only one who appeared surprised when I mentioned the babe."

"You're right," she mused. "That was very observant, Constable." Her admiration erased his earlier irritation, though he liked it far better when she called him Gavin. "Why would Mr. Harris not have said something when we encountered him at the church?" she asked.

"Kingsley had impressed upon him the need to keep Marianne safe. Since Harris didn't know you were Hannah's sister, he didn't wish to reveal his association with Kingsley, much less the reason for it." Another question formed in her eyes. Before she could voice it, he said, "Before you ask, I can tell you how your niece came to be in Cornwall in the first place." Mari's smile said he'd been correct in anticipating her question. "According to Harris, there was a witness to your sister's encounter with Lady Philippa."

Mari gasped, and Gavin explained. "Mr. Harris's cousin—a spinster lady by the name of Miss Thornton—was your sister's neighbor. Miss Thornton was tending your niece while Hannah visited the market that day. She witnessed what happened at the river, though she was too far to render any aid."

"Wh—what happened?"

Gavin leaned down. He wished to hold her hands, though he settled for holding her gaze as he said, "I don't think Lady Philippa meant to kill Hannah, but there was an argument and she shoved your sister. A struggle ensued. When Hannah fell into the water, Lady Philippa could have helped her, but she didn't. Miss Thornton, worried for the babe's safety, hid with her until Lady Philippa left. She was afraid to come forward after that, but she'd already made plans to visit her cousin in Cornwall, so she brought the child with her. 'Tis why Constable Bragg didn't find her when he went looking for witnesses."

"And why she was away from home when I went to Eventon," Mari said. "But there's a witness—that can only help the case against Lady Philippa."

"If it comes to that. Hannah's necklace is a strong piece of evidence. You were brilliant to confront her about it."

Mari smiled before her gaze turned speculative again. "Why did Lady Philippa hate Hannah so much? Why would she care what becomes of Marianne?"

"That is two questions," Gavin said. "As to the first, Beatrice shared that Kingsley broke off his engagement with Lady Philippa."

Mari started. "What? When?"

"A week before your sister's death. He meant to suffer any breach of contract suit her family might bring so he could marry your sister. It was only after Hannah's death that Lady Philippa persuaded him to resume their betrothal. I don't think he realized the lengths she'd already taken to secure her position."

A tear trembled on the edge of Mari's lashes, and Gavin hurriedly searched his coat for a hand-kerchief. It had not been his intention to cause her tears, but she deserved to know the truth.

"He really did love her," she murmured as she took the cloth from him. "I fear I've made the most horrid assumptions when I could have known him these last months. Hannah said nothing but good things about him in her diary. Had I but trusted that she knew her own heart—"

Before she could berate herself any further, Gavin spoke. "Your love for your sister and your dedication to finding the truth are admirable. Do not ever regret that."

She sniffed and attempted a pitiful smile through her tears that caused Gavin's stomach to twist painfully. He wanted nothing more than to go to her side and hold her tight against him. Instead, he retrieved a letter from his coat.

"As to your second question about Lady Philippa's concern for Marianne… When I began investigating Kingsley's death, I wrote to his solicitor to inquire after his affairs. I think his reply may provide an answer."

He extended the letter to her and, after a short hesitation, she unfolded it. He waited while she read, delighted to hear her little gasp when she reached the best part. Shortly after his marriage, Victor had instructed his solicitor to change his will, leaving what wasn't bound by the marriage settlements to his daughter, Marianne Talbot. It was a rather significant amount.

"Your niece," Gavin said, "is a lady of means."

———

MARI SAT, HER legs suddenly too shaky to hold her any longer. She didn't quite know what to say or where to look. It was all too much to take in. That she might know her niece in mere *minutes* was beyond anything she'd expected when she arrived at the inn's parlor that morning. And now, to hear that her niece was an heiress was another unexpected turn.

Frowning, she said, "Marianne will inherit, even though she's…?" *Illegitimate.* It seemed like an impossibly large label to put on such a tiny child.

Gavin heard her even though she'd not said the word. "Aye," he said, taking the chair next to her. "There will be some legal matters to attend—the court will require a male guardian, I imagine—but I can see that they appoint someone trustworthy."

Mari nodded, her mind rather numb to it all. Gavin watched her, his concerned expression finally breaking into her thoughts. Through the lump that had lodged in her throat, she said, "How can I ever thank you?"

"Thank me? For what?"

Mari spread her hands wide. "For everything. You've helped me find the truth about my sister's death. You've helped me find my niece."

His frown was immediate. "I didn't do it for your gratitude."

Of course he didn't. His every action he did because it was *right*. He helped her because he was a good man. He had a noble heart and a just spirit that was unlike any she'd encountered before, both inside and outside her Greek stories. He helped her because he'd been unable to *not* help her. The thought gave a painful twist to her insides, and she swallowed around a shaky smile. "I know you didn't."

He started at her agreement then wagged a finger. "Oh, no. I see the look in your eye."

"What look?"

"The one that says you think I'm noble or selfless or some rot. Pegasus or—"

"Perseus."

"Perseus. Right." He leaned forward, elbows on his knees. He looked from his hands to her and back again, as though she were a deep pool and he considered whether he wished to jump from a very tall cliff or not.

Finally, he spoke again. "Miss Talbot—Mari—I'm not noble and I'm certainly not the stuff of your Greek tales." His voice rolled over her name, sending a shiver to dance along her skin. "You seem to have a special talent for uncovering secrets," he said, "but have you not discovered my weakness?"

Mari's breath caught, and her eyes widened. "Your weakness?"

A commotion sounded beyond the parlor's open door. Gavin straightened, his expression tight as his young cousins entered.

"They're here," Matthew said breathlessly.

"Aye," Daniel added, "they just passed the lane above the church."

Mari's heart skipped a beat, and she forced the warm timber of Gavin's voice from her mind. She was about to meet her niece.

———

GAVIN SILENTLY CURSED his cousins to perdition, as

well as the Harrises and their abysmal timing. Though, to be fair, it was horrid of him to attempt a declaration when Mari's only thoughts were for her sister's child. Now, she paced from one side of the fireplace to the other as she waited for the Harrises' arrival.

A declaration. Was that what he'd been doing?

It was. He'd be foolish to call it anything else, even to himself. Their acquaintance hadn't come about in the usual way, it was true. There'd been no time for assembly dances or drives, and to be sure, they'd been at odds longer than not. But he couldn't deny the way her regard made him feel as if he'd grown ten feet.

Mari was his weakness. Like Achilles with his wounded heel, or Paris's passion for Helen. Or that bloke who died from staring at his reflection too long... Narcissus.

When Mari was near, his thoughts tangled, caught in the stuttering beat of his heart. He couldn't think of his own name, so intent was he on the deep shadows in her eyes. And, barmy fool that he was, her admiration. Ever since she'd first called him clever, he'd drawn her words in like the air he breathed. He'd never known anything like the confusion she made him feel, as if he were both weak and strong at the same time.

But there was nothing to keep Mari in

Newford—no family or acquaintances to lend their support. When she achieved her aim, she'd go, unless he gave her a reason to stay.

———

MARI TWISTED HER hands at the fireplace, her fingers tangling as the Harrises entered the Feather's parlor. Her breaths were shallow, as if her lungs couldn't quite expand enough to take in the air.

Mr. and Mrs. Harris entered first, their expressions guarded. Behind them came a young woman—the nurse, Mari presumed—and another female, a lady of middle years with her dark hair worn in a tight knot. She was rather angular, though her expression was kind, if a bit wary.

But what caught Mari's attention more than anything else was the blanket-wrapped bundle in the woman's arms, and the tiny fist that waved from it.

Mari didn't hear the words that were exchanged. She must have replied when Mr. and Mrs. Harris offered their greetings. Perhaps she even offered a polite smile, though she couldn't remember doing so. She was only dimly aware of their introduction to the lady holding Marianne—Mr. Harris's cousin, Miss Thornton.

Finally, Miss Thornton said, "Would you like to

hold her?"

Mari nodded, her throat tight, and Miss Thornton gently shifted her bundle into Mari's outstretched arms.

Baby Marianne's tiny face was just visible within her woolen cocoon. She was pink and healthy with a thatch of pale blond hair and the most delightful smell Mari had ever experienced. Mari was unable to speak, unable to think beyond the fact that she was finally holding her niece.

Marianne's tiny fist caught a lock of Mari's hair, and Mari breathed again, laughing as she disentangled herself. She adjusted the blanket and noticed a twist of delicate ivy on one corner. Hannah's ivy. Mari's tears came in earnest then as she hugged her niece tighter against her chest.

"Thank you," she said to the Harrises with a laughing sob. "Thank you for bringing my niece."

CHAPTER 24

MARI STOOD AT the window in her room and looked out on the high street. Newford was bustling with people coming and going from the baker's shop across the way. A pair of ladies marched along to the dressmaker's, and the apothecary was in conversation with Dr. Rowe as the surgeon swept his entry.

She'd seen little of Gavin over the past days, which was for the better. She couldn't think when he was near, and she wanted to remember every moment she had with Marianne.

The Harrises had taken rooms at the Feather so Mari might come to know her niece, who'd instantly captured the adoration of Gavin's female cousins. Mrs. Teague had turned to pudding over the infant and before long, Morwenna Williamson and relations Mari had never met began arriving at the inn. Babies, it seemed, were a rare sight in Newford.

But the Harrises would only remain for two more days as they were needed back at St. Lawrence, so Mari had two more days in which to decide her next steps. Forty-eight hours, which was not a lot of time to choose one's future, not to mention that of a child.

Though Victor's settlement meant her young niece would never lack for anything, it did nothing to solve the other, more pressing problem of who would care for Marianne. She couldn't remain at the parish home, no matter how kind the Harrises were.

Gavin had once asked if Mari considered the difficulties of caring for her niece herself. She had, and they were numerous for an unwed female. Nearly insurmountable, even. Both Mari and Marianne would have shadows on their reputations. There would be questions about Marianne's parentage—questions Mari would be unable to answer without dishonoring her sister or casting more of a pall on Marianne's background. She and her niece would be together, it was true, but they would have little respectability, and that was not the life she wanted for Marianne.

If that was the first of Mari's choices, it was the least palatable. The way she saw it, she had three remaining paths open to her, which should have been plenty but did nothing to quell the upset in her thoughts or her stomach.

The Harrises had offered to find a home for Marianne—a loving but childless couple, perhaps, who would raise her as their own. Mari had told Gavin she'd be content with such a course if she could only meet her niece. How foolish she'd been!

Now that she'd held Marianne, had counted each of her tiny pink toes and admired the cleverness with which she rolled from her front to her back, Mari couldn't let her go. She could no more leave her sister's child to be raised by others than she could leave her own arm behind. That option quickly went the way of the first.

Next, she considered widowhood—a *false* widowhood, rather. Like Hannah, Mari could take a cottage in a village where she wasn't known, posing as a widow to a man who'd never existed. Her life would be a lie, but that was a sacrifice worth making if it meant she and Marianne could enjoy a measure of respectability.

Her final choice, the one that caused her palms to grow damp and a flutter to set up behind her ribs, was marriage. A respectable marriage wouldn't erase Marianne's illegitimacy, but it would lessen the sting a bit. Society would be less inclined to question her background, were she under the protection of a respectable household.

Down below, as if cued by a Greek chorus, she spied Gavin striding confidently toward the Feather. He wore a dark suit, finer than any she'd seen on him before, and she wondered if they were his Sunday clothes.

He stopped when someone hailed him, spoke a few words, then continued his pace. He went on like this, past the farrier and the theater, pausing his steps to greet someone or answer a question before resuming his march toward the inn. He was coming this way.

She was not so naive or silly that she didn't suspect his intentions, given his near-declaration from days before. *Have you not discovered my weakness?*

She had, just as she'd found her own. Gavin was noble and honorable and heroic. Admirable traits, all, but they would drive him to make hasty promises. To offer himself in order to save her.

And she would be tempted to accept. If a valiant nature was his weakness, then an ignoble one must be hers, for she wanted nothing more than to remain in Newford and become his wife. But that was a choice for *her*, not for Marianne. And certainly not for Gavin.

If any other man were to offer marriage, she might accept, so long as he was possessed of a kind and even nature. But the notion of transacting such a marriage with *Gavin* left her with a sour stomach.

A short while later, a knock came at her door. She opened it to find Leo on the threshold. He wore a clean shirt and new shoes, the soles firmly stitched to the uppers and not a naked toe in sight. Mari smiled, relieved to know that, despite all that had occurred over the past days, Leo would be fine. He'd found a home at the Feather, and he would be cared for in Newford.

The boy thrust a paper toward her, which she took and unfolded. She read the constable's even script inviting her to drive with him. Despite her low thoughts and the twisting in her belly, she knew she must go, if only to thank him again for all he'd done for her and Marianne. If he took it in his head to be noble, if he resumed his declaration, she would stop him. It would be cruel to let him go on, and she had too much regard for him to treat him so shabbily.

"I'm s'posed to wait for yer reply," Leo said.

"You may tell the constable I will be down directly." Leo ran off, his footsteps loud in the corridor as Mari collected her courage.

Gavin was waiting for her at the bottom of the stairs. He'd removed his hat and turned the brim in his hands as she descended.

"Miss Talbot." He greeted her with more

formality than they'd used in recent days. It was both a relief and a sorrow that the easiness of their previous exchanges was gone.

"Constable."

"You're well?" he said, and she felt the heat of his gaze as it roamed her face. "Happy?"

"I am, thank you. I…"

"Yes?"

"I'm to join the Harrises and Marianne for luncheon in an hour's time."

"Then we'd best make the most of our drive." He lifted his arm, and she hesitated before laying a hand on his sleeve.

He led them out. The day was warm, the sun high on its path. A cart waited in the Feather's yard, the horse already hitched to it. Gavin handed her up as Peggy came bustling out of the inn. The maid adjusted her cap before taking the seat at the back.

Of course. In his honorable way, Gavin would have arranged for a chaperone. Perhaps this was nothing more than a drive, and she'd been foolish to worry.

He guided the cart onto the street and drove them past the harbor. They spoke of Marianne and Gavin's cousins, Wynne and Jory, who would each have babes of their own soon. Mari began to relax and enjoy their outing. The day was a fine one, and Newford was as pretty a place as she'd ever seen, with its flower-bedecked high street and homes large and small dotting the surrounding hills and vales.

When they reached the cliffs above the sea, Gavin shifted the reins to one hand. "Miss Talbot," he said, "we never finished the conversation we'd begun when the Harrises arrived. I should like to remedy that."

Mari swallowed around the lump in her throat. His tone was formal, his expression so earnest it nearly brought tears to her eyes. The time was now, before he said anything more. "There is no need," she whispered.

He leaned closer, his arm brushing hers as he said, "I beg your pardon?"

"There is no need to finish our conversation. I'll be leaving Newford soon, though I"—she searched her mind for something more to say, something pleasant and kind—"I should be glad to hear from you on occasion."

He sat straighter, away from her. The wind was cool against her arm where his heat had been. Oh, she was not very good at this. Hannah had always known just the thing to say to put gentlemen at their ease.

"I see," he said. Then, with a clearing of his throat, he added, "To be clear, you refer to our conversation in the Feather's parlor? The one where

I was about to declare myself"—Mari closed her eyes, hands folded in her lap—"and ask for your hand in marriage? *That* conversation?"

"Yes." The horse plodded on for several paces before she added, "Please, do not think I am ungrateful. You are the noblest of men—"

"Devil take it," he said with heat, halting Mari's words and causing her brows to hitch. "I'm not being noble. D'you think I ask every lass in need to marry me?"

Mari winced at his words. "Of course not," she said, "but therein lies the problem. I do not wish to marry you out of *need*." Her heart broke a little as she said the words, and at the stark expression on his face.

"'Tis not at all what I meant." His fist tightened on the reins and his gaze remained fixed ahead as he said, "D'you deny you've any tender feelings for me?"

Mari shook her head. She wouldn't lie to him. "I will not deny it, but…"

"Aye?"

"I will not deny it," she repeated, "but I cannot marry you." Oh, how she wanted to take her words back, but it was done. Given her uncertainties about her future, the notion of marrying Gavin, though all-too tempting, felt like an escape rather than a choice, and he deserved so much more.

He pulled a long breath through his nose. In a calmer tone, he said, "I do not wish to make you uncomfortable with my suit. If that is your answer, I must accept it."

Mari was unable to speak, so she simply nodded. The cart arrived at a wide place in the path, and he turned them back toward the Feather. Down below, the sea rolled endlessly, and a pair of gulls swooped in tandem to scoop fish from the surf. Mari's chest ached with an unbearable tightness until she thought she'd choke from it.

———

FOR ONE HALF of a minute, Gavin wondered if his confession at the cove, if his reading troubles, had turned Mari off the notion of marrying him. She was smart and no doubt had been accomplished in the schoolroom. Would she hesitate to align herself with someone like him? His old shame returned, twisting in his belly, before his reason asserted itself. This was Mari, and she would not hold such a thing against him.

But if that was not the reason for her rejection, then what was? Even as the question played through his mind, he told himself it didn't matter what her reason was. She'd declined him, and that was an end to it. He meant what he'd said—he didn't wish to make her uncomfortable with unwanted attentions.

Gavin stayed away from the Feather for two days. His absence, though, didn't mean he was uninformed. Thanks to Leo's service as courier, Gavin learned that Mari meant to set up a widow's house in Devon, of all places, and she'd persuaded Marianne's nurse, Sarah, to accompany her there. She would do well with Kingsley's funds to support her niece, though he imagined it would take some time for her to become settled.

Kingsley's solicitor would stand as guardian to the little heiress, and Gavin had to admit the man was an adequate choice. He was older, but not so old that he would die before Marianne reached her majority. More importantly, though, he was married, so he wouldn't be seeking Mari's hand.

Yes, Mari would be fine, and with no aid from Gavin.

He also learned from Wynne, who had it from Peggy, that the noise in the cart wasn't as loud as he thought it was. Peggy had overheard much of their conversation and reported that it was the most ham-handed proposal any lady would wish to receive.

Gavin couldn't disagree—he still cringed to think of their drive above the cliffs. Thank providence he'd stopped speaking before he began begging, though it had been a near thing.

But when the time came for Mari to go, he

couldn't stay away. He was waiting by the coach when she exited the inn with Marianne in her arms and the nurse in tow. To his irritation, a number of his cousins had also come to see them off. They were arranged round the inn yard, chattering amongst themselves as the coach was readied.

Mari paused to speak to each of them, thanking Wynne and Roddie for their hospitality and promising others she'd write to let them know how Marianne got on. Her step faltered when she saw him waiting for her, but she quickly recovered and walked briskly to the coach.

"Miss Talbot," he said when she reached him.

"Constable." Her eyes were shadowed by the brim of her bonnet as she gazed up at him. She'd acquired a new hat from Morwenna's shop, a fetching straw thing, though he was disappointed to see there were neither birds nor fish on the brim. The bundle in her arms squirmed, and Mari moved her niece to her other shoulder. "Though you won't like to hear it," she continued, "I do wish to thank you again for everything. Your aid, your belief in me when no one else would hear me, and your friendship, especially."

Gavin swallowed. "I wish you and Marianne the best," he said. Then, recalling his purpose, he withdrew a small purse from his coat. The coins jangled when he passed them to her. "'Tis your share of the reward for apprehending Kingsley's murderer. 'Twill help see you settled."

Her brows lifted in surprise. "A reward? I didn't know… thank you."

"Will you write and let me know when you reach your destination?" At her hesitation, he added, "I ask only in a professional capacity, of course."

"I will," she said, and he was gratified to hear a little catch in her voice. She was not unaffected by their parting, though how that knowledge was of any use to him, he couldn't say.

The nurse took the babe, and Gavin handed them in before turning back to Mari. He lifted her hand in his and even through her gloves, he felt the fine warmth of her skin. He would have continued holding her if not for the audience watching her departure.

"Good-bye, Gavin," she whispered.

"Godspeed."

CHAPTER 25

LATER THAT EVENING, Gavin stared into his cup as his cousins traded barbs at their table in the Feather's coffee room. They were a noisy crowd, but Gavin heard none of it, so absorbed was he in studying the loose ground that swirled at the top of his coffee.

"Gavin?" Alfie said, finally drawing his notice.

Gavin looked up. From the expressions on his cousins' faces, they'd been trying to gain his attention for some time. "Aye?"

"We weren't aware Carew had posted a reward for finding Kingsley's murderer. D'you think—"

"He didn't," Gavin said and, with a nod for the table, he collected his cup, pushed back his chair and left.

Over the next days, Gavin couldn't forget Mari's

words during their drive above the sea.

I do not wish to marry you out of need.

Not, *I do not wish to marry you.*

There was a distinction, but the devil if he knew how to bridge the gap. So, he did what no lovesick swain should ever do. He consulted Wynne, which was as good as consulting the entire female populace of Newford and half the males.

"Follow her to Devon and court her properly," was the ladies' consensus, followed closely by, "Arrest the lass," from more than one gentleman.

Pengilley's sage advice to "Name yer boat after 'er" was promptly refuted by Evans' loud snort. "When did such a scheme ever work fer an old lout such as yerself?"

In the end, it was Wynne's quiet suggestion to "Give her thoughts time to settle," that calmed his racing heart. Was that all Mari needed? Time to accept everything that had occurred in the last days and weeks?

Wynne only confirmed his thoughts when he cornered her later in the Feather's kitchen. A fire burned in the oven, and the scent of fresh pastry was heavy in the air as Roddie and Leo brought in wood for the bin. Wynne pulled a stool up to the table and slid a raspberry tart onto a plate for Gavin.

She took a long moment to settle herself upon the stool, her rounded belly hampering her movements until she propped her feet on a small crate with a sigh. Gavin watched this endeavor with wise forbearance until Wynne finally spoke.

"Only consider Miss Talbot's position," she said. "She is a lady of considerable independence and spirit. You rescued her from the sea and then you came to her aid again, with your help in sorting her sister's death. To agree to marry you now, out of a perceived necessity, might appear to her as another rescue, and no lady, no matter how she might enjoy the attentions of a hero, wishes to be rescued with marriage."

Gavin tucked his chin and paced, ignoring the pastry and certain he'd never understand the workings of the female mind. Roddie merely shook his head, so Gavin assumed he was not alone in his confusion.

Pausing to wipe a crumb from the table, Wynne continued. "Imagine for a moment that you find yourself in dun territory, without the benefit of family to aid you." At Gavin's scowl, she pressed, "Just imagine it."

"Aye..." Gavin said slowly.

"Now, a wealthy lady, whose admiration and affection you cherish, has proposed marriage."

"A lady would not propose—"

"Just imagine it."

Gavin sighed. "Very well."

"Now, would you not feel the merest pang of discomfort to think your marriage is one borne of need rather than affection?"

"But—"

"Mari's refusal means she loves you."

Gavin frowned. "How much longer d'you have 'til your confinement?"

Wynne tilted her head at him. "What does that have to do with anything?"

"It seems the babe is robbing you of your sense."

His cousin gave a sigh of long-suffering. "'Tis like this: if you were just another kind gentleman offering marriage, Mari would have accepted. That she did not means her feelings for you run much deeper."

"Bugger it, but that don't make a lick o' sense," Leo said. Gavin started, having forgotten the lad's presence.

"Mind the lady," he said, more from reflex than any concern for Wynne's sensibilities. His cousin could out-swear many of Gavin's sea fellows. He didn't argue Leo's assessment of her logic, though, until he stopped and considered her words.

Devil take it, but she was right. He'd pulled Mari from the sea then caught her again when she fainted in the smuggler's croft. He'd helped her sort the matter of her sister's death then brought her niece to her. Now, when she needed to build a respectable life for herself and Marianne, he'd suggested marriage. He'd even given her funds to see her settled. Thankfully, he'd had the sense to disguise them as a reward.

But of course, she would have viewed his offer of marriage as one more rescue.

Gavin paced the length of the kitchen. "What the devil am I to do now?" he said to Wynne.

She shrugged, which was hardly encouraging. "Grant her time, I suppose, and your patience. This is a decision she must reach on her own."

Gavin stiffened. "Time? You suggest I do nothing? When has anything ever been accomplished by doing nothing?"

Wynne pursed her lips and cocked an irritated expression at him. "This is from the man who's perfected the questioning silence? You manage entire conversations by 'doing nothing.'"

Gavin practiced his questioning silence now and was satisfied when she waved a hand between them and continued. "At any rate, when Mari returns—"

"What?"

"Oh, my. And I promised I wouldn't say anything." Wynne's attempt to look contrite was lacking in sincerity.

"Wynne…"

With a put-upon sigh, she said, "I understand she means to return in six months, to visit with the

Harrises and let us all see how Marianne gets on."

Gavin's heart calmed a bit. "She means to return… You might have started with that."

Wynne left her stool to see to the oven. When Leo returned with another armful of wood, Gavin called him over. The lad had been learning the ostler trade from the men in the Feather's stables and now, here he was toting wood. "How d'you like life on land?" Gavin asked.

Leo wrinkled his nose, and Gavin didn't miss how Wynne's shoulders tensed as she awaited Leo's reply. "I never thought to find meself a lubber," Leo said as he rubbed his nose with his sleeve.

"Aye, but d'you think you can make your peace away from the sea?"

Leo leaned close to Gavin. In a voice that wasn't as low as he thought, he whispered, "Mrs. Teague mothers somefin' fierce, and she's dunked me in the bath twice now. I reckon I'll be set if there's anyfin' you can do to make *that* stop."

Behind him, Wynne's eyes rounded as if someone had just suggested the Feather's linens had lice.

"Aye," Gavin said to Leo. "But I imagine that 'mothering' must come with plenty of biscuits and tarts."

Leo gave a pensive frown, clearly weighing whether Wynne's pastries were worth the trial of regular baths. "I s'pose that's awright then." Behind the lad, Wynne relaxed and returned her attention to her baking.

Gavin studied Leo's thin arms, now covered in a properly fitting shirt. He didn't know if he had the patience to wait six months for Mari to return, or if she'd even have him when she did. He'd best find something to occupy his thoughts. Standing, he replaced his hat and said to Leo, "Come find me when you've finished your work."

"Wot for?"

"'Tis time to begin your pugilism lessons."

"Me wot?"

Gavin clarified. "I'll show you how to throw a proper punch."

"Aye, sir," Leo said with a grin. "D'ye need me to fetch ye anyfin'?"

A lass, Gavin thought. If only you could fetch me a comely lass with Maid Marian eyes.

———

A WEEK LATER, as the morning fog lifted from Newford's cobbles, the routine of Gavin's day was interrupted by the clatter of hooves against the stones. Matthew and Daniel rode up to him, their faces flushed with anxiety, and Gavin's heart lurched.

Had they brought news of Mari? Was she ill?

His pulse only found its rhythm again when Matthew reined in his horse and said, "'Tis Evans and Pengilley."

"What have they done now?"

"Nothing yet," Daniel said. "But they're marching toward the Feather, and they bring a crowd with them."

Gavin's irritation with the pair climbed a notch. He'd already explained to them that Lloyd's was still reviewing the case of the *Destiny* before they decided on any salvage reward. He reached the high street to see a line of villagers trailing the determined figures of Bertie Evans and Trevik Pengilley as they advanced toward the inn.

Gavin hurried to follow and when he arrived at the Feather, it was to find the pair in the middle of the coffee room. They stood elbow-to-elbow, feet braced before the squire's table as the crowd filled the room behind them. A surprisingly *calm* crowd. Gavin watched uncertainly as Evans slapped a folded paper onto the squire's table.

"What's this?" Carew asked, eyeing the paper as he sopped his plate with a crust of bread.

"'Tis a petition," Evans said.

Pengilley clutched his lapels. "*I'll* be tellin' it. 'Twas me notion, after all."

"Then tell it," Evans grumbled.

"A petition for what?" Carew said. His brow

furrowed as he chased a pea on his plate.

"'Tis a petition," Pengilley explained, "to prevent ye from sackin' the constable."

Gavin's brows lifted in surprise. He leaned against the wall to listen, and Gryffyn and Jory joined him as he crossed one ankle over the other.

"Aye," Evans said. "Us 'eard ye mean to rethink 'is appointment—"

"*I* 'eard it," Pengilley corrected. "Ye were too busy contrivin' to woo the widow."

"Pengilley 'eard it," Evans allowed, "and when we tol' the others, 'twas decided. Ye can't ignore all them marks there." He indicated the paper, and several others in the crowd grumbled their assent. Gavin straightened from the wall, eyeing the men that had accompanied Evans and Pengilley—they'd *all* signed a petition to keep him as constable? To be sure, the squire was more bluster than bite, but the notion that they'd gone to such trouble on his account... It brought an unfamiliar lump to his throat.

Carew drained his ale, then lifting the napkin in his buttonhole, he wiped his mouth. "You're all mad," he said. "Why the deuce would I remove Kimbrell?"

"I 'eard yer shoutin'," Pengilley said. There were nods behind him from others who'd witnessed Gavin's public reprimand.

"Why would I remove Kimbrell," Carew repeated, "when the Admiralty has asked for him *especially* to consult on their cases? No other parish can claim such an esteemed constable."

Gavin's neck heated beneath the sudden force of his cousins' stares. "'Tis true?" Jory whispered.

"Aye."

"Carew will never let you leave now, even if you wanted to," Gryffyn said.

Gavin snorted a laugh, surprised at how little the notion bothered him. His next thought, though, sobered him, as he wanted nothing more than to hear Mari's opinion on the matter.

Three and twenty weeks to go.

CHAPTER 26

DEVON
THREE MONTHS LATER

THE AFTERNOON SUN shimmered through the parlor window, illuminating Mari's workspace with its warm light. The desk, a sturdy oak piece pulled from the attic, was cluttered with her paints and inks and half-finished sketches while her meager library, sent on by Mrs. Sherwood, barely filled one of the shelves behind her. The rest of the parlor held books that had come with the cottage lease. Mari thought it would take her and Marianne a lifetime to read them all, though Marianne preferred chewing the corners to perusing their pages.

Sarah, sat with Marianne opposite the desk in a chair near the stone fireplace. The nurse adjusted

Marianne's blankets and smoothed her wispy hair as she murmured to the baby with a quiet efficiency. The sound had become a familiar one to accompany Mari as she worked.

She bent over her desk, her quill scratching against a half-sheet. Mari had drawn and redrawn the same illustration of Perseus for weeks now, but she was never pleased with it. Though she'd captured a suitably fierce set to the hero's jaw, there was something off about his eyes. They were too… flat. Lacking in dimension. Lacking in warmth and kindness and wit. Her thoughts wandered again to Gavin, and her pen paused above the parchment.

A soft whimper from Marianne pulled Mari from her thoughts.

"I expect we'll be seeing that first tooth any day," Sarah said.

Mari smiled as her niece's little fist curled around the edge of her blanket. Setting aside her quill, she rose and crossed to the pair. Taking Marianne, she cradled her against her chest. The infant fussed, her legs kicking at the blanket.

"There, little one," Mari whispered. She pressed a soft kiss to Marianne's forehead, inhaling the sweet scent of her baby skin. Marianne's face lit up at the sound of her name, and Mari marveled at how swiftly she was growing. Just last week, she'd begun crawling about on her own.

Mari hummed the first notes of a lullaby, something her own mother had once sung for her and Hannah. Sarah gave her a cold cloth to ease the babe's gums, and Marianne's fussiness subsided, replaced by contented gurgles. Mari couldn't have been more pleased with her niece's pink, round cheeks and dimpled hands. She was thriving in their new home outside Plymouth.

Mari wished she could say the same for herself. She was finding her footing in this new life, it was true, but as she gazed down at Marianne's face, longing shot through her. How much more time must pass until this ache in her chest, this constant awareness of what she'd left behind, began to fade?

Sarah took the baby away for her nap, and Mari returned to her desk and a fresh sheet of parchment. The afternoon went on, sunlight slanting ever lower through the window. Mari occupied herself with her work, burying her thoughts beneath lines and shadows and perspectives. With careful strokes, she drew the hero's form then, giving in to her instincts, she addressed his eyes.

When at last she set her pen aside and studied the image, it was with a mixture of satisfaction and melancholy. Satisfaction because Perseus was perfect, melancholy because it was Gavin who looked back at her from the page. Proud, honorable Gavin, whose love she'd rejected.

She closed her eyes as she recalled their last drive above the cliffs. Even then, she'd recognized the love in his eyes, but she'd been too scared of her own emotions. Too scared of *needing* him to recognize that she wanted him.

Despite the turmoil of her emotions, though, she couldn't escape the feeling that she ought to have tried harder to explain herself. It was a regret that kept her awake nights long after she should have found her slumber.

She wondered what he'd been doing with his time. His cousins, who wrote with regularity, had kept her apprised of his still-unmarried state, a fact which caused her both sadness and relief.

Sarah returned as the last rays of sunlight slanted across the carpet. Mari looked up, roused from her contemplation to see that she carried a letter.

"This just arrived for you," she said, and Mari's heart gave a disobedient thump of anticipation that she quickly quelled.

She'd written Gavin on first arriving in Devon to let him know they were well, but aside from communicating his pleasure at the news through his cousin, she'd not heard from him. Not that she expected to. It would have been improper for him to correspond with her, no matter that she now went by the widow's name of Mrs. Stewart. And, it must be acknowledged, gentlemen didn't often carry on a correspondence with ladies who declined their offers of marriage.

She took the letter and recognized Wynne Teague's script rather than her cousin's. Enclosed was another, still-sealed letter. Frowning, Marianne read the innkeeper's words. Wynne explained that the enclosed letter had gone first to Mrs. Sherwood, then to Newford, before Mari apprised her former employer of her new direction in Plymouth.

She studied the sealed letter. The script was unfamiliar, though the paper was of the finest quality. She opened it, and her eyes widened when they found the signature.

Victor Kingsley.

———

MARI LIFTED THE window shade on the coach, and her heart rose with it to see they'd reached the cliff path. The sea stretched wide and blue beneath the small window as they bowled along. Newford wasn't far.

Despite the cold autumn air, warmth filled her cheeks to think she might encounter Gavin soon. She would never have wished for him to wait for her, but the fact that he remained unattached caused an ember of hope to burn in her chest.

Marianne squirmed, having grown tired of the journey an hour or more past. Reaching up, she tugged at Mari's bonnet strings. With long practice, Mari removed the ribbons from her niece's fist. She murmured nonsense at the babe as she thought of Victor's letter again.

It had taken her three hours to find the courage to break the seal.

In an ironic turn, he'd written it after Mari had already taken employment in his home. In his letter, he confessed how deeply he'd loved her sister and would always mourn her loss. He also explained that he'd hired a man to find their child and when he did, Victor hoped Mari might want to know Hannah's daughter. Above all, he regretted allowing anything to come between him and the love he and Hannah had shared.

Mari had wept for all that had been lost. She'd lost her sister and Victor, his love. Marianne would never know her parents. And Gavin—Mari had been so foolish to leave Newford. The lesson in Victor's letter was a hard one to miss. If she allowed anything as silly as pride or misplaced dignity to stand in the way of her love for Gavin, she deserved every ounce of regret she was sure to suffer.

After her tears, she'd refolded Victor's letter and stored it away for Marianne to have when she was older. The next day, she began preparing their things for the journey to Cornwall. There'd been no pacing, no hesitation. No doubts.

But now, as the coach rattled over the cobbles of Newford's high street, Mari's nerves stretched thin. Her breath was short and her palms damp by the time the coach rocked to a stop outside the Feather's stables. She remained inside while Sarah stepped down with Marianne. Then, with anticipation fizzing through her, she followed.

Two men came from the stables to see to the horses as another unloaded their trunks. Mari allowed Sarah to go ahead to the inn as she stood on the cobbles, drawing in a full breath of Newford's salty air. She wondered if she'd waited too long to return. What if Gavin no longer felt—

"Mari."

She closed her eyes, savoring the timber of his voice caressing her name. She turned and there he was, as tall and handsome as she recalled. The wind lifted his hair, and he tapped his hat once against his thigh. "Gavin," she said, though she could barely hear her own voice through the heavy thrum of her pulse.

"You're three months early." His voice rolled over her like warm cream. More stable hands arrived to tend the coach, but at Gavin's glare, they fell back.

Licking her lips, Mari said, "I've brought your twenty pounds." When his brow drew low in confusion, she added, "You didn't expect me to believe that nonsense about a reward, did you?" Inwardly, she cringed. What was wrong with her tongue? She'd not come to discuss the money.

His gaze slid to a point over her shoulder before he brought it back to hers. "I apologize for the deception—"

"It was a kind and lovely gesture," she hurried to say. "Truly. No apology is necessary."

"Constable!" Squire Carew stood at the door to the inn, waiting for Gavin.

"The squire is calling for you," Mari said unnecessarily. "I—you should go."

"Aye," he said, though he didn't move to leave her. Instead, his eyes traveled her face. "You're well? And Marianne?"

"We are both well," she confirmed. And then, before he could go, she hurried to say, "There is something I've been wondering, though."

"Aye?"

"I've been wondering what it might have been like..." His eyes narrowed on her face, and she nearly faltered. She pushed ahead before she lost her courage. "...had we met in the usual way of things," she finished.

The sun caught on his cheekbones, lighting his countenance. She held her breath until he moved closer. When the tips of his boots touched the shadow of her hem, he said, "As have I."

Mari's heart sagged in relief. "Do you think we would have shared a set at the assembly?"

"I imagine we would have enjoyed at least three dances by now—one for every month."

"Only one?"

"I wouldn't wish to presume, but would you have given me two?"

Tilting her head, she considered him before saying, "I think I might have."

"Three?"

Mari laughed. "That would be outside the bounds of propriety."

"I would have contented myself with two, then." He reached out and Mari was startled when he took her hand, right there in the inn yard. She allowed it, though, and their fingers tangled as he said, "I would have taken you driving, too, though I might have cast your ugly fish hat into the sea by now."

She snorted a laugh, unable to help herself. Behind Gavin, the Feather's door banged shut as someone pulled the squire inside. The rest of the inn yard was empty, the stable hands having found other tasks to occupy them. Mari couldn't say she minded as Gavin continued his imaginings.

"I would have taught you and Marianne to swim"—her brows lifted at that—"and I'm certain I would have stolen immeasurable kisses by now."

Mari's cheeks warmed. "Immeasurable?"

"Aye. It means a lot." Her lips twisted at his humor. "And if we'd met in the usual way of things," he continued, stepping still closer, "I would have made a proper proposal of marriage. You would have been so impressed with my cleverness, not to mention my person, that there wouldn't have been any reason for you to say no."

"No," she said. "I don't think there would have been."

His blue eyes lit. "D'you think you would have said yes?"

"Oh, Gavin," she whispered. "I have been so foolish. I should have tried to explain myself better."

"And I should not have been so certain of your agreement, but I will listen now if you've something you wish to tell me."

"It's not an easy thing to explain, and harder still to understand," she said in imitation of the words he'd spoken to her at the cove.

"I will try if you will," he replied with a soft smile.

She studied their joined hands as she considered her words. "Too much had happened," she began slowly. "In the matter of a few short months, I'd lost a sister and gained a niece. For weeks, I lived with another woman's name and a singular aim to find the truth of Hannah's death. Once I had it, though, I felt rather like a ship without a rudder. Without a clear course. I… I think I just needed to find my footing again." She licked her lips before she finished with her final truth. "But above all that, I didn't want to *need* to marry you."

Gavin's thumb stroked the back of her hand, the motion as soft as a whisper. After a long moment, he said, "Dare I hope you *want* to?

She nodded because she couldn't speak around the lump in her throat.

"Mari, lass—"

"Yes?" she whispered.

"May I finish my declaration?"

Something in the region of Mari's heart fluttered. She wasn't certain where to look, but the intense blue of Gavin's eyes held her anchored in place.

"I—if you wish it," she said.

"I do." He tucked his chin as if gathering his thoughts, then, holding her gaze with his, he said, "From the first time you landed in my arms, my emotions for you have been… engaged, even as they warred with my thoughts at times. Then the sight of the *Destiny*, ablaze and adrift, and the fear that you might be aboard, nearly caused my heart to cease its beating. I am enamored with your fierce spirit and your loyalty, your sharp tongue and your sharper mind. I admire your defense of the defense- less and your unwavering perseverance." He paused to draw a breath before saying, "I love you, Mari Talbot, and I earnestly wish to marry you, not because you need me but because *I* need *you*." She opened her mouth to speak, but he stopped her with a finger laid gently across her lips. "Before you say 'tis a poor bargain, know that I will agree. 'Tis un-conscionably uneven, with all the good to my side."

Gavin's gaze was steady on hers, his blue eyes unwavering. Mari couldn't look away, even if she wanted to. Instead, she placed both hands gently on either side of his face, feeling the roughness of his cheeks.

He stilled, and she suspected he held his breath much as she did. Then, licking her lips once, she said, "And I adore your intelligence and your honor. Your persistence and your valor, dear Perseus, have my admiration. I know that to love a hero, I must be prepared to be rescued on occasion. I cherish the way my stomach twists when you look at me, and how your kiss nearly melted my insides. I love you, Gavin Kimbrell, and I would be honored to become your wife."

He grinned, and his chest lifted as he pulled in a long breath. "Nearly?"

It took her a moment to grasp his meaning. Of all the things she'd said, *that* was what he heard? That his kiss had *nearly* melted her? "Very nearly so," she said, unwilling to give him the complete truth lest it go to his head. She could tell by the spark in his eyes that he recognized her words for the challenge they were.

He moved closer, and she slid her hands to his shoulders, feeling firm muscle beneath her fingers. He pulled her to him, cupping her cheek with one hand. His scent of warm salt and amber and the heat of his body folded around her, and his lips, when they finally touched hers, were soft and warm. She drew his breath inside as his kiss melted her quite thoroughly.

EPILOGUE

EIGHT MONTHS LATER

MARI GAZED UP at the sky, marveling at the clear blue brilliance of summer in Cornwall. The currents in this part of the cove were gentle now, the water smooth and placid as it lapped softly at her form. Closing her eyes, she allowed herself to drift.

She was truly at peace for the first time since learning of her sister's death. Just last week, with all the church and legal approvals finally complete, Hannah's grave had been moved from the crossroads above Drayton-Marsh to the churchyard in Newford.

Mari had made all the necessary applications to Squire Carew as well as the church officials and Mr. Petersham back in Somerset, with Gavin's support along the way. When she met with obstacles or delays, he was there to help her navigate the process.

His gift to her had been a lovely gravestone carved by his cousin Gryffyn. Together, they'd taken Marianne to lay sprigs of lavender atop the marble, though at just over a year in age, Marianne didn't realize the significance of the moment.

Lady Philippa, as the daughter of a marquess, had employed her father's influence to avoid the noose. Instead, she'd been quietly transported to New South Wales two months previously, where she would live out the remainder of her days. Given the complexity of her crimes and the separate jurisdictions in which she'd been charged, the process had been a lengthy one. When her sentence was finally read and it was not the hanging some expected, Gavin had asked Mari her feelings on the matter. His relief at her reply had been a tangible thing.

"Lady Philippa's death would not return my sister to me," Mari said. "Knowing she'll live out her days in that harsh land, far from everything she knows, shunned by all... it's enough. Hannah would want me to find peace for myself and Marianne, and I've no wish to bring bitterness into our home. I wish to look forward now, not back."

Gavin had pulled her tight against him and held her for a blissfully long time.

As she floated now, a shadow blocked the sun. She opened her eyes to see the grinning, dripping face of her husband. "Tip your head back," he reminded her.

"Then how will I see you?"

"You don't need to see me."

"But I *like* to see you. Especially when your hair is wet like that."

He shook his head to send a shower of cold droplets over her. She squealed and rolled over. Pushing off from the shallow seabed, she swam some yards before turning to splash him with both hands.

On the beach, Marianne squealed with delight and squirmed to escape her nurse. "Swim!" She made it as far as the surf's edge before Gavin caught her and swung her in an arc above his head until she landed with her toes skimming the water. More squeals ensued, high above the low rumble of Gavin's laughter. Mari hurried from the water in her shift, grateful for the warm towel Sarah swiftly handed her.

Her husband seemed pleased with his lot. Indeed, he appeared happier than she'd ever seen him, though he'd never been morose. But there was more light to him now, a vibrancy that had been absent. It was there in his eyes when he laughed, which he did readily now. Like floating, she'd not missed his laughter when she'd not known it, but now she couldn't imagine passing a day without her husband's smile.

He may have saved her numerous times, but she wondered if, perhaps, she hadn't saved him a little, too.

———

GAVIN HELD MARIANNE above the water, her toes dangling just beneath the surface. She squealed, blistering his ears, but he'd never heard anything so lovely.

Nor had he seen anything so perfect as his wife, walking out of the sea in nothing but her shift. He bridled his thoughts and dipped Marianne to her dimpled knees. He wondered if he ought to acquire a dog. Children loved dogs, didn't they?

The tide was beginning to turn, so he gathered his little family and they began a leisurely walk back to Newford. As they reached the lane above the harbor, his wife's steps slowed until they walked several paces behind Marianne and her nurse. Gavin took Mari's hand and twined his fingers with hers.

"Look at that," she said, halting their pace altogether and nodding toward Newford.

The street was busy with carts and riders, and a trio of ladies emerged from the chandler with their parcels, heads bent in conversation. At the far end, the church's square tower cast cool shadows in the afternoon sun as the Widow Chenoweth approached the apothecary. Trevik Pengilley and Bertie Evans spied her at the same time and tripped over their own feet to be the first to open the door for her. Aside from that, Gavin didn't see anything amiss. He leaned his head toward his wife to ask, "What am I supposed to see?"

"Home."

Gavin's eyes were struck with a sudden burning sensation, and he blinked. Home. She was right. Newford was sleepy and ridiculous at times, but it was his, and he wouldn't trade it for ten Truros.

THE END

AUTHOR'S NOTE

Saving Miss Swan is a book of fiction based on events, attitudes and practices of the period. Gavin learned his constable duties from multiple sources such as *The Constable's Assistant* (The Society for the Suppression of Vice, 1808), *The Office of Constable* (Joseph Ritson, 1815) and *The Magistrate's Pocket-Book* (William Robinson, 1825). Any errors are my own.

Below are a few more elements that influenced Mari and Gavin's tale.

*****Spoilers Ahead*****

Coffee. In the early 19th century, Gavin's favored beverage was gaining popularity as a fashionable alternative to tea. One receipt book from 1810 describes its benefits:

> The infusion… of the roasted seeds of the coffee-berry, when not too strong, is a wholesome, exhilarating, and strengthening beverage; and when mixed with a large proportion of milk, is a proper article of diet for literary and sedentary people. It is especially suited to persons advanced in years.

It then continues with this dire warning:

> By an abusive indulgence in this drink, the organs of digestion are impaired… and emaciation, general debility, paralytic affections, and nervous fever are brought on. [*The New Family Receipt Book*, John Murray, 1810]

It makes one wonder what, precisely, they were drinking.

Dyslexia. It's estimated that dyslexia affects about one in every five individuals, though degrees of the condition and the specific challenges it brings to each individual vary. It was first defined by the German ophthalmologist Rudolf Berlin in 1883, so it wouldn't have been recognized in Gavin's era.

Gavin wouldn't have had access to many of the learning aids and techniques used today, so he was fortunate to find something that worked for him. I imagine many others did not. I love how he turned his challenge to his advantage—given his lifelong study of words and letters, he was well prepared to identify patterns in handwriting, perhaps more than someone without dyslexia might have been.

Many people suspected of having dyslexia have become some of our most celebrated authors:

Agatha Christie, F. Scott Fitzgerald, and Jules Verne, to name a few.

[https://dyslexiahelp.umich.edu/success-stories/ famous-authors-with-dyslexia]

Ladies' Pockets. In the Regency era, ladies' pockets were small, detachable pouches worn under skirts and secured by ribbons tied around the waist. Sometimes embellished with embroidery, these were used to carry personal items and valuables. Unlike modern-day pockets sewn into clothing, these were separate and could be accessed through slits in a lady's gown. The design allowed women to keep their essentials close while maintaining the fashionable silhouette of the time.

Perseus. Perseus, who is best known in Greek mythology for his daring feats and virtuous character, was the son of Zeus and Danaë. While his most well-known achievement was slaying the Gorgon Medusa, he also rescued Andromeda, a princess chained to a rock as a sacrifice to a sea monster. Throughout the myths, Perseus is depicted as a symbol of courage, resourcefulness, and justice.

Gavin's rescue of Mari during the shipwreck mirrors the heroism and bravery of Perseus, while a less literal parallel can be found in his determination and courage in helping Mari find baby Marianne and the truth about Hannah's death.

Robin Hood. Though unplanned, this story ended up with a few Robin Hood allusions, some more literal than others. The most obvious, of course, is Gavin's comparison of Mari to the Maid Marian, who is often depicted as the noble and strong-willed love interest of the heroic outlaw, loyal and committed in her fight against injustice. Other parallels can be found in Gavin's causing Evans to contribute his gambling winnings to the children's fund and his fight against the corrupt sheriff of Nottingham, i.e., Squire Carew in this story.

Ship Careening. Before the prevalence of dry docks, it was common practice to intentionally careen a ship (lay it on its side) to make repairs to the hull, especially if the ship had sustained damage below the waterline. This could be done by beaching the ship at high tide and then allowing the tide to recede, leaving the ship partially or fully exposed on one side.

After repairs were completed, the ship would be refloated, often by waiting for the next high tide or using ropes and pulleys to pull it upright.

Ship Scuttling. The deliberate sinking of a ship has been a tactic employed throughout history for various reasons, some legitimate and others... not. Wartime vessels, for example, were scuttled to prevent their capture or to block strategic waterways. But scuttling has also been used to perpetrate insurance scams.

The events in this story are very loosely based on the 1802 case of Codling, Reid, McFarlane and Easterby, in which "Codling was charged with wilfully casting away and destroying the ship of which he was captain; Reid was charged with being on board aiding and assisting; and the two other parties, who were owners of the vessel, were charged as... having encouraged, counselled and engaged the captain to commit the crime."

[*The Trials of Patrick Maxwell Stewart Wallace, and Michael Shaw Stewart Wallace,* Williams and Son, 1841.]

Trengrouse's Device. The rescue device mentioned in this novel was the real-life invention of 19th-century Cornishman, Henry Trengrouse. Known as the "rocket apparatus," the device used a rocket to propel a line to or from ships in distress, allowing for the safe retrieval of crew and passengers.

My Pinterest Board (see below) includes a pin of *The Wreck of Jeune Oscar*, a painting depicting the use of the device. It even shows a person coming across in the chair. Trengrouse's own account published in 1817 describes the innovation like this:

> "Provided a stranded vessel should not go to pieces directly, a hawser may be hauled taut from the vessel to the shore on which a numerous crew may be landed—comfortably and quickly—by means of a *chaise rolante* conveyancer [literally, a wheeled chair], suspended to wheels which run upon the hawser. The *chaise rolante* is so portable that a child of three years old may with ease carry it under his arm." [Trengrouse, Henry. *Shipwreck investigated ... and a remedy provided in a ... life preserving apparatus*, 1817.]

Pinterest. If you would like to see my inspiration for Gavin, Mari, and some of the items above, be sure to check out my Pinterest board: https://www.pinterest.com/klynsmithauthor/saving-miss-swan/.

THANK YOU

Thank you for reading! If Gavin and Mari's tale brought a smile to your face, swept you away or simply provided a welcome escape, please consider leaving a star rating and/or review on your favorite book site.

Want more of the Kimbrell cousins? Subscribe at klynsmithauthor.com/dw and receive a free copy of the Hearts of Cornwall prequel, Discovering Wynne. It's a fun and flirty tale about innkeeping, smuggling and of course, swoon-worthy romance.

Don't miss the next in the Hearts of Cornwall series. Follow K. Lyn Smith on Amazon or BookBub or subscribe to her newsletter for new release updates.

BOOKS BY K. LYN SMITH

Something Wonderful
The Astronomer's Obsession
The Artist's Redemption
The Physician's Dilemma

Hearts of Cornwall
Discovering Wynne (Prequel Novella)
Jilting Jory
Matching Miss Moon
Driving Miss Darling
Kissing Kate
Saving Miss Swan
Charming the Captain
Engaging Miss Enderby*
Regarding Rebecca

Love's Journey
Star of Wonder
Light of a Nile Moon
Stars of Twilight Fair
Beneath a Brighton Sun

* Cadan's story appears in the
Hearts in Bloom Regency Anthology.
Visit klynsmithauthor.com
for the most up-to-date list of titles.

ABOUT THE AUTHOR

K. Lyn Smith writes sweet historical romance about ordinary people finding extraordinary love. Her debut novel, The Astronomer's Obsession, was a finalist for the National Excellence in Romantic Fiction Award, and many of her other titles have been shortlisted for honors such as the American Writing Award, the Carolyn Reader's Choice Award, the HOLT Medallion and the Maggie Award.

When she's not lost in the pages of a book, you can find her with family, traveling to far-off places and binging period dramas. And space documentaries. Weird, right?

Visit www.klynsmithauthor.com, where you can subscribe for new release updates and access to exclusive bonus content.

www.ingramcontent.com/pod-product-compliance
Lightning Source LLC
Chambersburg PA
CBHW031827310726
48972CB00005B/1192